THE DAUGHTER OF SHILOH

ENDURING HOPE

BOOK THREE

Terri J. Haynes

The Daughter of Shiloh

Enduring Hope
Book Three

YOU are the reason we do what we do here at Barbour Publishing. We promise that we will always use our God-given talents to produce content with you in mind—and that we will remain biblically faithful, no matter what.

Thank you for being the heart of our business.

Print ISBN 979-8-89151-199-6
Adobe Digital Edition (.epub) 979-8-89151-200-9

Cover Design: Kirk DouPonce, DogEared Design

Published by Barbour Publishing, Inc., 1810 Barbour Drive, Uhrichsville, Ohio 44683, www.barbourbooks.com

Our mission is to inspire the world with the life-changing message of the Bible.

Printed in the United States of America.

DEDICATION

To Dyara Henderson:
Thank you for loving me as a daughter.

CHAPTER ONE

Lealia Bevard reached the stairs of the chapel on the campus of Tuskegee Normal and Industrial Institute, her breathing heavy. She had spent so much time reading and rereading the letter in her pocket, unfolding and refolding it, that she had to run to make it to chapel on time. Her footsteps felt light, as if there were thick wool between her feet and the world.

The women's section of the chapel was only half full now, students coming in at a slow trickle. Lealia smirked as she walked quickly past near-empty rows of her classmates wearing the school's uniform of white blouses and black skirts. How the other students could be late for a required event she could not fathom. But, in the two years she'd attended, there were always late students. Scrambling in at the last moment. It baffled her. Chapel service was consistently held at the same time and place. It was too easy to be on time.

As she settled into a seat, her hand drifted to her pocket where the letter rested. The letter that was going to change her life, the reality of its words feeling like soap bubbles floating just beyond her grasp. Mr. Gadson, the Daily Bible Readings and English teacher, walked to the podium to begin chapel as they always had, with a scripture. The body of students stood as he read Psalm 23, his voice carrying through the building.

He finished the reading, and Lealia realized she had only heard "'The Lord is my Shepherd—'" and the "Amen" from the students around her. Her attention had drifted in the short time it took Mr. Gadson to finish. *You must be better,* she scolded herself. Other students lost their focus. Not her.

Mr. Booker T. Washington, the principal of Tuskegee, took the podium. "Students, I am pleased to announce that I will be giving a speech at the National Baptist Convention next week in Birmingham," he said.

He was going to be back home as well. Home. Although she had not been to Birmingham in years, Shiloh Baptist Church would always be home.

Mr. Washington traveling to speak was quite common. He was in great demand. But no matter how many trips and speeches he made, his focus was always on benefiting Tuskegee. Mr. Washington was building a good school here. Nevertheless, it was a school that could only be a starting point for her lofty goals. They could not be accomplished here.

She remembered when her brother, Nathan, had looked her in the eye and told her to leave Tuskegee as soon as she could.

"I will say nothing disparaging about my time at Tuskegee, but Mr. Du Bois has the right idea of moving us forward," he had said. "The Talented Tenth will show the way to the future."

She had heard her parents and brother talk so many times about the philosophy of Mr. Washington versus Mr. W. E. B. Du Bois. Mr. Du Bois was a Negro educator in Boston who believed that the race needed more than the type of education Mr. Washington offered.

He stressed that they needed a classical education the same as other students. . .white students. Only then would they be equal. Mr. Du Bois believed that from the classically educated Negros, a tenth of them would lead the race from poverty and ignorance.

Mr. Washington focused on upward mobility through labor and industry. On the surface, it seemed to have worked, at least in the town of Tuskegee. The students were well known for their ethics and the quality of their work.

Lealia agreed with Mr. Du Bois. The best way to ensure the races were equal was for both to have the same educational opportunities.

Mr. Washington continued. "Any student interested in accompanying me, please speak to me or Mrs. Robinson. It will be an opportunity to show Birmingham the greatness of the work we do here."

Under normal circumstances, Lealia would have jumped at the chance to join Mr. Washington and would have been selected first. Her grades ranked among the highest, and she did a considerable amount of extra work on campus—including teaching at the Negro Conference, an annual event during which farmers from the surrounding areas would come to take classes on everything from agriculture to hygiene. Lealia loved the Negro Conference because it gave her a chance to help the local farmers. There were so many of them who needed education, who had come through Reconstruction illiterate or unable to do simple sums.

But she need not go with Mr. Washington. She was already going to the National Baptist Convention as an invited guest, the same as he was. Not as elevated but just as important.

The National Baptist Education Board was going to give her a scholarship. A scholarship to get her to the school she dreamed of attending: Howard University. Once they met her, the scholarship would be hers. How could it not? She had listed all her accomplishments in the letter she had written to the Board. She was exactly the type of person the Negro race needed to hold up as an example of their greatness: an intelligent, hardworking woman who had pushed through many obstacles to maintain her grades at Tuskegee. That was another thing she had put in her letter.

And she would be going home to Shiloh Baptist Church to show them what their daughter had accomplished with the financial gifts they had given her. The entire time she had been at Tuskegee, her prayers had included thanks to God for the small congregation in Birmingham. They were the only reason she could afford her tuition here. Now she could truly make them proud. Tuskegee was a good use of the scholarship Shiloh had given her when she and her parents had moved there from Birmingham. The school, however, was just the first stepping stone to going to a classical university.

"Miss Lealia Bevard."

Her head whipped up.

Mr. Washington peered over the crowd. "Miss Bevard, where are you? Please stand up."

Lealia's knees wobbled as she stood. Why was Mr. Washington calling for her in the middle of chapel service? Did he somehow know about the letter in her pocket? They were told that their mail would be monitored when they enrolled. Had he read her letter and now was about to announce her news to the whole school?

"Oh, there she is. Without Miss Bevard's help, we would not have enough supplies for this semester's students at the Children's House." She exhaled and lowered her head to hide her smile. How could Mr. Washington know the contents of the letter? It was unopened when she picked it up from the school postmaster with her other letters. Mrs. Walden from Shiloh had written her normal monthly letter. Mr. Eves, another Shiloh member, had sent her a new copy of *The Birmingham Age-Herald* newspaper.

Lealia stood taller, lifting her chin as Mr. Washington explained how she had spent long nights studying the Children's House financial records and enlisting other students in writing fundraising letters. Mr. Washington's passion for education extended all the way down to the youngest of minds. The Children's House taught the local children beginning with kindergarten, starting their education young.

Lealia had heard through a classmate that there were more children this term than instructors had expected. When she went to ask how she could help, she found that the Children's House principal, Mrs. Dorsett, had no mind for sums. How she had her bookkeeping in such disarray and remained the principal baffled Lealia. In the end, Lealia had balanced the books, calculating the shortfall in funds, and asked Mr. Gadson to point out his best writers. Then she spoke with those students and asked them to write donation letters to businesses in downtown Tuskegee asking them to make up the difference.

It was easy to volunteer. She knew the kind of poverty the children lived in. When she and her family arrived in Tuskegee, they had little more than the clothes on their backs and the moneys Shiloh Baptist Church had given them. Part of it was Lealia's tuition for her first semester at Tuskegee, and the rest was just enough for her father to buy seed. Like many of the other Negro residents of Tuskegee, her father was a sharecropper, working ten acres of land.

If not for the money Shiloh Baptist Church sent her every term, Lealia would not be able to continue at Tuskegee. The least she could do was help others. The incoming donations to the Children's House would help this year's students' minds and stomachs, as one meal was provided by the school. When seeing the excitement in the eyes of the little ones in a neat line outside the Children's House at the beginning of the semester, she saw the good in what she'd done.

All the students in the chapel applauded. When the applause died down, Mr. Washington smiled at her. "Tuskegee has a great many needs, and your motivation would certainly be an asset to the school after you graduate."

She kept a smile pasted on her face.

After a song from the school choir and the benediction, some students crowded around her to ask her if they could help with the Children's House next time. She had to think of a vague answer fast, since she would not be here for the next time.

Mr. Washington stood directly across from her, surrounded by students. Likely all wanting to go to Birmingham. One of them broke from the group, a deep scowl on his face. She watched him a little longer. Was he in one of her classes? Then she remembered he was in the nursing program with her. Mr. Rafferty. He was two years ahead of her. They had had a class together in the spring. She could not have forgotten his name if she wanted to. Her classmates had giggled about how cute he was.

And he was cute. Tall but not towering. Lean and graceful in his movements. The summer sun had given him a richer mahogany skin tone than he'd had in the spring. Thick black hair and the beginnings of a beard. He had earned a reputation for being unflappable with even the most unsettling parts of their nursing courses, handling animal innards with ease. His steady demeanor and intelligence were the makings of a great doctor.

As she watched him, he looked up, and his eyes locked with hers. Then she remembered what she liked most about him. Mr. Rafferty constantly wore an expression of curiosity. As though the world was a mystery, and he aimed to solve it. Like now. He tipped his head to the side, and his forehead puckered a little, as if he was thinking hard. She squirmed under such an examination.

It seemed incongruent that someone would be so serious when she was so happy. Without thinking, she crossed her eyes.

His face broke into a grin, and his shoulders shook with laughter. That made her laugh too. She left the chapel with the same light steps she'd entered it.

Outside, the night air had cooled. The fields beyond the chapel stood in shadow, the trees catching a slight breeze. The smell of the warmed earth made her think of working the fields with her family. She would miss it all once she arrived at Howard.

Milton Rafferty had not expected to hear about Shiloh Baptist Church in chapel service at Tuskegee Normal and Industrial Institute. And to hear it mentioned in such a positive light. Shiloh was hosting the Negro Baptist Convention. Mr. Washington was going there to speak.

Better him than me.

Despite a very moving reading of Psalm 23 by Mr. Gadson, Milton's mood had turned black. He stood in Tuskegee's emptying chapel trying to pay attention to his friends' chatter. His thoughts, however, lingered on Shiloh. They had built a massive new building. His mother had told him through letters. Milton's mind was still on the 6th Avenue location. Where all his troubles had begun.

His friend Earnest Mickens tapped him on the shoulder. "Milt?"

Milton blinked. "Uh, sorry."

"You were lost in thought." Earnest picked up his satchel. "Thinking about that girl?"

"Girl. . ." Milton looked around.

Earnest let out a laugh. "The girl Mr. Washington recognized. Miss Bevard. The pretty one. You were staring with your mouth open."

Milton let out a nervous chuckle. "Oh, her. Yes, she was pretty."

When Miss Bevard stood up, Milton could not take his eyes off her. Rich brown skin, wide eyes, thick hair pulled into a neat bun at the back of her head. Her accomplishment caught his attention more. She cared for others, and that made her even more beautiful.

As he had applauded with everyone else, he recognized her somehow, beyond the fact that they had been in a nursing class together in the spring. Her familiarity went deeper than that. It was as if he could remember the sound of her voice. When she smiled, he was sure he knew her. He definitely remembered that smile. And then a note of caution sounded in his thoughts. The fact that he couldn't place her made him wary.

"So you were thinking about her?"

"Yes," Milton began. *Trying to remember how I know her.* "But not how you think. Did you hear what she did? It must have been impressive for Mr. Washington to recognize her like that."

Another friend, August Dixon, leaned into the conversation. "Leave it to Milton to see only a pretty girl's heart."

Earnest and August laughed. Milton stuffed his hands in his pockets. "Leave it to you two to see only how pretty a girl is. Bet her grades are better than yours."

August nodded. "Everybody's grades are better than mine."

"If not the girl, what were you thinking about? I called you twice, and you didn't hear me." Earnest folded his arms, a half smile on his face.

Milton picked up his satchel and started down the aisle, fighting back a grumble. Why were they so concerned about what he was thinking? "I was thinking about Mr. Washington going to speak in Birmingham."

"I am going to speak to him about going," August said. He nudged Milton with his shoulder. "You should too. You are from Birmingham, after all."

Milton shook his head. "I have too much classwork to do to be absent." And he had absolutely no desire to go back to Birmingham. The next time he set foot in that town would be to collect his mother and leave.

Earnest laughed. "Your grades are some of the highest in the school. A few days away ain't gonna change that."

Earnest was right about Milton's grades. He was one term away from graduating from the nursing program, the first leg of his journey to becoming a doctor. His grades would be higher if it were not for his agriculture class. He understood how to keep a human body alive, but he had less success with plants. "I have other work to do as well. My essay for the school newsletter is due, and I'm scheduled to cover the nursing department next week."

"If I were you, I would request to go simply to get a free trip home," August said.

Home. Two emotions surged in his heart. Homesickness. He missed his mother. Anger. He had tried to bury it during his time at Tuskegee, working hard to forget. But how could he? He was at Tuskegee because of the members of that church.

Before he could reply, he caught a glimpse of Miss Bevard. He watched her go down the aisle toward the door, smiling and greeting other students as she did. *Where do I know you from?*

Loud laughter from behind him jarred him back to the moment.

August and Earnest were nearly doubled over in laughter. Earnest took a deep breath and managed to say, "Sure, you weren't thinking about Miss Bevard."

Milton pushed ahead, letting out an exasperated huff, leaving them behind.

When he got to the door, he spotted Mr. Washington chatting with a group of students. Milton moved around the group. "I have noted all your names and will let you know soon. Shiloh Baptist is only providing travel expenses for six students." Mr. Washington looked up and saw Milton. "Mr. Rafferty, one moment please."

Milton stepped to the front of the group. "Sir?"

"I had planned to talk to you tomorrow," Mr. Washington said. "I would like for you to travel with me. I already have you recorded as one of my party."

No. Milton's jaw worked, but the word stuck in his throat. He did not want to travel with Mr. Washington. He did not want to return to Shiloh. "Thank you, sir, but I have quite a bit of work to do in the next week."

Mr. Washington patted Milton's shoulder. "The trip will only be a few days, and I will instruct your teachers to allow you to make up any assignments you miss. What better way to represent the school to the residents of Birmingham than one of their own?"

I am not one of their own nor will I ever be. While Milton fought to settle his thoughts, Mr. Washington moved on to the next student. He would have to go to Mr. Washington's office tomorrow and explain to him why he could not accompany him to Birmingham. Milton frowned. Maybe not explain.

He shouldered his satchel and turned to find Miss Bevard watching him. Or maybe she was watching Mr. Washington. Her eyes followed him. He knew he should look away but could not. Their eyes met.

Memories of her hovered just beyond his recall. *Where. . .*

But before he could finish the thought, Miss Bevard crossed her eyes, a cheeky look on her face.

It was so unexpected that he laughed out loud. Good thing his friends had already gone.

She turned and left the chapel with the brightest smile on her face. As if it had made her day to make him smile. It felt good to laugh like that over something silly. All his coursework had dragged his mood down in the past weeks. He was so close to finishing school. Closer to having the foundation of nursing to move on to medical school. When he had arrived at Tuskegee, his only goal had been to survive. He had so many more goals now. Get a position to earn enough money, rescue his mother from Birmingham, and never look back. He had no plans to go to Birmingham until he could accomplish just that.

CHAPTER TWO

By the time her dormmates rose, Lealia had bathed and dressed. She had tried to sleep, but her excitement only made her toss and turn. Then a frustrated grunt from the girl in the bed next to her made her get up. One of the other girls, Betty, looked her up and down as Lealia finished braiding her hair.

"You're quite happy for someone heading to class." Betty was always grumpy in the morning. As though getting an education was too much for her to be bothered with. All the girl talked about was getting her papers but was unhappy about doing the work to get them. Yes, they worked hard here, but how else could they excel? Lealia had offered to tutor her on several occasions, but Betty had always refused.

"I'm not going to class. I'm going to meet with Mrs. Robinson to cancel my enrollment," Lealia said with a smile.

"You're leaving?" Another girl, Amanda, gaped.

"Yes, I am going to Howard."

Several girls crowded around her, and Lealia sat perched on her bed, answering their questions.

"So the Education Board gave you a scholarship?" Betty asked.

"Not yet." Lealia continued to smile, but it dipped a little. They would give her the scholarship. How could they not?

Betty let out a laugh, putting her hand on her stomach. "Miss High-and-Mighty is just going to walk into the meeting and demand they give her a scholarship. She's gonna stand up like she did in chapel last night." Betty straightened her spine, lifted her head, and waved to the other girls like she was the Tuskegee annual parade queen. They all burst into laughter.

Amanda shook her head and continued dressing. "Chile, she was talking like she already had it." The rest of the girls went back to dressing with grumbles.

These girls had never liked her. Lealia would go as far as saying they were jealous, but they had to see how much harder she worked than they did. "You'll see," she said. "I'll be at Howard while you all are still here building tables and tilling fields."

"Or you'll be right back here with us building tables and tilling fields when they cover your full tuition for Tuskegee," Betty said, and the girls laughed.

Betty and Amanda began coming up with the most ridiculous scenarios of what the Board would offer her.

"Or they'll send you to Selma," Amanda said.

Lealia shuddered. Selma was a Baptist college in Birmingham many Baptist ministers and local teachers attended. The National Baptist Education Board preferred sending students there because the overall goal of the Board was to train more teachers and open more schools. These schools—which included Tuskegee—offered different types of education but were not the place for someone who wanted to excel in the classics.

She did not want to go to Selma.

As the girls continued teasing her, she realized that this was the exact reason more people needed to pursue a classical education. The race needed leaders. People who could show the way. If they had more leaders, these girls would think differently. See that the education they got here was inadequate to fight against prejudice. How could they be equal doing the same activities the Negro had always done? How could they be seen differently when they were still mostly laborers?

She finished her hair as quickly as she could and grabbed her hat. *Well, at least I won't have to see this bunch again.* Lealia left the room, the girls' laughter following her.

By the time she reached Mrs. Robinson's office, Lealia had managed to put her dormmates out of her mind. What did they know? They were satisfied with what they had here. No ambition.

Mrs. Robinson, the women's principal, welcomed her with a smile. "Good morning, Lealia. Have a seat."

Lealia sat down. "I received a reply from the National Baptist Education Board. They want me to come to the Baptist Convention to meet with them."

"Wonderful news." Mrs. Robinson smiled broadly. Lealia had discussed her intention of writing the Education Board with Mrs. Robinson, and the woman was as excited for Lealia now as she was then.

"I figured I'd go ahead and cancel my enrollment now."

"Before you get an answer from the Board?" Mrs. Robinson asked with a frown.

"Yes. They must be planning to give me a scholarship if they asked me to come all the way to Birmingham. I will be leaving from Birmingham to go straight to Howard."

Still frowning, Mrs. Robinson said, "This process may not move as fast as you are anticipating. Many times scholarships are awarded after they are discussed by several different boards. Just like they are discussed here at Tuskegee."

Lealia squirmed and changed the subject. "I have to find somewhere to stay first," she said with a forced laugh.

"That has been a bit of a challenge for the students traveling with Mr. Washington," Mrs. Robinson said. "Seems lodging is hard to come by once all the delegates arrive."

In her last letter, Mrs. Walden had written how she was taking in three lodgers and how the other Shiloh members were taking in just as many. If only her letter had arrived sooner, Lealia could have lodged with people she knew. Now she'd have to stay with strangers.

Mrs. Robinson tapped her cheek. "Maybe you could catch the train the day of your meeting."

And be frazzled and wrinkled by the train ride. "My meeting is the day of Mr. Washington's speech. The train will likely be crowded."

Mrs. Robinson brightened. "I nearly forgot." She rose and walked to the bulletin board outside her door. "Mr. Washington mentioned that a student traveling with him was from Birmingham. He said his mother had an empty room." She plucked a piece of paper from the board. "Mr. Rafferty."

Mr. Rafferty. Lealia found herself grinning at the memory of his smiling face at chapel. She quickly wiped the smile off her face when

Mrs. Robinson returned. "Mr. Rafferty should be heading to agriculture class next."

Lealia rose. "Thank you. I'll go there now."

"Miss Bevard." Mrs. Robinson stopped Lealia with a hand on her arm. "I know you have hopes of how things will go in Birmingham, but remember, God may have other plans. His ways are not our ways, you know."

Lealia stood up straighter, refusing to believe that God's plans were any different from hers. "I know."

"Regardless of His plans, they will be good, and I am sure you will excel in whatever you do."

Lealia nodded and smiled. What plan could God have for her other than success?

Milton pulled the book closer to himself and sighed. He normally enjoyed studying for his English classes. Hard to enjoy it now when he had so little time.

He had visited Mr. Washington's office first thing this morning, a speech prepared to inform Tuskegee's principal that he could not travel with him. He had too much classwork. Too many responsibilities. He had practiced it staring up at the ceiling of his dorm room after he and his other dormmates had gone to bed. He had walked into Mr. Washington's office, confident he could get out of the trip.

His confidence lasted less than five minutes.

Mr. Washington was so pleased that Milton would be accompanying him. Thought Milton was the perfect person to attend. He praised Milton for his grades and his dedication. So much so that Milton's desire not to go quickly turned to guilt. Mr. Washington wanted him to go because his presence might garner more financial support from the residents of Birmingham. An honorable cause. Milton was a Tuskegee success story.

Mr. Washington shook Milton's hand. "Also, I would be at your service if you helped another student in our party arrange lodging. Most of the inns are already full of delegates traveling to the convention. I have one more student that needs a room. Maybe he can stay with you if your mother has any available space."

That had made Milton's protest dry up in his throat. As much as he did not want to go back to Shiloh, he couldn't deny he would love the chance to see his mother again. "I'll send her a letter tomorrow. I'm certain there is an empty room at my house if a student needs it."

He was certain there would be an empty room because no one at Shiloh would recommend his house to the delegates. Shiloh would not risk exposing the delegates to scandal. But a student from Tuskegee would know nothing of his family's history.

He tried to convince himself that it might not be so bad, but failed. Going back to Shiloh was going to hurt. He could feel it.

Milton exhaled loud enough for the librarian to glance over at him.

Before him was the poem "The Vision of Sir Launfal," the first assignment for his grammar and analysis class. His eyes skimmed over the poem and the notes he'd taken. He had scribbled *iambic tetrameter*, and as soon as class was over, he'd rushed to the Carnegie Library to research the term.

But when he arrived to the quiet of the library, his eyes lingered on one section of the poem:

Joy comes, grief goes, we know not how;
Everything is happy now,
Everything is upward striving;
'Tis as easy now for the heart to be true
As for grass to be green or skies to be blue,
'Tis the natural way of living:
Who knows whither the clouds have fled?
In the unscarred heaven they leave no wake,
And the eyes forget the tears they have shed,
The heart forgets its sorrow and ache;
The soul partakes the season's youth,
And the sulphurous rifts of passion and woe
Lie deep 'neath a silence pure and smooth,
Like burnt-out craters healed with snow.
What wonder if Sir Launfal now
Remembered the keeping of his vow?

He reread the line *everything is upward striving.* He would have used that line to describe his life before Mr. Washington asked him on this trip. He was finishing his last semester, and his teachers had given him his school assignments for the next week. His other assignments sat unopened in his workbook. They had all agreed that he could turn them in late, but Milton was determined to turn in as many as he could before he left. He would not let this trip put him behind.

Everything is happy now,
Everything is upward striving;

He sat back in his chair, staring out the windows of the Carnegie Library, wishing he could feel happiness. Or remember what it felt like to be happy. All of his memories, especially those of his time at Shiloh, were not happy.

He had not traveled home to Birmingham once in the four years since he had left in the early morning dark for Tuskegee. He wished, like the poet, he could forget the tears he'd shed. He had hugged his mother tight as they stood on the train platform. He remembered the feeling of running away, leaving her to bear all the family's problems.

Running away like his father.

Although he was nearly twenty-one years of age, he'd still felt like a child that night. Uncertain, afraid. His mother had insisted that he leave before the taint of his father's shadow fell on him. Through tears, he'd begged her to come with him.

She had shaken her head. "I have to keep up the house now that your father's gone."

Milton had squeezed her tighter. "I can stay and work. Help you with the bills."

"No," his mother had said quietly. "You need to go and become the man your father never was."

Then she had kissed his forehead and put him on the train.

Even though it had happened four years ago, the memory of that night still stung. He had kept up constant correspondence with his mother, and she had been right. For some reason, all the fervor concerning his father died down once Milton left. His mother had never been the object of their anger. They pitied her. That anger was reserved for the male Raffertys. Once school was over, he'd graduate with the skills to support his mother the way his father had not.

He closed the book and returned it to the librarian. Agriculture was his next class. He forced down a grumble. Although he excelled in his other classes, he struggled with agriculture. He understood the principles, but in practice. . . He had killed every plant Mr. Carver had assigned him. To him, all plants looked happy, even the ones needing water and food.

As he made his way to the field where his agriculture class was held, he saw Earnest trotting from the opposite direction. He waited for his friend to catch up.

"Magic Man from Magic City," Earnest said, a little out of breath.

Milton chafed at the nickname. "No magic. Just hard work."

"There's got to be some magic in it. You got handpicked for the trip to Birmingham."

Milton clenched his jaw. *I would rather not be picked.* "It makes sense, since my mother is still in Birmingham." Milton walked at a slower pace to let Earnest catch his breath.

"That's not the only reason. When I talked to Mr. Washington, he said that he had already selected a group of exceptional students to attend. You are exceptional. Not me."

"Not true. You simply asked too late, and all the slots were full," Milton said, patting him on the shoulder. "You would have been chosen had you talked to him right after chapel." If Milton had known Earnest wanted to go, he would have offered him his spot immediately.

"Picked over the Magic Man? I doubt it." Earnest rubbed the back of his neck. "You are an exceptional student, Milton. And a good person. You deserve to go."

A tendril of discomfort wrapped around Milton's heart. "Thank you. But hold your praise. We've got agriculture class now."

Earnest clapped him on the back and laughed. "You excel even in that. No one has killed as many plants as you have."

Milton let out a long exhale.

Unfortunately, class went exactly as Milton suspected it would. He misidentified two plants and fed too much bonemeal to another. Mr. George Washington Carver, their instructor, gave him a sad look and shook his head. "Unexpected for a nursing student, Mr. Rafferty. You and plants do not get on."

Milton set the overfed plant aside. "No, we do not."

Class ended, and Earnest, who was far better at plants than Milton, let out a low whistle. "Well, will you look at that."

Milton did look.

Miss Bevard strolled across the lawn. She held herself like royalty, her hair braided around her head like a crown. Milton gawked.

"Since you would not go to her, she has come to you," Earnest teased.

Milton gave him a light shove. "It's just as probable she came for you. She likely has other business here. She is a student, after all."

"Uh-huh." Earnest picked up his satchel.

Miss Bevard walked past the students and went straight to Mr. Carver. Milton tipped his head. Mr. Washington hadn't told them who was going on the trip, but now he wondered if Miss Bevard would be in the party. She seemed to be an exceptional student.

She said something to Mr. Carver. Then Mr. Carver looked right at him and called his name. Milton blinked.

Earnest clapped him on the back. "Guess she is here for you."

Milton picked up his books. *What can she want with me?*

Lealia arrived at the field where the agriculture classes were held. She knew this part of campus well. It was her favorite refuge from a day of study. The fields were a comfort to her, reminding her of home. She had been tilling and toiling long before she'd come to the school.

Mr. Carver, the head of agriculture, had just dismissed the class when she approached. The students, all male, were collecting their things.

Mr. Carver smiled at her. "Miss Bevard. The class is over."

Lealia laughed. "I didn't come for class. Mrs. Robinson sent me to speak to Mr. Rafferty."

"Oh, you're just in time." Mr. Carver turned to the group. "Mr. Rafferty," he called out.

Mr. Rafferty startled, and a look of surprise crossed his face. The man standing near him broke out in a grin. Lealia straightened her spine to keep from squirming. It almost seemed they had been discussing her before Mr. Carver beckoned Mr. Rafferty over.

Mr. Rafferty picked up his bag and made his way to where she and Mr. Carver stood, eyeing Lealia all the way. Again, Mr. Rafferty gave her a very frank and open appraisal, his eyes flicking from her hair to her boots. *Does he know how unnerving that is?* Especially since his gaze held no malice or any other emotion but curiosity. Figuring her out. She felt that he could see all her secrets and fears.

Mr. Rafferty stopped in front of them. "Yes, Mr. Carver?" he asked, although his gaze again drifted to Lealia.

"Mrs. Robinson instructed Miss Bevard to speak to you." Mr. Carver motioned to Lealia. "Have you two met?"

"No, but I did hear Mr. Washington congratulate her in chapel last night," Mr. Rafferty said, giving her an approving look. The sun caught his deep brown eyes.

Oh my. Since she first arrived at Tuskegee, she had noticed that the men on campus had hard expressions. Not surprising when one considered their backgrounds. Many of them came from poverty and lack and were desperately clinging to the hope that getting an education would make their lives better. Their expressions were weary and closed.

But not Mr. Rafferty. Beyond his curiosity that did not seem like nosiness, he had a warmth in his face and his eyes. He must not have suffered the same hardships the other male students had. She avoided looking into his eyes by focusing on the top button of his shirt.

Mr. Carver began collecting his tools. "Very well. Always good to see you, Miss Bevard. Until next class, Mr. Rafferty."

After Mr. Carver had moved away, Mr. Rafferty leaned over a little to meet Lealia's eyes. "How can I help you?"

"Uh. . ." she began, her voice squeaking a little. "I'm heading to Birmingham, and Mrs. Robinson said you may be able to advise me on my trip."

His expression closed so fast Lealia almost expected to hear it snap. "Are you joining us?"

"Us?"

"The group of students attending the speech with Mr. Washington."

She cleared her throat. "No, but I am attending the National Baptist Convention. Mrs. Robinson said your mother might have a room at her house and that other lodging might be hard to find."

He shifted his bag to his other hand. "My mother wrote and said all the inns are full and delegates are staying in the homes of Shiloh members."

"I know. One member of Shiloh I know is taking in three lodgers, and she said others are doing the same."

His normal quizzical look turned even more questioning. "You know members of Shiloh?"

The question ended sharp, emphasis on *Shiloh*. "Yes, I lived in Birmingham before my family and I moved to Tuskegee."

Mr. Rafferty looked above her head at the trees. "Did you attend Shiloh?"

Lealia straightened. "Are these questions a requirement for lodging at your mother's house, or are you just nosy?"

He leaned back, his eyes narrowed. "Am I not allowed to ask questions?"

"Absolutely. Questions pertaining to my staying at your mother's home." She gave him an over-cheery smile. "Unless attending Shiloh gets me the room."

Mr. Rafferty's mood changed as quickly, like thick clouds building before a storm. "I have already written to my mother at Mr. Washington's request. I will inform you when I have more information."

Lealia shifted her weight from foot to foot and lifted her chin. "I expect to hear from you soon."

"You do? You're very confident," he said in a tone that left her wondering whether he was complimenting her or insulting her.

"Again, is there something wrong with that?"

He thought for a moment, chewing on the corner of his lip. "Nothing wrong with confidence, but too much of it is off-putting."

Anger heated her face and scalp. "Are you saying I am off-putting?" Her thoughts flashed back to her dormmates laughing at her.

He gazed at her for a full moment, that curious gaze looking past her anger and injured pride. He inhaled and said, "Yes."

Now her anger was full-blown, but Mr. Rafferty turned away. "I must get to my next class." He trotted across the field in the direction of Cassedy Hall before she could get in another word.

Mr. Carver stepped to her side. "Shouldn't you be heading to class as well?"

"I'm taking a break from classes."

Mr. Carver frowned. "Is all well?"

Lealia smiled. Mr. Carver understood that nothing but trouble could keep her from class. She'd not missed many classes, and the only time she'd been absent for a longer period was when her mother fell ill at harvesttime and she'd gone home to help in the fields.

"Yes. I am heading to Birmingham."

"Oh, for the speech?"

She shook her head and told him about the opportunity with the Education Board.

He broke into a grin. "That's wonderful. You are one of the few students I know who is suited for both vocational and classical education. Although I will be sad to see you go. Who will I recruit to do soil testing when you're gone?"

"You have lots of students. Mr. Rafferty seems like he could benefit from studying under you." She was proud that she managed to keep her voice level. Maybe Mr. Carver could teach him that confidence was not off-putting and it was not possible to have too much of it.

"Mr. Rafferty is a good person, but I would not trust him with my plants." Mr. Carver chuckled. He patted her shoulder. "Good luck, and I plan to see you at Howard next time I visit."

"Thank you, Mr. Carver."

She left, going the opposite direction of Mr. Rafferty, but she looked back at him walking across the field with his classmate. Mr. Rafferty was another person who seemed to have a problem with her and her plans to head to Birmingham. If she ended up not needing his help, she would never speak to him again. He would be here at Tuskegee, and she would be at Howard.

CHAPTER THREE

Lealia awoke at dawn almost as tired as she was when she'd gone to bed. She lay in her bed, staring at the ceiling and listening to her father moving quietly about. He would be in the fields soon, before the day got too hot.

She had arrived home yesterday by catching a ride with a kindly delivery man heading in the direction of her house. He'd even lifted her trunks onto the bed of the truck. Her parents had been so happy when she told them the news.

Supper felt more like a celebration than a separation. They'd lingered over dinner, talking and making plans.

"Maybe once you graduate from Howard, you and your brother can earn enough to get your ma and me off this land," Pa had said, beaming.

Lealia had sobered. "Of course. I'm sure Nathan would have done it by now if he could."

"We know he works hard, and we appreciate the little money he sends." The pride in Mama's words was evident.

Little money. Lealia had hidden her dismay at the small amount under her smile. Mama always had an excuse for it, saying how much more expensive it was for Nathan to live in the North compared to Birmingham. True, but it nagged her that her parents had sacrificed so much and still had so little.

When the talk returned to her trip, she'd told her parents how she still had not secured lodging.

"It's a good thing we kept in touch with Shiloh," her mother said. "We should ask one of them to help with the lodging."

"I had a letter from Mrs. Walden, and she said all the members' homes are full. There is someone at Tuskegee who is helping me with that. His mother still lives there. He said she may have an empty room at her house." As Lealia spoke, Mr. Rafferty's curious expression and his "off-putting" comment filled her mind.

"He?" Her father lifted an eyebrow. His reaction to Mr. Rafferty made her realize that she had not considered a relationship since she'd gone to school. She would not start thinking of one now with Mr. Rafferty.

Lealia patted her father's arm. "Mr. Rafferty. He studies at Tuskegee in the nursing program."

"How come we haven't heard about Mr. Rafferty before?" The corners of her father's lips tugged at the beginning of a smile.

"Because he is just another student at the school." Just another student. Yes, she'd thought him handsome at first. Thought maybe they could be friends.

"Rafferty. That name sounds familiar," Mama said.

But the conversation had drifted away from Mr. Rafferty and on to preparations for her trip.

Maybe once you graduate from Howard, you and your brother can earn enough to get your ma and me off this land.

Her father's words had resounded in her mind all night.

She very much wanted to get them into a place where they did not have to work so much. Nathan was supposed to get Pa off the land. Nathan was supposed to achieve great levels of success and make lots of money. He hadn't yet done that. What if she failed too? What if her journey to Howard took a longer road than Nathan's and her parents spent their older years working the land? And without her or Nathan nearby to help. What if their lives ended without them ever being free from the hard labor they had endured their whole lives?

No. She hopped out of bed. Her journey would not be like Nathan's. She was going to help her parents by getting an education.

But a small nagging voice continued the conversation. *How?* She tried to answer, but she couldn't guarantee anything beyond getting into Howard. The world at Tuskegee seemed so full of promise. But back here on the land, the view was much darker and leaner. Hope was less abundant here. She had noticed it when she first arrived home, but now, when she was rising before dawn to help in the field, hopelessness threatened to overwhelm her.

And then there was Nathan. He had accomplished what she was working toward. He'd gone to Howard. He'd become a lawyer. Or at least had gotten the education to be one. He was, in every way, exactly what Mr. Du Bois said leaders of the race would be, but the only advantage he seemed to have over others was that he had papers. Nathan had followed that path and was now only an underpaid law clerk. Would her path be the same?

She shook off the weighty thoughts and got dressed. Thankfully, she fell into a practiced rhythm in the fields, her hands working from memory. The work was not as hard as she remembered, and she knew why. The work at Tuskegee had conditioned her to work hard in a different way. In the fields, she could work and let her mind drift. At Tuskegee, she had to focus. If she daydreamed like this in her woodworking classes, it would end with disaster or injury.

They finished the first part of the day's work and returned to the house for lunch. Just as they finished eating, a knock sounded on the front door. Her father rose to answer it.

Lealia lifted a stack of plates from the table and heard a familiar voice come from the now-open front door.

"Hello, sir. My name is Mr. Rafferty. I am a student at Tuskegee and was wondering if Miss Bevard is here."

Her father glanced over his shoulder, giving Lealia a quizzical look.

"Remember I told you about Mr. Rafferty yesterday, Pa?" *And what is he doing here?* Embarrassment colored her cheeks. Having Mr. Rafferty here in their meager household, with his curious eyes, unsettled her.

Her father stepped aside, and Mr. Rafferty entered the house, nervousness coloring his features.

"What business do you have with my girl?" Her father crossed his massive arms across his chest.

Mr. Rafferty stood up straighter. "Sir—" His gaze flicked to Lealia. His eyes pleaded with her.

"Pa," Lealia said, adding a playfully scolding tone to her voice, "he's helping me with lodging in Birmingham, like I told you yesterday."

"At his house?" her father said. Milton shifted like he would run.

But it was her mother who broke the tension. "Milton Rafferty?"

Mr. Rafferty frowned. "Yes, ma'am."

"Is your mother Augusta?" Her mother was smiling now.

Mr. Rafferty's frown, however, deepened. "Yes, ma'am," he said.

Her mother clapped her hands and laughed. "You come in here actin' like a stranger. Don't you remember me? You surely sat next to me enough times in church."

"I—" Milton began.

"At Shiloh," her mother said with a tsk. "We attended Shiloh in Birmingham. You and your mother attended as well."

Mr. Rafferty's eyes widened, and he leaned back as if her mother had struck him. His eyes whipped to Lealia. "That's where I know you from."

Mama laid a hand on Lealia's shoulder. "Milton and his mother were good friends when we were in Birmingham. Milton used to run errands for me once Nathan went to school. How are you?"

Lealia stepped back, searching her memory. She did remember playing with a little boy who attended church with them, but her memories were hazy. Hiding under a bench to avoid having to go to Sunday school. Sliding down the center aisle of the church after the floor had been polished. Eating peaches from the tree outside.

"I do remember you," she said with a smile.

But Mr. Rafferty was not smiling. "I remember you too."

Her mother continued to fawn over Mr. Rafferty, but he grew more withdrawn by the minute. Lealia remembered that he'd had the same reaction when he asked her about being a member of Shiloh. What did he have against the church?

Milton cleared his throat and tried to fix his face, but he felt his mask slipping the longer Mrs. Bevard talked. He would have left except for the letter in his pocket from his mother. He exhaled. The letter was going to make things worse.

He had taken the chance in coming here to let Miss Bevard know that his mother had found a room for her at the home of one of her friends. She had also told him that no delegates were staying at their house, so they could enjoy their time together without interruptions. Milton could feel the sting of her words. Apparently, no one who had written to Miss Bevard had mentioned that his mother had an empty room. . .no, two empty rooms since no one expected Milton to be home.

Not only would it have helped the delegates that would soon flood Birmingham, it also would have helped his mother, since most of the delegates were willing to pay for lodging. At least he could prepare himself that nothing had changed. The members of Shiloh Baptist Church still held a grudge against his family. Four years later, and the black mark on his family name was still there.

And now he was standing in the home of former Shiloh members. Members who probably forced his mother to send him out of town.

He wished he had figured out who Miss Bevard was sooner, because he would have never offered to help her find lodging. His mother had already made it clear that he would be responsible for getting Miss Bevard around Birmingham. Now he wished he had not agreed so readily.

"Come sit down, Milton." Mrs. Bevard grabbed his hand and led him to the table. "Have you had lunch? How did you get here?"

"I walked, ma'am," he said, trying and failing to get his bearings.

"Oh, then you must be hungry." Mrs. Bevard turned to her daughter. "Lealia, get Mr. Rafferty some food and drink."

Mrs. Bevard beamed at him. "Tell me all about Birmingham. We've lost touch with so many of the people there. It's nice to ask someone who has more recent information than we do."

Milton shifted in his seat. "I can only share secondhand information my mother has written me."

Mrs. Bevard grinned. "Then we can compare notes." And they did, spending the time it took for Lealia to reheat some food talking about Birmingham and Shiloh. They talked about the new church clerk, Rodah. The growth of the church and the new sanctuary. New businesses in town, like Mr. Stokes' dry goods store. Mrs. Bevard beamed when he told her about the new Negro schools that had opened.

"That's what we need. More education," Mr. Bevard said, slapping his hand on his knee. "The only way out of all this work is education."

Milton folded his hands in his lap. "Education is an important part, but I do not believe it is the only part. We also need to be able to work and take care of our practical needs."

Miss Bevard set a plate of food in front of him. "So I see you believe Mr. Washington's philosophy when it comes to upward mobility of the race. I disagree, and so do my parents. That's why they've worked to send my brother Nathan to Howard, and I will be attending there too. I take Mr. Du Bois' side."

Milton leaned back and frowned at her. "Side? I am not taking anyone's side. After being at Tuskegee, I see that both philosophies are right. It just depends on the person."

"So you are satisfied to work hard all your life?" Mrs. Bevard asked. Her tone was not hostile but curious.

"Tell me how anyone in any field can avoid hard work," he said, leaning forward. "What does your son do?"

Mr. Bevard answered. "He's a law clerk."

"Sir," Milton said, quietly, "does your son not work hard?"

"Sure he does, but not like this." Mr. Bevard waved his hand toward the field.

"But with the discoveries Mr. Carver is making, your work could be easier," Milton said as he turned his attention to Lealia. "No, I don't mind working hard for the rest of my life, because there is honor in it and in being able to take care of my mother." His anger had loosened his tongue. He had not meant to mention his mother. He took a deep breath.

"You are mighty spirited about this topic," Mr. Bevard said with a chuckle. "Eat your food. All that passion works up an appetite."

As he ate, Miss Bevard sat across from him, studying him while chatting with her parents. Now, knowing she and her family were members of Shiloh, he noticed that her face had not changed much from what he remembered. She still had her wide eyes and bright smile. Once Mrs. Bevard had solved the mystery of her familiarity, his memories of Miss Bevard. . .Lealia. . .came back sharp and clear.

Happy memories.

Mostly that the two of them were almost always in trouble. Not because they were mischievous. More because they were curious. They never passed up an opportunity to figure out how something worked.

Or doing what they didn't realize at the time were scientific experiments. Exploring the church grounds for bugs and plants.

He remembered that Lealia was as fearless as she was funny. Unlike the other little girls at Shiloh, she wasn't afraid of getting her dress dirty gathering worms. She never backed down when he challenged her to a tree-climbing race. Even when she fell and skinned her knee, she walked with her head held high, tears in her eyes, to her mother for help.

She could always be counted on to be the first person to giggle when something funny happened. Bright, energetic, and fun-loving. He also remembered how the pastor of Shiloh had proudly read a letter from their "daughter" who would be starting at Tuskegee. He remembered all the members being so proud of her and how they were helping her with a donation to college. Sending money to her but not bothering to help his mother and him when they knew his father had spent all his paycheck on drink.

He almost wished he hadn't figured out who she was. He would have liked to rekindle their friendship for their remaining time at Tuskegee, but everything connected with Shiloh still stung. Even what little happiness he had from his childhood friendship with Lealia had evaporated. He was a kid then. He had no idea how fragile happiness was.

After he finished eating under the watchful eye of Mr. Bevard, he stood. "I must get back to the school, but I wanted to let Miss Bevard know that my mother found a room for her with some family friends." The Primm family were some of the few people who supported his mother after his father left. They had even sent goods and food to Milton at Tuskegee during his second year.

She beamed. "Thank you, Mr. Rafferty."

Her mother waved a hand. "So formal. You two were closer than two cows at a trough. You can call him Milton."

If he wasn't mistaken, Lealia blushed. Maybe he did too. Mrs. Bevard was right. They were, after all, peers. But something about calling her Lealia made his face heat.

She looked down at her hands. "Thank you, Milton."

"Mrs. Lenard, our drawing teacher, will be staying with the same family as you. She is a delegate from the Baptist church in town," he said, extremely aware of Lealia's papa's intense stare. "You can send a note to Tuskegee for me with your arrival times. I'll meet you at the Birmingham train station."

Lealia thanked him and gave him a wide smile. One he would have basked in before he knew who she was. He had been ready to guarantee Lealia a room at his mother's house. Thank goodness he had not.

Milton stepped off the train behind Mr. Washington and the other students in the Birmingham train station. His heart felt like he had never left. Yes, the train station had expanded and had been painted, but it was still the place where he had stood with his mother four years ago. A knot formed in his stomach. He was back here earlier than he wanted and for longer than he wanted.

After everyone collected their baggage, Milton helped Mr. Washington and the other students arrange for a wagon to take them to their lodging. They had taken the first train out of Tuskegee that morning, as Mr. Washington had additional business to take care of while he was in town.

"What about you, Mr. Rafferty? Maybe we can drop you off at home?" Mr. Washington asked as he climbed into the wagon.

"No, sir. I live very close. I can walk. Besides, you'll want to get settled to prepare for your speech."

Mr. Washington nodded. "Very well. See you tomorrow."

Milton lifted his luggage and started the trek to his mother's house. The changes in Birmingham became more evident as he walked. Downtown had its first skyscraper. He studied the architecture as he passed. It was nothing like the rows of low brick buildings on the rest of the block. As he approached 19th Street, his steps slowed.

His mother had told him about the construction of the new Shiloh Baptist Church in her letters. Had described it in great detail, down to the color of the bricks. Still, the sight of the church took his breath away.

It was far larger than the old clapboard building. It sat on an elevated platform and, with its prominent stained-glass windows, resembled a cathedral more than a church. The size, however, stoked his amazement the most. Mom had told him that the church could seat three thousand people, and he had struggled to believe it. She'd said this was the largest Negro church in the country, built entirely by Negroes. She'd said there were balconies inside. *I will see them soon enough.*

His anger boiled. Look how far they had come. This building and Lealia were proof that Shiloh could accomplish great things. However, the other side of the coin was also true. They could inflict hurt as well. They had wounded his family and moved on like it was nothing. He increased his steps, eager to see his mother.

He turned the corner, and the small house where he had grown up came into view.

Home. His mother had kept it well, although some of the paint was peeling and there was a small hole in the front-door screen. His heart weighed heavy in his chest. As much as he believed he had settled things, the conflict of his childhood came roaring back. This was a place of his mother's love and his father's abandonment.

Straightening his shoulders, he climbed the stairs and knocked on the door. He heard his mother moving inside and called out, "Ma, it's me. Milton."

In less time than he thought she could have reached it, the door swung open and his mother, who had visibly aged, stood on the threshold. She wore a wide smile on her tired face. Her welcome was big, warm, and loud.

"Milton!" She threw her arms around him. Tears sprang to his eyes, and he felt her shoulders hitch with sobs. He hadn't realized how much he'd missed her.

"Hi, Ma," he murmured into her shoulder, remembering the last time they had embraced like this. Very different now, with very different tears.

She stepped back, studying him from head to foot. "Oh, look how tall and handsome you've grown. You could have passed me on the street, and I wouldn't have recognized you."

Milton laughed, wiping the tears from his cheeks. "Yes, you would have. You would've known your son anywhere."

She took a deep breath and sighed. "I've missed you so much, Milton."

"I've missed you too."

Then she went into a flurry of activity. She pulled him inside so quickly he almost didn't have time to grab his bag. "Put your things down. I cooked. Do you want to freshen up? How was the train ride?" She said all this without stopping—and seemingly without taking a breath.

"Slow down, Ma," he said with a laugh. "I'll be in Birmingham until Sunday. We have plenty of time."

She gave him a sad look. "Not enough time for me." He moved to embrace her again, but she waved him away. "Take your things to your room."

He climbed the steps, warmth and familiarity cocooning him, although the house seemed smaller. It had not grown with him. It also held the same fear and anger. The last time he was here, they'd been afraid. Afraid of what the future held. Afraid of the anger of the church members.

His father had left town before they could extinguish the fire at the old 6th Avenue location. He had given them little reason and little warning. He'd just said that he had to leave.

His mother had screamed, "Leave? Where are you going?"

"Away from here," his father replied. He'd gone to the bedroom he shared with Milton's mother and pulled out a travel case.

Milton had stood in the doorway, tears blurring the scene in front of him, listening to his parents argue. Even then, he didn't have the best relationship with his father. The pain in his mother's voice had cut through his heart like a scythe. After he had packed, his father carried his bag to the door and then stopped to stand in front of Milton.

He looked Milton in the eye. "You will have to be the man of the house now."

Anger flared, and Milton clenched his fist. "No, that's your job, whether you stay or go."

His father had blinked, surely not expecting Milton's response. But still he left. Left his mother to take care of him and make do on the little they had left.

Milton exhaled. Things would be better for his mother if Shiloh had not taken their wrath at the father out on the son.

Things would be better if his father had been a different man.

CHAPTER FOUR

Nothing could have prepared Lealia for her arrival in Birmingham. She knew it wouldn't be the same as it was when she left as a little girl. Her memories had grown fuzzy, like a dream. When the train stopped in Birmingham, she felt as if the world had expanded to a size she was unable to grasp. It seemed that there were more people in the station than there were in the whole student body at Tuskegee.

Trains whistled and rumbled, and people called to one another, moving around Lealia as she waited for Mrs. Lenard to climb down. She followed Mrs. Lenard to the end of the platform, weaving between other passengers, and then spotted Mr. Rafferty. Milton. He stood with another man who was shorter and stouter. He and Milton chatted animatedly. Milton's movements made Lealia smile before she could catch herself. He had always struck her as a very serious, thoughtful person. He had been quite intense at her parents' table as he talked about work. Now he was smiling and laughing with the man beside him.

Something else struck her as she got closer. Milton's ease now was different than the tension he seemed to carry at Tuskegee. He seemed happier. Likely because he was home again with his mother. It was clear that he loved her deeply.

But his seriousness had not completely vanished. Every few seconds, he scanned the crowd. Lealia's stomach did a small flutter. He was looking for her. *Stop. He's supposed to be looking for you.*

But once he spotted her, the flutter screeched to a halt. His smile dimmed, and his demeanor sobered. Lealia let out a huff. When Milton was at her house, she'd seen him undergo the same transformation. He'd been much friendlier when he first arrived. She tried to understand what had changed. It seemed he would be more friendly knowing her family had also been members of Shiloh, not less. Shiloh was a warm and friendly congregation. Her mother had once told her that Lealia had been everyone's favorite baby, that all the women had wanted to hold her during services. She'd been the church's baby.

She remembered Milton being a typical boy. No matter how she searched her memory, she couldn't find any reason she and Milton stopped being friends other than she moved away. Maybe she could find out what happened to Milton at Shiloh while she was here in Birmingham. She could try to be his friend now. . . She reined her thoughts in. There was no point when she would be going to Howard, not back to Tuskegee.

With a wooden smile on his face, Milton moved forward. "You made it safely," he said as he easily took both their bags. "This is Mr. Primm."

Mr. Primm's greeting was much warmer than Milton's. "Hello, ladies. My wagon's this way."

As they moved through the crowd, a small brown boy selling *The Birmingham Age-Herald* cried above the din. She handed the boy a penny. After she read the newspaper, she would send it to her parents. They would be as fascinated as she was with the growth of Birmingham.

"Must be the National Convention delegates," Mrs. Lenard called over her shoulder.

"Yes. Some came in last night, and there'll probably be more tomorrow," Milton said as they broke through the crowd.

"Is this normal?" Lealia asked. Baptist Conventions were important events of worship, education, and organization. She had never seen this many people in one place outside Tuskegee. And this was only the train station.

The train had been crowded too. Mrs. Lenard had told her that this was unusual. The train was all abuzz about the Wizard of Tuskegee coming to speak in Birmingham. Not all the talk, however, was positive. There was still deep hurt in the Negro community surrounding a speech he'd given in Atlanta seven years ago. It was later called the Atlanta Compromise because many thought Mr. Washington intended to keep Negroes subject to the white men in the south. The anger at the perceived degrading of the Negro had lasted years.

Lealia's years at the school had changed her opinion about Mr. Washington's speech. She could see her parents' and Nathan's position, but she could now understand Mr. Washington's. There was no way to survive in the south without some kind of positive relationship with the whites. Those living in the community had done much to support the school. Mr. Washington promoted the idea that upward Negro mobility also included friendship with the white race. He had proven that with the school he built. A school uplifting Negro students and training them to help the community around them.

That friendship had worked. Maybe she could try and be on friendly terms with Milton while she was here.

Mr. Primm lived only a short distance from the train station, but he took the wagon down 19th Street to show Lealia and Mrs. Lenard the site where the convention would be held. Lealia gasped when she saw it. It was the largest church building she had ever seen. Very different from the two-room building Shiloh used to congregate in before the fire.

It sat on a slight rise with stone stairs leading up to the front door. Two steeples sat atop the church, and windows decorated the front of the building. Two rows of windows circled the church. Lealia shielded her eyes to take it all in.

From the corner of her eye, she saw Milton watching her. When she met his eyes, he tipped his head toward the church. "Your Shiloh."

Lealia heard the sour note in his words but was so in awe of the building she lacked the words to respond. It was magnificent. Pride for the Shiloh members swelled in her chest. They had always been generous in their giving. The grandeur of the church suggested they'd reaped what they sowed. She turned in the wagon to watch the church as they drove away, not taking her eyes from it until it was out of sight.

They arrived at the Primm house, and Mrs. Primm, a round, happy-faced woman, met them warmly at the front door. "Welcome. We're honored to have you here."

Milton helped Lealia climb from the wagon. His grip was firm and warm. Polite and nothing more. Lealia straightened her hat once she was down, pushing the feel of his strong fingers from her mind. She would not give him any more notice than needed.

Mrs. Primm gave Milton a very warm hug and a kiss on the cheek. "Good to see you again, Milton."

Mr. Primm patted Milton on the back. "Our boy is all grown up. A man now."

Lealia watched Milton accept the Primms' praise, and he seemed to loosen up again. "It's been four years."

After introductions were made, Milton stepped back. "I'll be going now. My mother is expecting me for dinner."

Mrs. Primm grinned. "Give her my love."

"I will," he said, smiling. He forgot to turn that engaging smile off when he turned to Lealia. "If you or Mrs. Lenard need anything, the Primms know how to reach me."

Lealia blinked, hoping he couldn't see her flushed face under the brim of her hat. "Thank you."

She wanted to watch Milton as he walked down the street, but Mrs. Primm drew her and Mrs. Lenard inside and took them upstairs.

"Here is your room, Lealia." Mrs. Primm opened the door to reveal a small but well-appointed room. "Sorry, it's the best we can do." Mrs. Primm stood at the door, wringing her hands.

"This is very generous, and I appreciate it," Lealia said. "I had not realized that every room would be taken for the convention. I am very glad Milton"—she cleared her throat—"Mr. Rafferty spoke to you on our behalf."

"Milton was the sweetest boy. Always eager to help. It's good to see that his heart for people has remained unchanged. Even after—"

Lealia studied the woman. "Even after?"

"Well, I will only say that young man has had a hard start in life."

Lealia, curious now, gave Mrs. Primm an encouraging smile. She shouldn't care about Milton's history, but if Mrs. Primm was willing to tell it to her, Lealia would be willing to listen. "I suspect many of our race would say the same."

"Yes, but Milton's problems were not of his own making."

"I see. Still, that can also be said of much of our race."

Mrs. Primm smiled, and Lealia could see that the woman would reveal no more. "Yes, very true. Like all of us, Milton has overcome. Get settled in, and I will collect you for dinner shortly."

Once the door closed, Lealia took off her hat and sat on the edge of the bed. The window afforded a view of row after row of corn. The newspaper she'd purchased lay on the bed next to her. She picked it up, opened it, and skimmed the first few pages. Her eyes slowed at a story about a fire. She folded the page back, leaning forward.

> *Authorities continue to investigate the fire at Stokes' Dry Goods. The owner, Alfred Stokes, believes that the fire is the work of an arsonist. Mr. Stokes states that his store will reopen as soon as he receives the insurance payout. He added that his business has proudly served the Negro population of Birmingham for years and he looks forward to serving them again.*

Lealia set the paper aside. She remembered Mrs. Walden's letters mentioning the Negro-owned dry goods store in town. Too bad it had burned down. If the store did that much good, it would be a shame if it was not rebuilt.

There were so many new Negro businesses in Tennessee since Reconstruction. Of course, many of the newly freed had returned to familiar work in sharecropping, but other businesses had opened as well. Shoemakers, banks, insurance companies. Even the new pastor of Shiloh owned a brickyard.

Her thoughts drifted to her fellow students at Tuskegee. Negro-owned businesses would continue to increase with the skill-based instruction they received at Tuskegee. That was one of Mr. Washington's goals: to cultivate skilled students who could contribute to the rebuilding of war-destroyed economies.

But since Mr. Washington had a plan to rebuild the communities, and he had plenty of students to do it with, she would take another track and be an example of how higher education could also rebuild communities.

It had been many days since Milton had smiled this much.

His mother had indeed cooked a feast for him. The table was spread when he got back from escorting Lealia and Mrs. Lenard to the Primms' home.

Lealia was still as pretty as ever, if a little overwhelmed at Birmingham. Today, she had worn a hat pulled down low over her eyes. So when she had looked up to speak to him, her beautiful brown eyes and smile appeared like a sunrise. He'd had to glance away a few times to collect himself before he responded to what she was saying.

But as they got closer to the church, he remembered that Lealia was loved by Shiloh. Not her fault, but they chose her over him. Nothing about her life seemed extremely difficult or challenging. They had named her their "daughter" and left their son to fend for himself. He had been angry, at who exactly he couldn't tell, until they reached the Primms' house and Lealia put her small, strong hand in his as he helped her down from the wagon. Of course she was strong. She performed the same work at Tuskegee that he did.

His mother leaned forward into his view. "What are you pondering?"

He debated responding for a moment. "Do you remember the Bevard family from Shiloh?" He watched her face closely.

It brightened into a smile. "Yes! They had two children, Nathan and Lealia. Lealia was cute as a little doll but fierce as one of the boys. You and she used to cut up something terrible in church."

Milton hid his surprise that his mother had any positive memories of the people at Shiloh. "Lealia is one of the women staying at the Primms."

His mother clapped her hands. "Why didn't you tell me? I would love to see her."

"You will likely see her at the services. She has a meeting with the Education Board to get a scholarship to leave Tuskegee and go to Howard."

"I thought I heard that her brother went there."

"Yes. Her parents told me that when I had lunch at her house."

His mother grinned wider. "You had lunch at her house?"

"Not you too," he groaned, remembering his classmates' ribbing. "Yes, I went to let her know about the room. I met her parents while I was there."

"Hardworking family," Mom said with a sigh. "Most of the members only had two pennies to rub together, but we could make something out of nothing. Alberta was a good cook, and we enjoyed anything she brought to Sunday dinners."

Milton thought of the plate of food Lealia had given him. "That seems to still be the case."

"Is Lealia as pretty as she was as a child?" Mom asked just as he was taking a sip of water.

He swallowed too quickly and choked.

His mother patted him on the back, laughing the whole time. "Then she must be lovely."

Once he caught his breath, he frowned at her. "She is pretty, but she—" He stopped when he saw the expectant look in his mother's eyes. Lealia was borderline arrogant, and the only thing that made it tolerable was that she actually had the skills and intelligence to back up her ego. "She's excited about going to Howard." That should dim his mother's prodding.

And it did. Mom reluctantly changed the subject and caught him up on the happenings around Birmingham.

"Do you remember when I wrote you about Mr. Stokes being so kind to me?"

His mother had written Milton an entire tearstained letter about what Mr. Stokes had done for her. Mom had been sick and missed a few days of work. That meant she lacked the money for food. Mr. Stokes had let her purchase food on credit and then "forgot" about the debt when Mom went back to pay.

"Yes, I remember."

"His store burned down," she said, the sadness in her voice catching him off guard.

"That's terrible. How?"

"No one knows. The fire department said it looked like arson." Mom wrung her hands in her lap. "I'll confess, my first thought was that your father had come back to town."

Milton swallowed. "Did someone accuse him?"

"Not directly." Her shoulders slumped. "It did start all the talk again. I felt bad because everyone was talking about my rotten husband and not Mr. Stokes' loss. He was so kind to so many in town."

Milton curled his fingers into a fist. "So our name will immediately be attached to every fire in town?"

Mom reached over, placed her hand on his, and worked her fingers to loosen his grip. Then she clasped his hand. "You're still too angry, Milton. You have to forgive and leave it in the past."

"I'm still angry because we are still suffering."

"You can't change other people's fears, Milton. But you can change yours."

He took a deep breath. "I cannot accept that all these years have passed and they're still afraid of our family. Papa has been gone for years."

"Forgive me. Let me say this a different way." Mom squeezed his hand. "When unexpected things happen, people want an explanation to help them feel safe. Blaming your father gives them a sense of security. And it lets them feel morally superior. They can feel good about themselves because they believe they're not as bad as your father."

"That's not fear. That's cruelty."

"People who are afraid can sometimes act in very cruel ways."

"So does that mean my father was afraid?"

She dropped her head. "I believe he was."

Milton pulled his hand away. "What did he have to be afraid of? We weren't yelling at him. He didn't have to hide from us. We hid from him."

"He was afraid of failing as a husband and a father," she said with a sigh. "I can see it more clearly now that he's gone."

Milton gaped at her. Did she truly believe that?

"That was one of the reasons I worked so hard to pay your tuition at Tuskegee. So you would succeed. So you wouldn't become cruel," she said quietly.

All of Milton's anger evaporated. He had suffered from his father's bad behavior, but his mother had suffered more. Week after week, she had faced the people who said negative things about their family, but she never lost her faith. She never stopped being faithful to church and giving to those in need.

He had escaped to Tuskegee. He had no right to be angry if she was not. The realization didn't erase his feelings, but it did cool them a little.

He asked her about the preparations for the convention. As she began to talk, he realized he would get no comfort from this subject either. She spoke of Shiloh as a tight-knit congregation, not people who judged her for what her husband had done.

She stopped speaking and shook her head. "Now, Milton."

"I didn't say anything," he said, shifting in his chair.

"You didn't have to. Your expression says it all."

"It's hard listening to you talk so warmly about Shiloh," he said. "After everything."

She laughed. "Shiloh is a different church now. The sanctuary holds three thousand people, and we have at least half that in regular attendees. Most of the old members from 6th Avenue have moved on. We even have a new pastor. And Mr. Stokes is a member of Shiloh."

"I didn't consider that."

"Give them a chance is all I ask." His mother reached across the table and grasped his hand again. "I am so proud of you. You've turned into quite a wonderful young man."

"I have you to thank. I couldn't have done this if you hadn't worked so hard to pay my tuition."

She smiled, tears shimmering in her eyes. "It's my joy. Sometimes it's the only thing that keeps me going when I have to work two shifts."

Milton sighed. "I wish it could be easier for you."

"That was always your father's responsibility. Not yours."

Milton squeezed his mother's hand. "Have you heard from him?"

"No. After all this time, I don't expect to." She returned the squeeze. "I know you said you don't want to come back after you finish at Tuskegee, but are you sure? Things have changed around here."

"I'm sure," he said. He clenched his jaw. "Things have changed, but not truly. Once I graduate and make a little money, we can move north. You're all I care about here. You're the only family I have."

"I was hoping you'd meet someone at Tuskegee to start your own family with."

Lealia's face flashed through his mind. Not her. She was going to Howard with her lofty accomplishments in hopes of becoming a part of the Talented Tenth. There was no reason she wouldn't get there somehow. If she endeared herself to the Education Board like she had a whole church, she'd likely be heading north on the next train. Lealia was out of his reach in many ways.

He slid his glass across the tablecloth. "Not much time for meeting between classes."

"I had hoped that you would be ready to build a family of your own. No need to avoid marriage because of mine," she said with a snort.

Milton laughed. "I'm not avoiding it. I truly haven't met anyone. I want to be sure and make a good choice."

She patted his hand. "Smart man."

Lealia was surprised to see that there were already people gathering around Shiloh when she arrived for her meeting with the Education Board. Likely hoping to get a seat for Mr. Washington's speech as soon as the doors opened. The speech would not begin for another hour.

She climbed the steps and saw a pretty young woman waiting by the doors.

"Are you Lealia Bevard?" the woman asked.

"Yes, I am."

"Hi, I'm Rodah."

"Rodah, the new church clerk?"

Rodah's eyes widened. "You know who I am."

"Mrs. Walden wrote to me and told me about you."

"And I know who you are. Everyone has been talking about you." Rodah led her into the foyer.

Lealia had expected the inside of the church to be grand, but she was not prepared for how grand. Rodah led her through the sanctuary, and Lealia could do nothing but stare in awe. The pews were deep mahogany, as was the altar rail. The choir loft was elevated behind the pulpit. One small round and three arched stained-glass windows created dots of color on the pews. Three electric chandeliers hung over the center section of the sanctuary. "Wow."

"It's beautiful, isn't it?" Rodah slowed her steps so Lealia could take it all in.

"Yes."

"You attended the 6th Avenue church. This is much nicer."

They passed through a door to the right of the choir loft and into a long hallway. "You must be so excited to be going to Howard. I'm taking classes at Selma," Rodah said, excitement in her eyes. "Not as great as Tuskegee and Howard, but I'm on my way to getting a degree in arithmetic. I love math."

"Me too," Lealia said, the excitement in her voice matching Rodah's.

"Reverend Walker says that once I finish school, I can work here as the full-time church clerk. Right now, I'm only here part-time."

A flicker of uncertainty checked Lealia's smile. If she were in Rodah's situation, she would already be on her way to getting Mama and Pa off the land. She could help now if she had a part-time position. Rodah already had a job lined up after school. Lealia's mind drifted to what Milton had said to her parents. How he was working hard so he could be in the place to support his mother. Shouldn't Lealia be doing the same?

As they walked the hall, several Shiloh members greeted her. They remembered her and said they were amazed at how much she'd grown up. Her heart warmed. Then she thought of Milton again. He clearly did not like Shiloh or its members. Why? She would have to find out.

Rodah led her to a small room near the back of the church where the board was meeting.

"Godspeed. I know you'll do well," Rodah said as she opened the door.

"Thank you." Lealia resisted the urge to press her hand to her middle to stop her stomach from churning.

Inside what looked like a Sunday school classroom sat six men and four women who greeted her with smiles. The Education Board. All of them degree holders. All of them professionals. She sat down in a chair they had placed facing them, grateful to be off her wobbly legs. She nearly slumped but then remembered why she was there. What she needed to accomplish.

She straightened her spine and put on her best smile.

Her nervousness ended up being unwarranted. The people in front of her were dedicated to providing opportunities for Negroes seeking education. They asked very ordinary questions. About her family and the land. One of them, a Reverend Massey, asked her about her time at Shiloh. She was happy to tell them of the church's generosity.

They asked about her life at Tuskegee and her goals. They were particularly interested in her involvement with the farmers around the school. "You seem passionate about the Negro Conference that's held annually at Tuskegee," Mrs. West commented.

"It's an important program. Growing up on my papa's land, I saw how devastating crop failure or drought could be. Teaching at the Negro Conference, I'm able to share ways to diversify crops, identify good seed, and do soil adjustments. It's a way to help."

"We see that you enjoy it. Your expression lights up when you talk about it," another member, Mr. Wheaten, said with a laugh.

"It makes a big difference to people who have so little in means and education."

Then they asked her about her future goals at Howard. She talked about becoming a lawyer like her brother or going into nursing. As she talked, however, she could hear the difference in her excitement level. She talked about Howard like she was reading from a rehearsed script. But isn't this what she wanted?

Reverend Massey steepled his fingers. "You have such a diverse set of skills. You would make a wonderful teacher. Have you considered education or attending a normal school? That is likely the best place to use your skills. Let someone else go to Howard."

Lealia ground her teeth. She remembered her first teachers. They were always in great need, traveling from town to town, lodging with the families of their students. It was a hard living. *If he thinks I'm going to Selma, he's in for a surprise.* She sat up straighter. "Yes, I do have many skills, but I also have intelligence. I can use it to help uplift the race."

Mrs. West leaned forward in her chair. "You would like to be a part of the Talented Tenth? Even though you attend Tuskegee?"

"I attend Tuskegee because I've had no other opportunities." Lealia pushed her shoulders back. "But if I had the resources, I would choose differently. I believe this is a defining moment for our race and the development of our culture. This cannot be done with a vocational education alone." She made sure to stress *vocational.*

"I see," Reverend Hawks said. "We applaud your discipline and desire to further your education. Your accomplishments alone were enough to grant you a scholarship, but now that we have met you in person, we are even more convinced that you deserve any opportunity we can provide."

Joy, pride, and shock swelled in her heart. She had done it. She was going to Howard. "Thank you."

Mrs. West made a note on the paper in front of her. "We will inform you of the details after the convention concludes."

Lealia's chest hitched. The convention closed on Sunday. "After?"

"Yes. The pastors and the delegates will be bringing donations. Once we've collected them all, we'll better know how much assistance we can give you. We have a slight administration problem right now and need to clear that up first." Reverend Hawks smiled at her. "Once we tally our funds, we will send you the scholarship in November."

November? That was over a month away. "I understand. I will be in Birmingham for the duration of the convention."

"Good to hear," Reverend Hawks said. There was a shuffling around the room that signaled the meeting was over. Lealia rose, thanked the board, and managed to walk out of the room without crying.

The tears came once she reached a bench in an open garden next to the church. November. She had given up her room at Tuskegee. She hadn't considered a delay. Where would she stay until she received the scholarship money? Of course, her parents could help her, but it would be a burden. Or she could return to Tuskegee and work. Mr. Carver would find her a place in the agricultural department.

Then she chastised herself for crying. The Board had given her good news. This meeting, however, was supposed to end her toiling and the waiting. Now she had to wait another month for an answer from the Education Board.

She looked up and saw a man cross the street and walk toward the garden. She soon recognized Milton's frame and swiped her tears.

"Hello," he said as he approached the bench. He was dressed in a dark blue suit, different from the black suits the men were required to wear at Tuskegee.

"Hi, Milton." She stood and added as much cheer to her voice as she could.

"Is everything all right?"

"Yes," she said. His kind tone disarmed her. Every other time he'd spoken to her since she'd arrived his words had been clipped.

He peered down at her, his eyes searching hers as though he could discover the cause of her distress. "It sounds as if it's not."

"I got the scholarship to go to Howard."

Milton's face brightened. "That is good news." Then his face fell. "But those don't seem like happy tears."

Lealia took a deep breath to keep her lip from quivering and returned to her seat on the bench. "No. I mean yes." She took in a shaky breath. "The Board has not decided how much the scholarship will be, and I have to wait until November to get it."

Milton took the seat beside her. "I assume you wanted this process to move faster."

"Yes, I miscalculated. I didn't foresee a delay."

"But it's a short delay," Milton said. "You can stay home. A month feels like a long time, but it's not. All is not lost."

She looked up from her hands and into Milton's eyes and saw real concern there. "You're right. I'm despairing for nothing."

Milton smiled. "You are. The delay doesn't change the fact that you were smart enough to get this far. And you will go even farther."

Her sadness decreased a notch. "Thank you for the encouragement and for making lodging arrangements for me. The Primms have been excellent hosts."

Milton softened, giving her a real smile. Like he had in chapel when she'd made him laugh. "You're welcome." He glanced in the direction of the church. Since they had been talking, the crowd of people waiting to get inside had grown. "We should probably go in. It's a big church, but from all the talk, it will be crowded soon."

He offered her his arm, and she took it. Milton was right. Her life had changed today. Maybe not in the way she wanted, but tomorrow would be the beginning of very different days for her.

CHAPTER FIVE

Lealia reluctantly removed her hand from Milton's arm when they stepped into the sanctuary. She had tried not to enjoy the strength of it as they walked up the front stairs. It was nice having him by her side. His presence calmed her, smoothed out the wrinkles of her disordered emotions. How did he do that? She stole a glance at him. When she did, she saw to Milton's right one of Shiloh's members (she could not remember the man's name) glaring at Milton with a look of disgust on his face.

Maybe I've had it wrong. Maybe Shiloh disliked Milton and not the other way around. Why? He was prickly at times, but it was clear he was not unkind. Mr. Carver had said he was a good person. If she had known that he was this interesting, she would have done more than giggle with her classmates about how cute he was.

Another Shiloh member frowned at him as they reached the top of the stairs, but Milton held his head high and ignored them. Lealia glanced around and noticed several more disapproving stares directed at Milton. Her jaw worked to ask him why, but she could not utter the words. Not when Milton was obviously working so hard to ignore them.

Shiloh loved her, but they seemed to hate Milton.

"Mr. Washington has requested that Tuskegee students sit together. I am sure you could probably sit with me and the others." He lingered once they reached the sanctuary, having to stand close to her because of the steady stream of people coming through the door.

"I already promised Mrs. Lenard that I would sit with her. I should look for her."

"Oh." He glanced to where the other students sat near the left front side. "I guess I'll see you when Mr. Primm takes you back to the train station on Monday. I'll be spending the time with my mother, but if you need anything from me, you only have to ask."

"Thank you." She watched him make his way down the aisle, resisting the overwhelming urge to follow him and let Mrs. Lenard find her own seat. The church was filling up fast, and latecomers might have to stand.

There was space on a pew in the middle section of the sanctuary for both her and Mrs. Lenard. A spot where Mrs. Lenard would be sure to see her when she arrived. It was in the middle of the pew, and she had to squeeze down the row to get to it. *Mrs. Lenard needs to hurry, or she will not get in*. As she looked around for Mrs. Lenard, she caught a glimpse of Milton glancing back at her. A strange warmth bloomed in her stomach before he turned to face forward.

Someone tapped her on the arm. She shifted to face the woman to her right, who wore a deep frown. "Are you Lealia Bevard?"

Lealia nodded, a smile beginning to form on her lips. "Yes."

"All grown up since the last time I saw you." The woman's expression did not change.

"I'm sorry, but I don't remember you," Lealia said, unsure of the woman's reaction.

"Well, I remember you." She poked Lealia's arm with her finger. "And him. Why were you speaking with Milton Rafferty?"

Her thoughts completely disarrayed, Lealia folded her hands in her lap. "We attend Tuskegee together."

"You would think after what his father did, no Shiloh member would speak to him. I know the Primms do, but they are new to the congregation."

Lealia glanced at Milton. He was chatting with the man next to him. "What did his father do?"

The woman tsked. "Milton Rafferty Sr. burned down the 6th Avenue meeting place."

Lealia rocked back. "What?"

The woman nodded. "They found his father outside the burning church, sloshed, staggering, and cackling like a madman."

Is this what Mrs. Primm had hinted at? About Milton's problems not being of his own making? "My family and I moved before the fire."

"Yes, I remember now." The woman grasped her hand. "But some friendly advice. The men in the Rafferty family are trouble and always will be. Just because Junior has gotten an education doesn't mean anything has changed."

The service was about to begin, and Lealia had to surrender Mrs. Lenard's seat to another person since the sanctuary was so full. The conversation around her made it clear that many people had come to the convention just to hear Mr. Washington speak, but her mind was on what her neighbor had said, her stomach sick. The woman's words and the stares Milton got when they arrived.

How could Shiloh members blame Milton for something his father had done? She looked in his direction again, and he happened to glance back at her at the same moment. He gave her a smile, but there was unease in his posture, as if he wanted to run from the sanctuary. *Poor man.* She did what she knew would lift his spirits. She made a funny face, this time widening her eyes and poking out her tongue. It worked. She could see him still laughing after he turned to face forward.

The service started and redirected Lealia's attention. After a song from the choir and Baptist Convention formalities, Mr. Washington rose. Excitement seemed to charge the air as he stepped to the podium. He cleared his throat and began to speak. Lealia leaned forward although the sanctuary was silent. He spoke the same way he did at Tuskegee, but this was different. As he encouraged the listeners to get an education and learn trades, Lealia could feel his words' impact on the crowd. Whatever hostility anyone had toward him concerning the Atlanta Compromise seemed to evaporate under his straightforward, commonsense path to upward Negro mobility.

It impacted Lealia even more because she had lived his plan for the past nearly four years. She had seen firsthand the results of what he was saying. It was true that they received industrial training along with math and philosophy. That training had changed many communities because of the teachers and students he had sent out from the school. They had taken the education they received and benefited the farms and families in many states.

In that moment, she decided to think of her time at Tuskegee as her brother did. She would never say another disparaging word about it.

Mr. Washington was met with great applause, Lealia's included. The whole church was standing and clapping. Lealia glanced at Milton and wondered if he and the other students from Tuskegee felt the same pride in their school and their education as she did. Mr. Washington took his seat, and the service went on.

Lealia took a moment to search for Mrs. Lenard, whom she spotted in the very top corner of the balcony. When Mrs. Lenard looked her way, Lealia waved, and Mrs. Lenard gestured to the crowded space around her and shrugged.

A small commotion at the front of the church near Milton caught her attention. She could see him and his fellow Tuskegee students looking in the direction of the stage.

"Fire!"

The voice came from in front of her. It was muffled, but because of the design of the sanctuary, it carried all the way to where Lealia was sitting and beyond. The whole church seemed to stop, as if all the collected people paused. Lealia held her breath. *Fire? Where?* That could not be true.

Then, louder, from the front of the church, "Fire!"

Lealia sprang to her feet to see, but her view was soon obstructed by others standing.

Like a ripple in a pond, murmuring floated over the sanctuary. Then a louder voice screamed, "Fire!"

The room erupted in pandemonium.

Lealia's heart slammed in her chest as she looked around her. The pew where she stood was crowded on both sides. The aisles were also starting to fill as people pushed their way toward the door.

"God help me," she moaned as the swell of the crowd grew. Screaming echoed off the ceiling, and voices clamored from the choir loft. Lealia stood on her tiptoes to see the exit. There was such a thick crush, she could not see the door anymore.

I have to get out. No sooner had she thought it than she was knocked forward by someone climbing over the pews. Before she could recover, another person pushed her hard, followed by someone's foot connecting with her head. She stumbled, pressing her hand to her head as she tried to push up from her squatting position.

Using her legs to push off the floor, she got her head above the back of the pew and found herself facing the rear of the sanctuary. Around her, women and children were screaming. There were men standing on tables, waving their arms. And the people. . . It was as if the aisles had been turned into rushing water—except the water had stopped flowing at the rear of the sanctuary as people piled up in the doorway.

"Oh, God. Help us." Lealia tried to fully stand, but now there were two people wedged in beside her and there were people streaming over her head, stepping on both pews and bodies. She ducked and saw Milton on the other side of the church. He was pushing through the crowd, and she soon saw that he was moving to a woman and child pinned against the far wall. He grabbed the little girl, whose face was streamed with tears, put her on his shoulders above the crowd, and wedged himself between the woman and the crowd pushing against him. She lost sight of him then as another wave of people pushed toward him from the front of the church.

More people came over the pew from behind her, and their weight buckled her knees. She went down with a cry. Her head caught the edge of the pew as she did, and her vision swam. She grappled for anything to pull herself up, but there were only limbs to grab. She tried to crawl. More crushing weight pinned her to the floor, and the only space she could find was under the bench. She tried to pull her whole body under, but her ankle wrenched, and pain seared up her leg.

She tried to scream, but the space beneath the bench was so crowded, so tight, she couldn't draw air into her lungs. Her throat closed, both panic and tears fighting to erupt.

But they had no place to go. In this tight space, she could not even cry. Or scream. Or move her leg because there was someone lying on top of it. Or pray.

Her breaths came shallow.

I am going to die here.

The thought sent ice racing through her veins. *I'm going to die here, and none of my planning or smarts is going to change that.* She pressed her face to the cool wooden floor.

"Fire!" Milton jolted to his feet. *Oh no, not again.*

He had just sat back down after applauding Mr. Washington's excellent speech. Now others joined him, standing and peering around.

"Fire!" The scream came from the front of the church. He looked around for his mother, but her seat was empty. *Where did she go?* There was no smell of smoke in the air. No sign of a flame. He craned his neck to see if his mother was in the crowd standing at the back of the sanctuary, and when he didn't see her, his dread spiked.

Then at once, the whole congregation surged. Screams rang out as people began running down the aisle. Milton turned to his fellow students. "We need to go!" he screamed over the din. They didn't seem to hear, so he grabbed the arm of the nearest student. "We need—"

His words were cut off by someone slamming into his back. He exhaled hard and stumbled forward into the aisle. The person who ran into him rushed past him and pushed Milton into the wall. His heart in his throat, he steadied himself against it. The congregation boiled and swelled like waves around him. The screams of women echoed around the sanctuary. Mr. Washington was on stage, frantically waving his arms, but it was obvious few saw him. The whole congregation seemed to be single-minded in their purpose to escape the fire Milton couldn't locate.

He scanned the crowd, looking for the glow of a fire, but didn't see it.

His gaze drifted to the other side of the church. He spotted Lealia, and his stomach dropped. She was standing, her back to him. She was in the middle of a row. His pulse hammered in his ears. She was trapped.

"Lealia!" he screamed, but another rush of people coming down the aisle knocked the wind from him. Several people fell to the floor and disappeared under the feet of the crowd.

"Dear God," he heaved as he fought to stay on his feet in the crush. He pushed his back against the wall and glanced up the aisle, but it was packed with bodies. The people at the rear of the sanctuary looked as if an unseen hand had lifted them and stuffed them in the doorway. Limbs and heads dangled out of the mass in unnatural positions. Milton's stomach lurched. Where was his mother? *Please God. Let her be in the balcony and not down here.*

A scream rang out near him. He looked to his left and saw pinned against the wall a woman and her child. The woman was screaming for help, but her voice couldn't travel far in the din. Milton pushed off the wall, sliding his feet along the floor to avoid stepping on the people there. He had broken out in a sweat by the time he reached the woman.

"Give me the child!" He screamed over an usher on a table yelling at the crowd to be calm. The man was soon tipped off the table and disappeared into the crush.

The woman, with tears streaming down her face, handed the girl to him. He placed her on his shoulders, since he was taller than most people and that was the only place the child would be safe. The men and women around him were packed in, most of them upright. He used his arms to create a frame around the woman so that he took most of the shoves of the people trying to get by.

"Hold on to her!" he yelled, and the woman reached up and grabbed the child's legs. He leaned forward so that the little girl was balanced on the back of his head. She grabbed two handfuls of his hair, and although it was painful, Milton was relieved that the child had a good grip. He turned his head to try to see Lealia.

She was gone. *Did she get out?*

The woman in front of him was praying in a continuous stream. "God help us. God help this young man. God save us."

Milton took another blow to his back, then another, that one sending a sear of pain up his spine. His arms began to tremble in the effort of shielding the woman.

He joined in her prayer. *God save us. Help my mother. Help Lealia. Help us all.*

And then, everything stopped. The push to get out halted as abruptly as it began. An eerie quiet filled the sanctuary. Even the child had calmed to just a whimper. Milton managed to turn his shoulders so that one braced against the wall. He couldn't move any more, because of the press.

"Is it over?" the woman asked quietly.

"I pray so."

But now how were they to get out?

CHAPTER SIX

Lealia lost track of time waiting for death. Waiting for the air to run out. Her breaths hitched in her chest. Shallow. The air had grown warm.

Her thoughts drifted to her mother and father and Nathan. Would her parents blame themselves for her death? That they pushed her too hard to go to Howard? She wanted to cry but the weight of the bodies above seemed to force all the space out of her, including any room for her emotions. She lay there, her face pressed to the floor and what felt like someone's shoulder in her back. What little she could see blurred as her head spun and throbbed.

Then a slight shift in the weight above her. A lightening. Then a muffled voice above saying, "We need more help."

Lealia felt another shift. Maybe they were moving the people above her. With every movement, however, her ankle protested with more pain.

From somewhere in front of her on the floor a man moaned. She could hear him grunting, as if he was straining to move. "Someone help me," he wheezed.

Lealia turned her head as much as she could in the direction of his voice. "Sir, save your air."

He grunted again, "I must get out."

She took a breath and realized it was a little easier. There seemed to be more air in the crowded space. "Sir," she said to the moaning man, "hold on. Help is coming."

He grunted again and then cried out, "Someone is on my leg. I can't move!"

"Calm down, sir. Help is coming. My leg is pinned as well. If you try to move, you may injure yourself more. Just try to be still."

A scripture popped into her mind. *He leadeth me beside the still waters.* Through the growing fog of her brain, she recognized Psalm 23. She squeezed her eyes closed, trying to recall the rest. "'He leadeth me beside the still waters…'" Her head throbbed, and her stomach pitched. "'The Lord is my shepherd—'" she got out, and the weight shifted above her once more. "'The Lord is my shepherd,'" she murmured again.

And in the darkness, a voice replied, the groaning man she thought, "'I shall not want.'"

The shoulders of the person on top of her turned, and the darkness seemed to lighten. "'I shall not want,'" she repeated. "'He maketh me to lie down—'" She started the next line, and suddenly the shoulders lifted from her back and the weight lifted off her ankle. Light flooded the dark space, and clean air rushed in. She took a deep breath.

"We need more help!" someone cried again from above. Then hands, reaching down, pulling her up. An initial burst of relief filled her, and then the room tilted sideways and an excruciating pain sliced up the side of her head. Her vision began to narrow, and then all was black.

Relief came from behind Milton. He had lost track of time, trying to keep his eyes closed against the horror of the crushed bodies around him. Suddenly, the little girl let out a cry, and someone lifted her from his shoulders. He stumbled backward at the absence of the child's weight.

"We got you, sir," a voice sounded from behind him. He turned to see several police officers clearing the aisle.

"There is another exit this way," the officer holding the child said. He handed the little girl back to him. She buried her face in Milton's chest, clutching the lapels of his jacket in her little fists. "Can you carry your daughter and make it out on your own?"

Milton looked at the woman. "This is her child."

The officers moved forward and carefully extracted the woman from against the wall while Milton tried to soothe her daughter. When the woman's footing was clear, she swayed, and Milton and the officer steadied her.

"Come this way, ma'am." The officer held her arm as she cautiously moved toward the pulpit.

She turned to look at Milton. "Thank you, Mr. Rafferty."

Milton nodded. "Be careful."

He watched her until she safely moved through a door he hadn't noticed before. Around him, moans sounded in the calm of the church. The contrast of the chaos to the calm made him feel lightheaded. It was as if he had lived through a strong storm and now it had passed, leaving destruction in its wake. He surveyed the sanctuary once more. Very few people had stayed to assist in getting others out.

He would not turn his back on Shiloh in its moment of need, no matter how much they disliked him. He turned to the officer. "How can I help?"

"Are you hurt?"

"Just bumped around," Milton said, rubbing his spine where he'd been hit.

"We need to move these people out. Assist the ones still standing."

For the next hour, Milton led person after wobbly person down the aisle toward the door. The officers continued the work of detangling the bodies, and as they did, Milton's constitution barely held. Each time he thought he would break, strength came from someplace. It came and was just enough for him to help with the next person.

His nursing classes had trained him to tolerate the dead animals they dissected, but they hadn't prepared him for dead people. It was clear some of them were dead, although there was very little blood. The way their bodies were positioned broadcast that they were no longer in this world. Milton assisted the living with shaking hands, trying to shield them from the corpses being carried out around them.

But then there were no more living.

There were no stretchers, so Milton had to carry some of the bodies by their arms while an officer carried their feet. Still, his nursing training did not abandon him. He glanced at the bodies, assessing them. The blue tint of their fingers and lips told him that they had died from lack of air. Tragic, because there was plenty of air in the church. There was, however, no space for rib cages to expand, for lungs to inhale.

Milton worked this way for a half an hour, his heart breaking with every trip outside to where the dead were being laid. When they pulled a woman from the bottom of the pile, her flat eyes looking in his direction, his knees buckled.

Hands grabbed him. "Sir, let me help you out."

This time he submitted and let the officer led him to the rear of the sanctuary. He did not need to be told that the bodies would be at their worst the closer they got to the back door. The side door led to a flight of stairs. People sat on every step. Some moaned in pain. Uninjured people were handing out cups of water. Milton carefully stepped around them and to the ground floor.

He stepped to the door and stopped cold.

He had resigned his assistance because he was unable to look at more dead bodies.

Hundreds of people lay sprawled out on the grass around the church. He clapped his hand to his mouth to keep from sobbing. Some were unconscious and others were weakly moaning.

"Jesus, have mercy," he prayed as he staggered to the front of the church.

There were more bodies lying on the lawn, but one glance at them told him that these were the dead from inside. The police were carrying another body down the front stairs. A crowd had formed on the other side of the lawn near the gardens. A scream cut through the darkness as a woman spotted her loved one. Milton could see he was dead and being carried from the building, the grim scene lit by lanterns and the sanctuary's lights through the tall windows. The woman ran and gathered the man in her arms, rocking him and sobbing. Tears rolled down Milton's cheeks.

"Milton!" a voice screamed from behind him. He turned to see his mother sprinting across the lawn, her skirts lifted. When she reached him, she threw herself into his arms, nearly knocking them both over.

"Oh, God. Oh, God," she said as she squeezed him. "You survived."

Milton's tears flowed freely now. "I was so worried about you. I couldn't find you—"

She cupped the back of his head, pulling him down into an even tighter embrace. "I left early because it got too crowded. I was sitting out here waiting for you."

She released him and wiped his cheeks, but more tears quickly followed. "There are dead people, Mom. They—"

She pressed her hand to his lips. "I know, baby. I know. Come sit down."

He pulled away from her. "I'm not injured. I should go back to helping. I need to locate my classmates and Lealia." He could not bear the thought that she was still trapped inside. He had watched for her but hadn't seen her leave the church. Or be carried out.

"They are getting water to the injured and can use help." She squeezed his hand. "Be safe, and I will see you at home."

Milton eyed the way back into the church, and his steps faltered. He could not make his feet go inside even though that was where his help was most needed. He slowly walked past the rows of injured, building his courage. He had to do this. If he was going to be a doctor, he would be called to help with horrible events like this. He had the skills. He needed to go.

Halfway down the row, he spotted a familiar form.

Lealia.

He rushed to her. She lay on her back with her eyes closed. He noticed right away that her ankle was twisted. She was among the living. Relief shook him to his core. He ran to her side. Kneeling beside her, he softly called her name, but she lay there, still as stone.

One of the officers came up behind him. "Sir, do you know her?"

"Yes, she's my classmate."

"Do you see her family?" the officer asked. "We're trying to connect the injured with their families."

"Her family is not here. She lives in Tuskegee," Milton said. She was breathing. He gave her a quick and gentle examination, checking her pulse, looking for bloodstains. He ran his fingers lightly along the back of her head, and she moaned but didn't open her eyes. A head injury. He checked his fingers. No blood.

The officer handed him a piece of paper and a stub of a pencil. "Can you write her name on this and put it on her where it can be seen?"

Milton looked around and saw that other injured people wore the same scraps of paper. "I—" He spotted his mother carrying cups of water across the lawn. "No need. I'll care for her."

The officer nodded and moved to the next person.

"Mom!" Milton called out.

Despite the noise, she caught his voice and turned in his direction. He waved her over. When she arrived, he motioned to Lealia. "This is Lealia Bevard. Can you stay with her, please?"

His mother gasped and pressed her hand to her lips. "Oh, sweet Jesus."

Milton pushed himself to his feet. "If they come to move her, tell them she has a head injury and her ankle is twisted."

His mother sat next to Lealia. "Yes, Son. Go."

Milton took a deep breath. He had found Lealia. How many other people could he identify? His other classmates? Where were they?

He turned, resolve straightening his shoulders, and headed down the row of the injured, praying as he went.

Lealia opened her eyes and saw night sky.

Where am I?

She moved to sit up, but pain in her head made the world seem to tilt.

"Oh, honey. Stay still," a soft voice said from above her.

"Where am I?" She tried to open her eyes again, but the stars swirled, and she closed them.

"Outside. You're safe."

She frowned, tried to focus. *Safe?* Her hurting head clouded her thoughts. "Outside?"

"Outside the church. A doctor is coming to check on you soon."

Outside the church. The memory of being trapped, the wood floor against her face, flashed in her mind. She moaned. She was trapped in the burning church. So were Milton and all the other members of Shiloh. "The fire," she said weakly.

"You were injured. Don't try to move."

Lealia took in a deep breath, half expecting to be unable to, but the air came freely. Not trapped. Outside the church. Not trapped inside.

Darkness closed in on her again.

This time she awakened to someone gently lifting her head and something being pressed to her lips.

"Here, dear, take some water," the same soft voice said.

Lealia tried to swallow, but the pain in her head made her moan, and most of the water ran down the side of her neck. It did help to focus her mind. She opened her eyes to see the lovely face of an older woman framed by the night sky. "Did everyone get out of the fire safely? Milton Rafferty? Did he make it out?" Her mind flashed a memory of him crushed against the wall before she fell under the bench. Her memory, however, did not contain heat or smoke. Where had the fire been?

"Don't fret yourself. Rest."

Lealia lay back on the grass. She must be on the lawn in front of the church. As her other senses returned, she noticed she was cold. She heard no coughing. Actually, she heard nothing, the night silent and grave.

Then she could hear someone speaking above her. She forced her eyes open. The woman was speaking with a police officer. She nodded and returned to Lealia's side.

"Lealia, it appears that all the hospitals are full. It is getting too chilly for you to stay here. We're going to move you to my house." Lealia felt arms, maybe the police officer's, wedge underneath her. "Brace yourself."

Even though she did, it did not prepare her for being lifted off the ground. Pain pulsed like a heartbeat in her head and her ankle. Hot tears trickled down her cheeks.

"Please," she whimpered, unable to scream. "Please, it hurts too bad."

"Just a little farther, dear. You can make it."

Lealia squeezed her eyes shut, her roiling stomach and pounding head both screaming at equal pitch. Sweat poured down the back of her neck, and she began to tremble, but not from the cold. "Please," she moaned again.

"Almost there."

She heard voices talking, but she couldn't catch their words. Pain muffled them. She leaned her head against a solid chest. The person carrying her? It steadied her head a little, but she was panting as if she were running.

"You did well. Now the last step. We're going to lift you into the wagon."

"Please—" Lealia started, her words thick and sounding foreign to her ears. She grasped the back of the jacket of the person carrying her. Milton. . .no, Milton was still inside. *Oh, God. Milton is still inside.* She held on, fighting to get the words out. "Someone. . .please. . .help Milton."

In the clamor of her pain, she heard a deep voice reply, "I'm here."

Then she was being lifted, and the world pitched so violently that the edges of her vision closed in until only dark remained.

She was in a bed.

Lealia lay very still, the memory of her head throbbing keeping her from moving suddenly. She could feel the pain still, dull and waiting in the shadows to flare again. There was a pillow under her head and another under her ankle. She opened her eyes to look around but promptly shut them against the light from a lamp on the bedside table.

"Hello, dear." The same soft voice.

"Where—where am I?"

"At my house. I am Mrs. Rafferty."

Lealia frowned. Did she know Mrs. Rafferty? "What happened?"

"There was an accident at the church. You got hurt."

Lealia's throat closed. Trapped. She was trapped. Her ankle. . . She moaned.

"Be calm. You are safe. You bumped your head, and you twisted your ankle. I sent for the doctor. He is very busy, but he is on the way. Would you like to try some water?"

Lealia moved her head to nod, and the pain flared a little brighter. "Yes," she croaked.

Instead of a cup, Mrs. Rafferty brought a spoon of cool water to her lips. Lealia wanted to gulp it down her dry throat, but there was only a sip. Mrs. Rafferty kept spooning the water until Lealia's stomach started to churn.

"Thank you," she managed to say.

"You're welcome, Lealia. Please rest. I will wake you when the doctor arrives."

Lealia yawned. The little she'd done had already tired her out.

There was an urgency to her thoughts. Despite her exhaustion, they seemed to claw at something just beyond her reach. Something more had happened today. What? What had happened?

She drifted off to sleep, thankful for the relief darkness brought.

Milton helped carry water and the wounded until the sky started to lighten. He also identified a number of the wounded, including two more of his classmates and a deacon at Shiloh. The scene around the church grew quieter after the living were moved. The hospital had quickly filled up, and they were sending the injured to anyone who could house them. Many of the church members who were not injured took in total strangers.

Milton had carried Lealia to a wagon. Her head rolled to the side when he lifted her, and she whimpered. He had walked slowly, keeping his steps as even as he could on the grass so as not to jar her. At one point she had rested her head against his chest, her eyes closed. His heart broke when he lifted her into the wagon. She cried out in pain and lost consciousness.

Thankfully, she did not awaken during the entire ride or on the trip up the stairs to the extra bedroom. He thanked God that his mother had not taken in any delegates for the convention. Lealia could stay there as long as she needed. He'd kissed his mother and returned to Shiloh.

As he walked back, his mind replayed Lealia's words before she passed out again. *Someone please help Milton.* He tried to make her understand that he was not inside, but she had fainted. He wondered if she heard how his heart hammered at her pleading for someone to help him.

He hadn't had long to consider her words. There was still a good deal of activity in the church's yard. He assisted the Primms, both injured, back to their house. He made arrangements for other out-of-town injured to go to local houses. There were so many Shiloh members offering help that it became a matter of entrusting the injured into their care and taking note of where the person lived. Milton, inspired by the police officers labeling the injured, had grabbed his notebook when they took Lealia to the house. He recorded the names of all the injured, a description of their clothing, a brief description of their injuries, and where they were being taken.

Once the injured were hospitalized or housed, all that remained was the silence of the dead. Some women had tried to cover as many of the bodies as they could, but they were too numerous. Some were only covered by jackets and coats. Milton felt the heartbreak, but his tired body could not cry. In the darkness, his sorrow felt like a heavy blanket on his shoulders. He felt he would never stop if he started crying now.

He stood there on the lawn, looking for another way to help but knowing there was nothing else he could do. His eyes drifted to the row of the deceased. Men and women alike were there. At the far end of one row lay a man with a bloodstained shirt. Milton's mind fractured. So there *was* blood. He remembered someone mentioning that some of the people fleeing had fallen down the stairs after running through the front door. If the man had struck the stone stairs. . . He squeezed his eyes tight.

He milled round with the others helping, snatches of conversation drifting beyond his focus. He noticed the coolness of the night air for the first time since he had come outside. As the sky brightened, someone gripped his shoulder, and he started like he had been awakened from sleep.

He turned to find Reverend Walker, the pastor of Shiloh, looking as tired as Milton felt. "Milton Rafferty?"

"Yes, sir," Milton said.

Reverend Walker gave him a weak smile and extended his hand. "I thought that was you. You've done well, Son. Go home. I'm sure your mother is worried sick."

Milton shook the man's hand, unable to say more. He staggered to the edge of the lawn where someone, he could not focus his eyes to see who, helped him into the back of a wagon. He sat down heavily on the bed, letting his head rest against the wooden planks. He must have drifted to sleep, because the next thing he knew, someone was rousing him awake.

"Junior, you're home."

Milton sat up to see Mr. Hamilton, one of the men of the church, offering him a hand. "Thank you," Milton croaked. He slid off the back of the wagon, and his feet screamed in pain.

His mother opened the front door as he slowly made his way up the walkway.

She hugged him. "Oh, Son."

He shuffled into the house to the sofa. His back protested as he sat, and he remembered the blows he had taken in the press. "We cleared all the injured. The dead. . ." He swallowed hard. "The dead are still there. How is Lealia?"

"Still unconscious. I've sent word that we need a doctor for her, although I suspect they are all very busy."

"They and the morticians." Milton closed his eyes at the thought of the twisted bodies. The man covered in blood. "I can look at her ankle tomorrow. It's a miracle she was not—" He swallowed again. Her seat was in the middle of the row. He had helped move bodies from that section. He ran a hand over his face. *Thank God she's alive.* He imagined her parents' horror if something worse had happened to her. They had such high hopes for her, not to mention her own dreams and goals.

"Thank God that He gave you strength. Let me get you some tea." His mother eased a pillow behind his head. "I'll just be a minute."

He closed his eyes, exhaustion overpowering the screams from his memory, and drifted into a heavy sleep.

CHAPTER SEVEN

When Lealia awakened again, the room was brighter and someone was softly calling her name. She cautiously opened her eyes and found they could bear the faint light coming through the window. Mrs. Rafferty stood by the side of her bed.

"The doctor is here to see you," she said.

Then Lealia noticed the tall, lean man standing behind Mrs. Rafferty. He looked as exhausted as she felt.

"Hello, Lealia. My name is Dr. Briggs. How are you feeling?" Dr. Briggs moved around Mrs. Rafferty and set his bag on the floor beside the bed. Mrs. Rafferty moved to stand by the door.

"Tired. My head and ankle hurt," she croaked.

"No great wonder," Dr. Briggs said. "You took a nasty tumble in the church and hit your head."

Lealia's mind sharpened.

The church. The fire.

"You were trapped in the stampede for about half an hour." Mr. Briggs moved to the foot of the bed. "Let's start with your ankle."

He gently examined her ankle and applied a splint. "You should refrain from walking on that for a little while. It is strained and swollen."

"I will not be walking with my head spinning like this." Lealia unclenched her teeth as he lowered her ankle to the bed.

"We'll check that next." He glanced at Mrs. Rafferty. "Unfortunately, I will need to look at the back of your head."

Lealia swallowed a groan as Mrs. Rafferty moved to the other side of the bed. The woman gently braced Lealia's shoulders as Dr. Briggs slowly turned her head. Lealia bit her lip and clenched the bedsheets to keep from screaming. The pain was like nothing she had ever felt before, sending angry lightning from the top of her skull down the back of her neck. Added to that was the nausea and dizziness that came with moving.

"Good job," Dr. Briggs said softly. "You have a good-sized knot, but there's no blood." He straightened her head, slow and gentle, but the room still swam in her vision. "You should start to feel better soon. I'll leave some powders for your head, but you cannot take them just yet. The injury is too new. Try to lie still and rest as much as you can. No vigorous activities."

Lealia could only give him a weak "yes" while she fought to keep her stomach from rebelling. She heard Dr. Briggs and Mrs. Rafferty leave, but they must not have gone far, because their voices carried to her.

"Your son was right about her diagnosis. Keep her comfortable. Give her some broth and bread if her stomach can tolerate them," Dr. Briggs was saying. "And keep the room dark and quiet. She may be able to move around in a week."

Lealia's eyes popped open. *A week?*

"You look very tired. Can I fix you something to eat?" Mrs. Rafferty asked.

"No, I had something at the Davises' house, and I still have more houses to go. I suspect everyone is going to keep me fed."

Mrs. Rafferty sighed. "So many injured."

"My job is nothing compared to the mortician's job. More dead than all the nearby funeral homes can hold."

"Do we know how many?" Mrs. Rafferty asked.

"Present count is about eighty, but I expect that to grow. There are some gravely injured. Your friend here is in better shape, though her injuries are serious enough."

Lealia's chest tightened. People were dead? Hot tears formed in her eyes. She remembered waiting for death, but it had passed over her and claimed others.

"God have mercy on their souls," she prayed as she cried.

Milton sat bolt upright in his bed, his heart hammering in his chest.

In my bed. His breathing slowed. How did he get up here? His last memory was sitting on the couch with his mother.

He rubbed a hand over his face, but when he closed his eyes, the night before filled his mind. *God help us.*

That had been his prayer for most of the night. He had lost count of how many people he'd carried. How many wounded he had helped. Sleep had given him a reprieve from the memory of bodies.

He let out a shuddering breath, his hands trembling.

He slid off the bed, realizing he still wore his blue suit from the night before. The only evidence of what he had gone through was that his jacket was very wrinkled. There was no blood. Almost none last night except for people who had fallen down the stairs trying to escape.

The tremor in his hands started again.

He stripped off his jacket and splashed water on his face from a bowl on his dresser. He grabbed the towel next to it and dried off. His breath caught, the towel darkening his vision enough that in a second, he was right back on the church's lawn. He dropped the towel and gripped the side of his dresser, his trembling increasing. He squeezed his eyes shut. *So many injured. So many dead.*

A soft thump sounded on the other side of the wall. Lealia.

He fought to slow his breathing. Was she all right? Had the doctor come? He needed to get himself under control and check on her.

He was sweating now, but he couldn't get his fingers to release the dresser.

He lowered his head, grasping for a prayer. For any help.

A soft knock sounded on the door. "Milton?" His mother.

He swallowed hard, the room seeming overbright, and straightened. "Come in."

The door opened slowly, and his mother stood on the threshold with a mug in her hand. "I thought you might be awake. Did you rest at all?"

"I collapsed. I have no memory of coming up here last night." He took the mug from her, managing to keep his hand steady. He took a sip of the hot, sweetened tea.

"The doctor just left from examining Lealia. You were right about her head and ankle. Dr. Briggs says she should rest for a week."

Milton exhaled, but the tension in his shoulders remained. "Good news."

"Yes." Mom put her hand on his arm. "Are you injured?"

"No." His answer came too quickly, and his mother narrowed her eyes. "No. Not like Lealia. I was struck in the back, and it's still sore, but nothing some warm towels and rest won't cure." He forced his speech to be more measured.

She put her arm around his shoulder and kissed his cheek. "I'm glad you're well and your friend is well. I'll see if Lealia will tolerate some porridge and bring a bowl for you as well. She's asked about you."

He closed his eyes, remembering Lealia's pleading to help him. In her pain and confusion, she had thought of him. . .twice. "Is she well enough for visitors?"

He asked the question but knew he would have to calm himself before he went to see her. Stop the trembling. He had no doubt that if she noticed it, she would question him about it. He needed to keep this from her and his mother.

"Not yet. We'll see after breakfast."

After she softly closed the door, Milton sat on the edge of the bed, the mug of tea in his hand. He breathed in the steam, and his head felt better after he took a few more gulps. He understood how it helped. The sugar helped stabilize him. It did nothing, however, for his racing thoughts.

I should have refused to come. I should have stayed in Tuskegee. As tears rimmed his eyes, anger—at whom or what he could not place—filled his chest. He had come back to this place of pain only to suffer more pain. And the pain had spread. To his mother, his classmates, Mr. Washington. Lealia. He should have told Mr. Washington of his past. But if he hadn't come, who would have identified his classmates and Lealia? The other uninjured members would have had one less person to help at a time when they needed all they could get.

He stared into the mug. Why had this happened? Why, when he had come back after all this time, had the most horrible thing imaginable happened? People had died in the same room where he and others had listened to Mr. Washington's speech. Why? Lealia had dreams of going to Howard, and now she was severely injured, unable to even go home. Of all the ill that he felt toward Shiloh, no church deserved to have this happen in its most sacred place.

His hand shook so badly that he had to set the mug on the nightstand.

He forced his thoughts to quiet enough to finish the tea. His mother returned with the porridge. He heard her go to Lealia's room first. But two bowls sat on the tray she carried when she entered his room.

Milton eyed them, and she gave her head a sad shake. "Lealia said the smell makes her nauseous."

Milton took a bowl.

"Mr. Washington stopped by while you were sleeping," Mom said as she sat on the bed next to him.

Milton leaned back in surprise. "He did?"

"Yes. He wanted to check on you and Lealia. He also said that your two classmates have only minor injuries and will return to Tuskegee with him. He said the two of you can return to Tuskegee when you are healed."

"I am uninjured."

Mom looked at him for a long second. Long enough that he was sure she saw the real cause of his pain. "Mr. Washington said he is very proud of you. That you acted with honor. I attribute even more honor to you, since Mr. Washington does not know our history with Shiloh."

Milton stared at the bowl. "I did what was right."

"Yes, and I am proud of you too." She gently put her arm around his shoulder.

"How is Lealia?"

His mom gave him a smile, her eyebrows raised. "You asked me that already."

"I mean, when you went in to see her." He shifted on the bed.

"I already told you," she said, her smile spreading.

"Mom."

"She is very pretty."

"I know." How could he not know? When she had looked at him, tears in her eyes after getting the news from the Education Board, his heart had done a little flip in his chest. She was pretty enough to make a man forget his words.

Then he remembered her lying on the grass, eyes closed. He stood. "I think I need to get cleaned up."

Mom stood also. "I'll be back in a bit to check on Lealia."

Once his mother closed the door, his shoulders sank. Why did this happen? Why here?

Lealia lost track of the hours. She would wake to a room without light to give her an indication what time of day it was.

Mrs. Rafferty did her best to keep things quiet. She also had to go through several kinds of food before they found something Lealia could tolerate. As the doctor had instructed, Lealia did not exert herself. Not that she wanted to. Even the slightest movement sent both her head and stomach pitching again.

Guilt added to her discomfort as a result of the many meals she was unable to eat because of the smell. Mrs. Rafferty had brought her some roasted chicken and potatoes, and before she could get it in the room, Lealia felt like retching.

"I am so sorry for wasting food," she said when Mrs. Rafferty returned with broth and bread.

"It is not wasted. I'm cooking for my son as well."

Lealia frowned. "Your son?"

"Yes. Milton. He's still here. He hasn't returned to Tuskegee yet."

Relief brought her up off the pillow. "Milton is here?" Then her vision swam, and she lay back down again.

"Be easy."

Suddenly the fog in her brain cleared. She didn't need more than the pain as confirmation of her concussion, but if she did, this would be another. "You are Milton's mother." Now that she was focused, she could see the resemblance. Milton had gotten his thoughtful eyes from her. "You told me that."

Mrs. Rafferty chuckled. "I did. You have been out of it since you were injured."

"I didn't realize," Lealia said, pushing back the memories of that day in the church. The press of bodies, the lack of air. She swallowed. "Was he injured?"

"Not much. A few bruises from being squeezed in the crowd." She stood. "He's here now. Would you like to talk to him? He knows he must be quiet."

Tears stung in her eyes. "Yes, I would like to see him."

Mrs. Rafferty left, and a few minutes later, Milton stood in the doorway. He looked tired, but his exhaustion had not, to her joy, robbed him of his warm expression. He appeared to be happy to see her. Lealia sobbed, ignoring the growing throb in her head. "You are all right."

"Hey, hey. No crying, or Mom will put me out." He moved to sit next to her bed on the chair where Mrs. Rafferty had sat, and took her hand.

"Please forgive me, but I'm happy to know that you were not injured."

"And I'm unhappy to know that you were."

They sat in silence for a moment, Milton rubbing small circles on the back of her hand with his thumb, and she wondered if his memories were as dark as hers.

"I heard the doctor say people died. The fire must have been bad."

Milton tipped his head. "Fire?"

"In the church." Lealia lifted off the pillow an inch to look him in the eye.

"There was no fire."

Lealia frowned. "I am not sure I understand. In the church—" She swallowed down the memory. "In the church, someone yelled 'fire.'"

Milton gave her a sad look and shook his head. "It was not a fire. It was a fight."

"A fight?" Lealia raised her voice and tried to sit up. As soon as she did, the room swayed. The pain in her head that had become almost bearable fired across her scalp.

"Shh." Milton gently grasped her shoulders and guided her back to the pillow. "If you move too quickly, you will hurt yourself."

He was right. Her head was throbbing now from both pain and shock. "I simply cannot believe all of this happened over a fight."

"A fight between two delegates," he said. "You were not the only person who heard 'fire' instead of 'fight.'"

"There were so many people rushing to get out. I believed it was a fire. They were screaming." She swallowed again. "People were standing on the tables, screaming."

Milton eyed her. "Maybe this is not the best subject for you right now."

"But I want to know."

"I know. But maybe this is not the best time. For both of us."

Her heart sank. She wanted to know, but Milton had been inside the church that night. He had seen the horrors too.

"True." She closed her eyes, the magnitude of the stampede weighing on her heart. People died because of a fight? To think that her life could have ended, all her work to get into Howard nullified, and her family's hearts broken because two people had a disagreement.

He took her hand and gave it a light squeeze. "You are getting better. I asked my mother yesterday if I could come talk to you, but she said you were not well enough."

"She has taken excellent care of me."

"I was worried about you. When I walked past and saw you lying on the lawn with the injured, I asked my mother to stay with you until I got back from clearing the"—he swallowed hard—"until I was done helping with the recovery." A dark shadow passed over his countenance. She watched as he struggled to brighten his expression again.

"So that's how I ended up here."

"Yes. I helped carry you to the wagon."

She blinked, surprised. "That was you."

He gave her a sad smile. "Yes. I suspected you did not realize."

He carried me like I was made of pillow stuffing. Tuskegee had made him strong. "Thank you."

Milton would not make eye contact with her. "Thank you for trying to convince me to help myself."

"What?"

"When I was carrying you. You asked me to go help Milton." He smiled.

"Well, did you go help Milton?" She tried to make her expression like Mr. Carver when he asked them a question in class.

He chuckled. Although the sound made her head pulse, she laughed with him. "No, I am afraid I did not."

Once their laughter died down, she felt the prickle of tears in her eyes. "This is all so horrible. I keep thinking it's a dream."

He took a long inhale and trembled as he exhaled. "Me too."

Mrs. Rafferty reappeared at the door. "All right. Visit over."

Milton stood. "Glad to see you're recovering."

"Glad to see you're all right," she said, her voice cracking.

"Milton, did you make her cry? That will hurt her head." Mrs. Rafferty put her hands on her hips and scowled at him.

He gave his mother an exasperated look. "I did not make her cry. She did it on her own."

A giggle bubbled out of Lealia's lips. "He did not make me cry, Mrs. Rafferty."

She eyed them both. "Still, time for Lealia to rest."

Although she would have protested before, her mind begged for the relief only sleep brought. Mrs. Rafferty pulled the covers up to her shoulders, and Lealia was drifting to sleep before the kind woman left the room.

Then the nightmares began.

Lealia awakened screaming at some point in the night. Her dreams had been filled with fire and bodies. People crying out for help and someone quoting the twenty-third Psalm.

The room was dark, and she didn't realize she wasn't trapped in the church until strong arms wrapped around her.

"Lealia," someone said. It took her a moment to recognize the sound of Milton's voice over her pounding heart.

"The people were trapped—" She broke into sobs.

He sat on the bed and pulled her closer. "You're safe."

She heard other movement in the room but did not raise her head until the tears stopped flowing. In the dim light of a candle, she saw Milton sitting on the edge of her bed in a nightshirt and pants and Mrs. Rafferty standing at the door with a hastily thrown-on housedress.

It hurt Lealia's eyes to look at the light, so she lowered her head. "I'm sorry. I was having a nightmare."

"I know," Milton said. His words held the weight of understanding. Was he having nightmares as well?

"I'll fix us all something warm to drink. Milton, help her lie back down."

Milton did, and she focused on his curious eyes assessing her movements. "There," he said as he averted his eyes and handed her the sheet.

She pulled it up to her neck. "My dream seemed so real," she whispered.

"It must have been. I heard you screaming from down the hall." Milton sat in the chair.

"I've awakened the whole house."

"It's all right," he said. "Mom has had one ear out for you since you arrived. She has not slept through the night since we brought you here."

"I'm so sorry for being such a bother to everyone."

"You are not a bother to her or me," Milton said, rubbing his eyes. "We're just glad we had space for you. There were so many people injured in the stampede, the hospital was full. Members of Shiloh had to take the injured into their homes."

"So many."

Milton sat back and sighed. "Yes, but the local injured went home, which made a little space for people like you who couldn't go home."

Home. "My family. I need to notify them."

Mrs. Rafferty stepped through the door with three steaming mugs. "Mr. Washington already returned to Tuskegee and paid them a visit to tell them you were too injured to be moved."

They piled pillows behind her head so she could sip her tea. Lealia dreaded when it was gone because then she would have to return to the darkness of sleep and dreams.

CHAPTER EIGHT

Milton stayed in bed most of the next day, unable to sleep. The night before, he had just drifted off when Lealia started screaming. He had run down the hall, not wanting her to live through another second of the nightmare. His mother met him at the top of the stairs with a candle. She opened the door and peeked in, calling Lealia's name. Seeing Lealia thrash and hearing her cries made Milton's knees weak. He pushed into the room and awakened her, and she collapsed into his arms, sobbing. He was grateful for the darkness because it hid his own tears.

Once he calmed her and was back in bed, his exhaustion made falling asleep easy. He drifted off and then woke with a start. He expected to see his dormmates at Tuskegee around him. Then he remembered where he was, and his mind laid out all the horror of that dreadful night.

He was still in Birmingham. The stampede at Shiloh had killed people. Some of them Shiloh members.

His breathing quickened as he got out of bed. It felt as though, whether waking or sleeping, he had spent the last two days trapped in the church, surrounded by the dead and injured. By the time he was dressed, sweat had broken out on his forehead, and he was panting. He opened a window, letting in a breeze of warm September air and the smell of the fields.

He closed his eyes, and the first image that came was the church. It had been two days since the stampede. He could hear the church bells ringing all over the city. Today was Sunday. People would be gathered to worship. But not the members of Shiloh. Surely not.

He inhaled and held his breath until the memory of walking down the rows of the injured faded. But then another, just as terrible, took its place. An image of the dead.

He had to get out.

He grabbed his jacket and hat and then stuffed his sketchbook into his pocket before heading downstairs. His mother smiled when she saw him and fixed him a plate of food. "Good morning."

"Good morning," he said, as he sat at the table.

"You have a little more color than yesterday. Do you feel better?"

He lifted his fork, unable to form an answer. He didn't remember yesterday. Mom would be worried if he told her that though. "How is Lealia?"

"Improving every day," Mom said, putting her hand on his arm. "I'm very proud of you, Milton. I believe I could not have lasted as long as you did."

Milton swallowed. That night was a blur—how long he had helped was a blur. The only thing imprinted clear and raw on his mind was the dead and injured. "I think I need to get out of the house."

His mother looked at him with surprise. "Where are you going?"

"To the church. To see if I can do anything else to help."

"You have helped enough," his mother said, giving him a pleading look.

She was right. He had helped until he collapsed. But if he stayed shut up in the house much longer, the trembling would begin again. "I'm sure there is more to do."

She watched him for a little longer, and he avoided her gaze, shoveling food in his mouth.

Finally, she said, "All right, but bring back updates. I have been unable to leave because of Lealia."

He nodded. "I can do that."

He finished his breakfast, put on his hat, and stepped out on the porch. The relief of being outside nearly buckled his knees. He breathed deeply before he went down the stairs and started up the street.

He was walking at a good clip as the church's steeple came into view above the houses. His breathing quickened, and the muscles in his shoulders tightened. When he reached the front of the church, he exhaled. He'd been expecting to see the covered bodies still lying on the ground. It was hard to believe that it was the same site. To someone who had not seen the stampede, it looked like a quiet, majestic church. The grass was trampled on the right side, but there were no other signs of the tragedy. Milton's mind overlaid the bodies onto the peaceful scene, and he closed his eyes.

"Mr. Rafferty, you are still here." Reverend Walker approached him. "I thought you would have gone home with Mr. Washington."

"One of my injured classmates is at my mother's house," Milton said. "It would be best if I stayed to help her and anyone else who needs it."

Reverend Walker sighed. "There is so much need. The injured are scattered all over the city. The hospital is full. All the boardinghouse beds as well."

Milton turned to him. "How did this happen?"

Reverend Walker shook his head. "I still don't know. From our vantage point, it looked like chaos. We saw the fight and knew that there was no fire. I guess folks are still sensitive."

Milton squirmed. He was still sensitive too, but for a different reason. "Is there any way I can help?"

Reverend Walker rubbed his eyes. "I cannot fathom where to start. The people are so scattered."

"Actually..." Milton pulled out his sketchbook, flipped it open, and handed it to the reverend. "I recorded most of the names of the injured and where they were taken. Especially the out-of-town visitors."

Reverend Walker took the book, awe in his eyes. "In all the tumult that night, I never thought to record anything."

Milton shrugged. "The police gave me the idea. They were writing the names of the injured on pieces of paper and affixing them to the victims. I figured that eventually someone would need to find all of them."

"Very good, Milton." Reverend Walker handed the book back to him. "And that's where you can help. Can you go around to see if the people on your list are still where they were and if they've recovered?"

Milton stood up straight. That task would keep him out of the house all day. "Yes, I can."

"Of course, I realize you will be assisting your mother also, so just please report back to me as soon as you can."

"Yes, sir."

Reverend Walker gave him an encouraging look. "Thank you."

Milton's eyes smarted. Why did this man's words matter so much? But he knew the answer. The reverend looked at him the way he hoped the other Shiloh members would.

He told his mother about the reverend's commission over dinner.

"Are you sure about this, Milton?" she asked. "It means you'll be talking to a number of Shiloh members."

He had considered that after he had given Reverend Walker his word. "I doubt they'll be worried about me after what we've all lived through."

"But the similarities. They thought it was a fire." There was such weariness in her voice.

"But it wasn't a fire. They know that."

"They think your father set the fire at 6th Avenue," she said.

Milton sighed. "I know." He remembered the glares he got when they walked into the convention.

"You said nothing has changed. Why do this now?"

Because I can't sit in the house and think about this all day. "Because they need help. Some of the injured were delegates from out of town."

His mother dropped her head into her hands. "I never wanted you to have to bear this burden."

"It's the right thing to do." *Something my father never did.* Milton had never understood why his father hadn't simply said that he didn't set the fire. That he was just walking home drunk again. But even if he could have convinced them that he hadn't set the church aflame, he definitely couldn't escape the fact that he'd done nothing to help put it out. Maybe if he had been sober, he could have extinguished the flames. But no, he simply stood there and laughed.

That was how the fire department found him. Soaked in alcohol and hysterically laughing. That was the end of what little peace Milton and his mother had. Not that they had much. His father drank and caroused every weekend for years, spending much of his paycheck. Then his drinking became a nightly event. The yelling started too. Milton and his mother did their best to stay out of his way on those nights.

Milton shook away the memories and looked at his very tired

mother. "I'll wash the dishes. You should go to bed and try to get a decent night's sleep."

"Are you sure? What if Lealia needs something?"

"She only needs rest like you do. I'll manage. I am a nursing student after all."

His mother stood and stretched. "I thank God every day that you're here."

He stood and hugged her. "Me too. Rest well."

After his mother climbed the stairs, he cleaned up the kitchen and then went to his room. He would hear Lealia through the wall if she called out for assistance. He prayed that neither of them would be screaming in their sleep tonight.

Lealia nearly cried as she sat up in bed but not because of the pain.

She had sat up by herself.

Mrs. Rafferty normally came at first light to help her sit up and perform her ablutions. This morning, her head felt clearer. Some of the fog had dissipated. The sun shone through a small crack in the shade.

She would be forever grateful to Mrs. Rafferty and Milton for nursing her so well. She longed to see the sun. Feel the breeze on her skin. Then she would finally feel like she was alive.

For so many nights she had lain in bed and cried. Cried for the dead. Cried for the injured and cried for herself. She had not lost her life, but her life had come to a stop. The feeling of being unmoored had kept her feeling low. Mrs. Rafferty had to see it, although Lealia tried to hide it. It was hard to keep her spirits up when she could do nothing but think.

Sometimes the image of the bodies piled at the door was so sharp in her mind that her breath quickened as if she were still trapped. At night, the cries of the injured filled her dreams. She had stopped waking up screaming. Now she awakened with tears on her cheeks. Then there were times when her thoughts were filled with questions for God. Why had this happened? Why had He let her live? Surely some of the people around her had died. Maybe even the man she tried to comfort. Why was she alive? But she never found an answer in the darkness.

Her greatest times of relief were when Milton visited. He never stayed long and always looked exhausted. She cried, and he held her hand. Sometimes he cried with her. There was comfort in knowing he understood her tears. That he had lived through what she had.

Now she was sitting upright in bed. Her head swam a little but improved after she closed her eyes for a moment. Then she opened them and looked around the room. There was little furniture, just the bed, a small desk, and a table with a water jug on it. She was covered by a quilt with stitching that would rival the neat stitches she was taught at Tuskegee. She rubbed her hand over it, wondering if Mrs. Rafferty had stitched it.

"Oh my goodness," Mrs. Rafferty cried out from the door, making Lealia's vision blur. "Forgive me, but you startled me. I had not expected you to be sitting up on your own."

"I felt better today and thought I would try," Lealia said.

Seconds later, Milton appeared behind his mother. His shirt was unbuttoned at his throat, and he had shaving cream on one side of his face. "What happened?"

"Nothing. Lealia sat up by herself and startled me." Mrs. Rafferty set the tray on the desk. "I guess you're better."

"I would like to see if I can tolerate some sun."

Mrs. Rafferty and Milton looked at each other. "Are you sure?" Milton asked.

"Just a little. I have been in the dark so long." Lealia tried to sound strong, but her voice cracked.

Mrs. Rafferty stepped to the window. "We can try, but promise to tell me if it's too much, all right?"

"I promise."

Mrs. Rafferty opened the curtains a crack. Milton stood behind her as if he was ready to prevent Lealia from jumping out the window.

The angle of the light only reached the end of her bed, and Lealia sighed. It was just enough. She had spent so many days outdoors with her father and at school. She never imagined there would come a time when she would be unable to go out and see the sky.

"Thank you. That's perfect."

Milton grinned at her before he disappeared out the door.

Mrs. Rafferty brought the tray to the bed. "Maybe you can feed yourself as well."

Lealia lifted the spoon beside the bowl, dipped it into the porridge, and slowly brought it to her mouth. She nearly cheered when she managed not to spill it. She ate the whole bowl that way, one slow spoonful at a time.

When she was done, Mrs. Rafferty gave her a watery smile. "You did it."

Lealia took a deep breath to fight back her own tears. "I did. I would very much like to lie down again. That took a lot of effort."

Mrs. Rafferty lifted the tray from the bed. "You've made good progress. Maybe it's time for another visit from the doctor."

Lealia smiled at her from her position on the pillow. "Yes. Or maybe when Milton comes back, I can try and stand up."

Mrs. Rafferty paused. "Oh no. My heart isn't ready for that yet."

Lealia laughed. "We'll be careful," she said.

"Shall I leave the curtain open?"

"Yes, please." Lealia wiggled her toes underneath the blanket. Her ankle was in less pain, and she was sure she could attempt to stand on it. It was her head that still buzzed and throbbed. She felt better. Maybe she would be well enough to stand soon.

Lealia was awakened by voices downstairs.

She listened, not recognizing any of them. She smelled food, and her stomach grumbled. She grinned. Another milestone. The smell of food did not sicken her.

She heard footsteps on the stairs, and a moment later Milton came through the doorway with a tray. "Dinnertime."

"Good. My stomach was growling." She very slowly sat up.

Milton didn't move from where he stood until she was completely upright. He gave her a quirky grin. "That was impressive."

She huffed at him and closed her eyes until the room righted itself. "Your face says different."

He laughed. "Just watching to make sure you don't need assistance." He set the tray in front of her and sat down.

"Is there someone downstairs?" She picked up her fork.

"Some of my mother's friends who live in town." Milton rolled his eyes, causing Lealia to laugh a little too loud. "Shh. Mom will accuse us of making too much noise for your head."

"Sorry." She put a small bite of chicken into her mouth. "They sound like fun."

Milton sat back in his chair and eyed the door warily. "They love to pinch my cheeks and tell me how cute I am."

Lealia laughed. "Is that why you delivered my dinner? To get away from them?"

He gave her the most pleading look. "Can I stay until you finish?"

"Yes." She giggled, holding her fork up like a sword. "I will protect you."

"I should go and find Dr. Briggs. He should know how well you've progressed."

Lealia put her fork down. "He reminds me of you."

Milton's eyebrows rose. "Me?"

"Well," Lealia said, avoiding Milton's eyes by looking at the tray in front of her. "Remind isn't the right word. He's how I imagine you're going to be as a doctor."

"That's a great compliment. Dr. Briggs has been the community doctor since I was a kid." Milton's voice pitched a note higher as he spoke.

"And you plan to be a community doctor as well?" she asked.

"I plan to work at a hospital after graduation. Or at least I want to," he said. "I may not be allowed."

Lealia looked up. "Why not? You are an excellent nurse."

"Some hospitals have no Negro nurses. No Negro doctors either. I may have to find a clinic to work at."

"No, you should try for a hospital. This is exactly what Mr. Du Bois suggested. We should be recognized by the white race for our intelligence and talent and work alongside them."

Milton huffed. "He believes that, but I do not."

Lealia's eyes widened. "What?"

"I do not believe the whites will ever let us be their equal," he said. "Ever."

"That's dismal thinking," Lealia said. "They have to recognize us when we are highly educated and skilled."

Milton gave a sour laugh. "There are many Negroes who are already skilled, but we still have to ride in our own cars on the train away from the white passengers. Dr. Briggs is a wonderful doctor, but he practices out of his house, not at the hospital. All his skill does not matter."

Lealia frowned. "My brother, Nathan, is a law clerk in Washington. He's showing how skilled we are."

"And does the firm he works for serve whites or mostly Negroes?"

Lealia pursed her lips, knowing her answer would prove Milton's point. Nathan's letters detailed how almost all of his clients were Negro.

Milton's look softened. "I know you believe in the power of the Talented Tenth, but I think our goals should be more realistic."

"You mean my goals?"

Milton stood and lifted the tray. "Your goals are ambitious, Lealia, and to be admired. But they are too lofty for the conditions we live in." He moved to the door. "You should rest."

Lealia sat for a long moment, staring at the door after he left. Lofty goals that did no good now. But did it matter when she couldn't even stand on her own? She carefully returned to her pillow and fought back tears.

Even though he had anticipated the episode, it still tore through him like an angry beast. Milton had lain in bed, shivering as if he were in an icebox. Sweat stung his eyes. He had awakened, heart racing, but he couldn't recall his dream. Images swirled together. The weight of dread pinned him to the bed despite the urgency pumping through his veins to get up and help.

That urgency drove him from the bed once he had calmed.

He yawned as he went down the stairs. His mother was sitting on the couch, reading the newspaper. "Good morning."

He put his arm around her shoulder and planted a kiss on her forehead. "Morning."

"There is breakfast in the kitchen," she said. "And there's an article about the stampede in the paper."

He loaded a plate with bacon, eggs, and potatoes before he returned to the table. *I have to appear somewhat normal.* The last thing he needed to do was worry his mother. "Any news?" He didn't want an answer, but it would be odd not to ask.

"Just that there are several unidentified dead," she said. "My heart breaks for those families."

"We can pray that someone identifies them soon," Milton said, putting a bite of food in his mouth. At least his appetite still worked. "How is Lealia?"

"She was quiet for the night. I took her some tea after you went to sleep."

I would not call that sleep. "I believe she will continue to recover. She's strong and healthy." And, like him, she was full of hope and determination. Or at least he had been.

"Are you going to the church today?" Mom asked.

"Yes. I want to talk to Reverend Walker in regard to how to go about caring for the injured," Milton said. "I also want to take him a copy of the names in my book."

His mother gripped his arm. "You are a good man."

For the first time in two days, he felt a little lighter. "You raised me to be a good man." She had done it all after his father left, including paying his tuition at Tuskegee. He was grateful when he started receiving payment for volunteering as school medic. His mother no longer had to bear the load alone.

If I had died—

Milton shot out of his chair. "I should go."

His mother stood and kissed him. "I love you."

He fought back tears. "I love you too."

He arrived at the parsonage at the same time as the reverend, feeling a little revived by the walk. "Good morning," Reverend Walker called. He waved and then waited on the sidewalk until Milton reached him.

"I want to say again how much I appreciate this," Reverend Walker said.

Milton only nodded, a cold sweat forming on the back of his neck. He steeled himself, but Reverend Walker walked across the lawn toward the parsonage. Milton staggered under the relief of not going inside the church. He'd thought he was ready.

The parsonage had been decorated to serve as an extra office and meeting space. It was warm and bright, and Milton felt himself relax.

"I know I have to go back into the church, but I've been working here for now." Reverend Walker led Milton down the hall to what would be a bedroom in a regular house. "It's peaceful over here."

They reached the reverend's office first, and there was a man sitting there. He appeared to be a little younger than Milton. He wore a white shirt, dark brown pants, and a cap over his black hair. He looked as tired as Milton felt, and there was a sadness about him.

"Good day," Reverend Walker greeted him with surprise.

The man snatched the cap off his head. "Are you Reverend Walker?"

"Yes, I am. This is Milton Rafferty." Reverend Walker sat across from the man. "Is there something I can help you with?"

"My name is Evan Stokes. I'm looking for my father."

The young man's words were like an electric charge down Milton's spine. He took his notebook from his pocket. "What is his name?"

"Alfred Stokes. We live here in town. He is missing."

The reverend's eyes widened. "Missing?" He motioned for Milton to sit.

"Yes, sir. A couple days now."

"My mother told me he was quite kind to people in need in the community," Milton said as he searched the list of names in his book. He couldn't find Alfred Stokes. He glanced up to see both Reverend Walker and the young man looking at him hopefully. He checked again. *Mom is going to be devastated if Mr. Stokes is dead.*

"When did you last see him?" Reverend Walker asked Evan.

"The night of the disaster. He said he was coming to hear the speech, but then he never came home. Someone told me to come here because there was a man who was writing down the names of the injured that night." He wore his distress and worry on his face.

"He's not listed among the injured that I know of," Milton said as gently as he could.

"Is there anywhere else he could have gone?" Reverend Walker asked him.

"I have an aunt in Virginia, but he hasn't seen her in years. My grandparents are dead, and we got no other family." Evan's voice broke. "I don't have any other family here, and we were already in bad shape since his business burned down." He wrung his cap in his hands. "My father wouldn't leave, because he was waiting for the insurance payout to reopen the store."

Milton studied the young man. He was about the same age Milton was when his father left. Had he looked this way when he'd arrived in Tuskegee? Did Mr. Washington see his pain like Milton could see Evan's pain? His father's abandonment was an old wound, but seeing Evan, it felt fresh.

"I'll ask around for him," Milton said. "Where are you staying?" *I will find information if I have to search the whole city for it.* Milton recorded Evan's information in his book. "As soon as I know something, I will contact you."

Evan took a deep, shuddering breath, as if he was relieved to not have to bear the burden of his missing father alone. "Thank you. I've been so worried."

"We'll pray that he is found quickly," Reverend Walker said.

Milton started praying before Evan left the parsonage.

CHAPTER NINE

Once she was standing at the top of the stairs, Lealia's confidence wavered.

Milton looked at her, kindness in his eyes. "You can go back to bed if you like."

Can he see how afraid I am? She swallowed to wet her dry mouth, but it did no good. "No, I would like to try."

Today she felt the best she had since the stampede. Her head swam only a little when she sat up to eat. She had, although she knew she should not have attempted it alone, been getting out of bed and standing with the help of the desk. The doctor had told her that she would start to feel better in a week, and he was right.

Now she stood at the top of the stairs, Milton two steps below, gripping her forearms. Mrs. Rafferty stood behind him at the bottom of the stairs. "You can do it, Lealia. Just go slow."

She took a deep breath and stepped forward. She wobbled a bit on the first step, but Milton increased his grip on her arms. "I won't let you fall."

She smiled at him. That she knew. From what she'd learned about him in the time she'd been in his home, he had proven he could be trusted. Being this near him in the closeness of the stairwell, however, made her cheeks flush. Refocusing, she slid her foot off the first step. Her ankle felt stiff from being abed for so long, but it held. She brought her other foot down, and Milton descended one step also.

In this slow way, they progressed toward the floor below. Milton gave her a huge grin. "One more step."

She tried to smile, but sweat beaded at her brow and trickled between her shoulder blades. *One more.* She stepped—or more like fell—into Milton's arms.

"You did it," he said, righting her.

She glanced back at the steps. "I did," she panted.

"Just stand here for a moment and get your bearings."

The room in front of her was warmly decorated. A dining table sat near a door, a kitchen beyond, and a couch to her right.

Mrs. Rafferty retrieved one of the chairs. "Here, sit down." Her smile was as wide as Milton's.

Seeing them so happy and knowing that she had only accomplished what she had done almost every day of her life, her eyes smarted.

Milton's smile fell. "Oh no. It was too much. Maybe we tried too soon."

"No," she sniffled. "I'm not in pain."

Mrs. Rafferty disappeared into the kitchen and returned holding a glass of water. "Here," she said. "Drink this."

Lealia drank as much as she could, but the tears did not stop.

"Tell me what's wrong." Milton squatted in front of her.

"A month ago, I was helping my father seed a whole field. Carrying hay. Before I left Tuskegee, I was collecting the Children's House donations and helping Mr. Carver with his classes. And now. . ." Her heart sank. How could she be a leader and an innovator if she couldn't even stand on her own?

"You were injured. No one expects you to come running down the stairs. Your healing will take time," Milton said, his words soft. "You're progressing better than some of the other people who were injured."

Her sadness shifted to anger. "That doesn't make it better. I'm still unable to walk downstairs without assistance, whether others are better or not."

Instead of anger or disappointment, Milton's face softened even more. "Forgive me. You are correct."

His apology was so easy, Lealia felt bad for getting angry. "No, forgive me. I'm frustrated, and I shouldn't take it out on you."

Milton smiled. "Remember the lesson where the teacher told us that people will lash out at their nurse because they cannot stop the pain."

She blinked at Milton, shame twisting its way around her heart.

She shouldn't have snapped at him. He had been nothing but kind. "It still doesn't make it right."

Milton stood. "I've suffered through worse. There was a student who fell into the briar bushes behind the school. He was covered from head to foot, and it took three of us to remove them all. I never heard a student use language like that." He comically widened his eyes.

Lealia laughed. "Oh my."

"Indeed." He cupped her chin. "You have done well coming down the stairs. It's natural to be frustrated."

"Thank you," she said. He was going to make a wonderful doctor.

"Now." He clapped his hands. "Are you ready to go back up?"

She groaned.

"I jest. Can you make it to the couch? There's a better view of outside from there." And in the same careful way he helped her down the stairs, he guided her to the couch. It faced the field behind the house.

"This is a better view. Are those your fields?"

Mrs. Rafferty sat next to her. "No. Our property ends at the fence."

Lealia studied it. "There's still plenty of room for a kitchen garden."

"I planted a few things in my garden, but I need assistance. Milton is no help. He's an outrageous plant killer."

Lealia pretended to scrutinize him. "So that's why Mr. Carver said he wouldn't trust you with his plants."

"He said that?" Milton's outrage widened his eyes.

"The day I met you." Lealia laughed, and Mrs. Rafferty joined her.

Milton sat in the armchair next to the couch. "If I pass that class, it will be by Mr. Carver's grace."

His words sobered her. School. Would she ever attend any school again when she couldn't even get down the stairs on her own?

Milton stood. "We should get you back upstairs."

Lealia groaned. She had noticed that the more tired she became the more her head ached. "I'm unsure I can make it on my own."

"I can carry you," Milton said.

Lealia's face flushed. "I will not allow that."

He laughed. "How do you think you got up there in the first place?"

"I thank you, but I will go by myself. Just let me sit here for a minute."

Being close to Milton coming down had already been unnerving. Being in his arms would be even more so.

Milton had to carry Lealia back up the stairs in the end. She sat chatting with him and his mother for half an hour before her eyelids started to droop. Milton had watched her closely for any signs of pain, but the more she talked like her old self, the more he forgot to worry about her. She sat, her legs curled under her on the sofa, teasing him and smiling, although her words came a bit slower than usual. His heart swelled, seeing her better.

There was so much pain in this world, but the return of her smile was a good thing he could focus on.

Once she fell asleep, his mother instructed him to take her upstairs. He lifted her off the couch, noticing another good thing: The pain in his back was nearly gone. It had slipped his attention, his trembling hands occupying his mind. The trembling started when he awoke in the morning, and he had discovered that if he gave himself time for it to pass, he could function for the rest of the day.

Lealia awoke just as he reached the top step, her sleepy eyes focusing on him. "Milton. . ." She said his name so softly, it sent prickles racing across the back of his neck. "You were not supposed to carry me."

"How else would you have made it up here?"

"I could have flown."

Chuckling, he navigated the room with care. But Lealia nearly stole his focus when she wrapped her arms around his neck. Milton rebuked himself for the warmth that bloomed in his chest when she did. *This is not appropriate, no matter how good it feels.*

He got her settled as fast as he could, and to his relief, she drifted to sleep almost as soon as he laid her on the bed. He went back downstairs as quietly as he could.

His mother was sitting on the couch where Lealia had sat. She gave Milton a smile. "I knew she wasn't going to last long."

"Me too. It's good that she tried. Maybe she can come down without assistance soon." Milton sat next to her, and she took his hand.

"What about you? Are you better?"

Had she noticed his shaking hands? "I am. Just restless. I'm not used to sitting still."

She sighed. "I still cannot believe that this has happened. Sometimes I forget and wake up and am halfway through cooking breakfast before I remember."

Milton looked out at her garden. "I wish I could forget."

She squeezed his hand. "I'm sorry."

They chatted about other news stories for a bit. He noticed that his mother avoided discussing the disaster. He suspected she was trying to avoid causing him pain, but her other choice of subjects didn't help. She asked him about his nursing classes. He told her, although he would have rather not talked about what his life was like before the stampede.

A knock sounded on the front door. Milton rose and opened it to a familiar-looking man, but he was unable to place where he'd seen him. "Good afternoon, are you Mr. Rafferty?" the man asked.

Milton swallowed. *Junior or senior?* "I am."

"I am Reverend Massey from Shiloh Baptist. Reverend Walker sent me to talk to you."

Milton stepped aside, the tension leaving his shoulders. This was not someone looking for his father. "Come in."

The man stepped inside and spotted Mom. He straightened. "Hello, Mrs. Rafferty. I guess this is the long-lost son. Has he spent all your living and returned home?"

Milton clenched his fist at the acid in the man's tone. Another Shiloh member judging them.

"He is not long lost," Mom replied without a greeting. She stood with her back straight and her shoulders braced for a fight.

His mother's response surprised him. Milton had his issues with Shiloh members, but she tended to be more forgiving. Other than the snide comment about Milton being the long-lost son, what else had this man done to warrant Mom's dislike? It rolled off her in palpable waves. She went through the normal courtesy of offering food and drink but spoke through pursed lips. She did not smile, and if he was reading her right, she'd rather Reverend Massey leave than have to give him food.

Reverend Massey refused refreshment but did accept the offer to sit in the living room. "Thank you. I need to ask Mr. Rafferty some questions."

If Milton had hidden his tension, his mother did not. "About what?" she asked with a clearly hostile tone in her voice.

"The incident. The stampede," Reverend Massey said.

Milton glanced toward the stairs. Was Lealia sleeping soundly enough not to hear this conversation? He had not told her everything about his family, because he had not had the heart or peace to do so. "What questions?"

"Reverend Walker said you kept a record of all the injured," Reverend Massey said.

Milton felt his mother relax a little at the question. "I did," Milton replied.

"Did you happen to keep track of the dead?" Reverend Massey asked the question quietly, but it felt as if he had yelled it. As if the question were a brick from Tuskegee's brickyard and the good Reverend had lobbed it at Milton and struck his target with force.

"No, I—" Milton began, and the images flashed in his mind. His breath lodged in his throat, and he swallowed. "I helped with the injured, and then Reverend Walker sent me home before the mortician came."

Reverend Massey exhaled. "I was hoping you had."

"Why? What happened?" Mom asked.

"Nothing to worry yourself about," Reverend Massey said. "There are some irregularities, and we were hoping Mr. Rafferty could clear some things up."

"I had not thought to record them. There was so much chaos with getting the injured care. They seemed like a priority." Milton remembered that night. The living needed help. It was too late for the dead. He let out a shaky breath.

Reverend Massey rose. "Still, it would have been easy enough to write down the names of the dead too, if you had truly wanted to help."

Milton's jaw dropped. "Easy?" he asked, hearing the building anger in his own voice. *Easy.* Milton's hand trembled.

Mom sprang from her seat. "What were you doing that night, Reverend Massey? Why did you not record the names of the dead?"

Reverend Massey took a step toward the door. "I was assisting as well."

Mom continued, her voice rising. "Then you know how horrible that night was. Nothing was easy that night. Nothing."

Milton stood and grasped her hand. "Mom, I'm sure Reverend Massey realizes that."

Her jaw tightened. "I'm not sure he does."

With mumbled words about needing to get back to the church, Reverend Massey left.

As soon as the door closed, Milton returned to his mother's side. She hadn't even walked the man to the door.

Before Milton could speak, his mother's eyes flicked over his shoulder and her expression softened.

Lealia's voice sounded from behind him. "Who was that?"

Milton turned. "Lealia, you should not come have come down by yourself."

She quirked a smile at him. "I'm not incapacitated." She moved to sit on the couch. "I woke and realized I was hungry. I stood at the top of the steps calling for you."

"Lealia—" Milton began.

She wrinkled her nose at him. "No need to lecture, Milton. I used the rail to come down."

He exhaled and returned his attention to his mother. "Now what was that all about?"

Lealia leaned forward. "Indeed. I haven't heard you speak that angrily since I came here."

Mom exhaled and let her shoulders sink. "Let me get Lealia some food." She moved into the kitchen. "That was Shiloh's newest minister."

"He's on the Education Board. You don't care for him. Why?" Lealia asked.

"He is pompous and arrogant," Mom said, returning from the kitchen with a plate of food.

Milton extended a hand to Lealia to help her to the table. Once seated, Lealia gave Milton an encouraging look and tipped her head toward his mother. As if to say *Get on with the questioning while I eat.*

Milton nearly laughed. "What did he do to make you think that?"

Mom sat up straight in the chair, her fingers curled. "He came to us from another church as an appointee from the Baptist Board. He came in like he was in charge. Talking about the changes he wanted to make. The nerve of him."

Milton stifled a chuckle. His mother was one of the most kind-hearted and forgiving women he knew, so to see her this mad at someone was amusing. Reverend Massey must have really angered her.

"Can you send him back?" Lealia asked softly. Her tone sounded as if they were discussing a badly mended garment.

The tension broke as she, Milton, and Mom burst into laughter. "I wish we could, my dear," Mom said when her laughter slowed. "I wish we could."

A very tired Dr. Briggs visited the following afternoon. Lealia was excited, watching his relieved expression as he checked her ankle and then the back of her head. She had gone downstairs that morning and was sitting on the couch when he arrived. "Excellent, Ms. Bevard."

"I have excellent caregivers." She beamed at Milton and Mrs. Rafferty, and they looked as happy as she felt.

Dr. Briggs turned to Milton. "Did you tell me that you were a nursing student at Tuskegee?"

"Yes, sir. As is Lealia."

Dr. Briggs gave Lealia an approving look. "I wish you were uninjured. I could certainly use both of you. There are a lot of injured, and there aren't enough doctors who will see Negro patients. They're spread out all over the city, and no one knows where they are."

"I do," Milton said.

Lealia studied him. "You do?"

"I made a list that night when they were moving the injured. I thought someone should know where they all went in case more care was needed."

Although she had no claims to him, Lealia was proud of Milton. In that horrible moment, his unflappable demeanor had kept his head clear enough to write a list. "Good job, Milton," she said.

He looked down at his shoes. Was he blushing? "Thank you."

"I would like to see that list," Dr. Briggs said.

They moved to the kitchen table, and Dr. Briggs and Milton went through the little sketchbook. As they did, Dr. Briggs had Milton make notations in his book, as if Milton was working as his triage nurse. Milton even gave suggestions on Dr. Briggs' treatment plans for some of the minor cases. Milton would have the latest knowledge of medical practices, since he was still at Tuskegee.

Lealia couldn't help but grin. If there was one person who perfectly embodied Mr. Washington's vision for his students, it would be Milton. He was using his Tuskegee education exactly as expected. But when Lealia looked at Mrs. Rafferty, the woman had tears in her eyes. Lealia remembered that something bad had happened to this family. She needed to find out what it was.

When they had finished going through the book, Dr. Briggs looked at Milton. "I was serious about needing your help."

"Reverend Walker has commissioned me to visit the people in my book and report back to him," Milton said. "I haven't started, because I wanted to make sure Mom didn't need help with Lealia." He left unsaid his secondary reason: The tremors had left him so exhausted most days that he struggled to go out. He couldn't face the victims of the stampede like this. He told himself he only needed a little more time before he started.

"I would like to go with you," Lealia said. That would give her a way to help others like Milton and Mrs. Rafferty had helped her.

Milton frowned. "No. You need to rest."

Lealia folded her arms. "Dr. Briggs just said I was better. You will need a nurse if you come across someone still injured."

"Me?" Milton asked, his eyes widening. "But I am a nurse."

"But you are further along than I am by two years. You will be the doctor, and I will be your nurse." She couldn't fight the excitement of being useful again. "It will be good to have two of us."

"She speaks the truth, Milton." Mrs. Rafferty nodded.

"I approve. She needs to get some exercise on that ankle or it will grow stiff." Dr. Briggs turned to Lealia. "As long as you rest when you're tired."

He then addressed Milton with an amused look on his face. "I'm committing this patient to your care."

Lealia gave Milton the brightest smile, and when his expression became more worried than happy, she laughed. "I promise to be careful, Milton."

Milton exhaled. "You have to tell me as soon as you get tired, so I can bring you home."

She was sure that he had not intended to call this house *her* home, but she understood. "I promise."

Dr. Briggs stood. "Keep me posted on anyone who needs my care."

"We will," Lealia said.

After Dr. Briggs left and Mrs. Rafferty went into the kitchen to prepare lunch, Milton sat next to her. "I don't like this. What if something happens to you?"

She would have made a joke or tried to make him laugh, but his expression was serious, worried. "If something did, how would either of us prevent it?"

Milton swallowed, and in that moment, Lealia saw something else in his demeanor. A struggle being covered by a huge dose of self-control. Milton was hiding something. "You would be safe here at the house."

"You don't know that. We thought we were safe at the church." She reached across the table and grasped his hand. It trembled a little. "Helping the injured is more important than the possibility of something happening to me. They need help. That is what's certain. Tuskegee prepared us for this. Besides, I have nothing else to do."

She probably could travel home, but the thought of the loud train station made her shudder. The Education Board. What happened to its members? Were they injured? They'd told her that they would have a better idea of their funding by the Sunday following the speech, but no one had to tell her that they had been unable to meet. After all her plans, her life had come to a screeching halt. She needed to do something.

Milton closed his eyes. When he opened them, he gave her a weak smile. "We'll start visitations tomorrow."

"Great." Lealia returned his smile, gratitude filling her heart. She was recovering. Now she could help someone else.

CHAPTER TEN

Mom prepared him and Lealia a meal as if they were heading to harvest.

Lealia had come down to breakfast wearing a dress she had borrowed from his mother, her hair freshly braided. Other than her clothes, she carried herself as though she were going off to a day of classes at Tuskegee. Milton's heart did a happy little dance seeing her like this, and he hid his smile behind his hand as he dug into the food. "We will go to the Primms' first."

He had written the names of the injured in a second notebook so he could give the first copy to Reverend Walker. He added space to take notes on the condition of the people he and Lealia visited and what they might need, just as Dr. Briggs had asked him to.

They stepped out of the house into the warming September morning after Lealia had fetched her hat. She stood on the step and inhaled, then exhaled slowly. Milton smiled. He remembered that feeling, the first time he got out of the house after the stampede. Unlike Lealia, who was just happy to be able to move about again, he'd felt as if he had been released from jail. A very small, dark jail.

They walked slowly to the Primms' house. Lealia asked him a few questions, but it was clear she was concentrating on walking. He watched her closely. Then, out of the blue, she said, "I can't go home."

He glanced at her and saw tears in her eyes. "You can. We can ask Reverend Walker to cover a train ticket—"

"You miss my meaning," she sniffled. "I can go home, but to do what?"

"Go back to school," Milton said, frowning.

She shook her head.

"Why not? Mr. Washington is already expecting me to return. Why not you?" His mind drifted to the chapel service when Mr. Washington commended Lealia and indicated he wanted her to work at Tuskegee after graduation.

Lealia turned her face away. "You don't understand."

He placed his hand on her shoulder. "Help me understand."

She looked at him, parted her lips, and then said, "What happened to you at Shiloh?"

"I was just bumped around. I think I avoided the worst of it because I was near the front where there were fewer people."

"No," she said quietly. "Before."

His mouth went dry. He knew what she was asking, but her question prompted pain on top of pain. Shiloh had hurt him again. Not like before, but the pain was real. "It's a long story. The Primms' house is just there."

She studied him a second longer before she looked forward. *She's not going to let this go.* He probably should think of the least painful way to tell her his sordid history.

They climbed the stairs and knocked on the door. As they waited, he could hear heavy steps inside the house. When the door opened, a very haggard Mr. Primm stood there.

"Milton. Lealia," he said with a weary smile.

"How are you doing, Mr. Primm?" Milton asked.

"Could be better." He stepped aside. "Come in."

The house was nowhere near as tidy as Mrs. Primm liked to keep it. He noticed Lealia looking around as well. Mr. Primm, limping heavily, sank into a seat at the table. "Nice of you two to check on us."

"We are visiting the injured on Reverend Walker's behalf." Milton reached to slide a stack of newspapers off the table. He placed them where Mrs. Primm normally kept them by the door.

"You don't have to do that, Son," Mr. Primm said, a flicker of shame in his eyes.

"It's all right," Lealia said. She began collecting the dishes from the table.

Milton collected the rest and followed Lealia into the kitchen, only to find the sink full already. He rolled up his sleeves. Without speaking, Lealia began sorting what was in the sink. In minutes they had most of the dishes done, falling back on the cleanliness routine they had learned at Tuskegee. "How is Mrs. Primm?" Milton asked when they returned to the living room. Lealia took a cloth with her and cleaned the table.

"Still pretty bad off," Mr. Primm said.

The sadness in his voice made Milton's heart ache. "Does she need a doctor?"

"One's been 'round. Dr. Briggs. He says she needs to rest, but her arm's painin' her pretty bad."

"When is he due back?" Milton asked.

Mr. Primm sighed. "I didn't think to ask."

Lealia touched Milton's arm. "I'll make tea. You go check on Mrs. Primm."

Milton smiled at how right it felt working with her. "If you agree," he said to Mr. Primm, "I can examine Mrs. Primm's arm. My nursing training might help."

Mr. Primm looked away but not before Milton saw the sheen of tears in his eyes. "That would be a big help. She is in such pain."

Mr. Primm went up to prepare Mrs. Primm, and Milton helped Lealia arrange the tea things. "There's almost no food here," she whispered to Milton.

"I saw. Neither of them have been able to go out for any."

She tapped his arm. "Write that down in your little book."

By the time Milton finished the notation, Mr. Primm had returned. "She's excited to see you both."

Lealia took the stairs slowly behind Mr. Primm and Milton, and Milton kept glancing behind him. She was closely watching each of her steps. He wanted to take her home but realized that he needed to let her be the judge of when she had reached her limit.

Mrs. Primm was lying in bed with her right arm propped on a pillow. Where Mr. Primm hid his tears, Mrs. Primm's fell freely down her cheeks. "Milton and Lealia," she said, her voice warbling. "It is so good to see you both. I was so worried."

Milton sat in the chair that was next to the bed.

"How are you, Lealia?" Mrs. Primm asked. "I understand you were injured."

"I was, but I improve more each day," Lealia said with a smile.

Milton saw her eyes drift to Mrs. Primm's swollen and purple arm.

"What did the doctor say about your injury?" Milton asked.

"He said he thinks it's fractured and he would come back later. He left some powders but has not returned." Her voice was strained with pain.

"It is fractured, and you need a splint." Milton had put splints on many a student at Tuskegee. Not only did he study nursing, he also served as a medic for minor injuries at the school. "I must warn you, it will be painful when I put it on."

She let out a huff. "Can't be much more painful than it already is."

Milton, with Lealia's help, collected the supplies he needed. When he touched her arm, Mrs. Primm winced.

Lealia placed her hand on Milton's shoulder. "Maybe she should take a dose of the pain medicine the doctor left."

Milton saw the concern in her eyes. "Can you bring a bit of food and tea?" He hated to send Lealia back downstairs, but he didn't want to send Mr. Primm. The man looked as stricken over his wife's arm as Milton had felt over Lealia's injuries.

Milton breathed a sigh of relief when Lealia returned. She was panting slightly and was a bit flushed, but she put a smile on her face. "Here we are."

She is going straight home after this, Milton thought as she helped Mrs. Primm eat and drink.

"Since you're here, I want to hear about your time at Tuskegee," Mrs. Primm said to Milton. "Lealia told me all about hers."

"I learned a lot." He began applying the splint, with Lealia handing him each item as he needed it.

"Like doctoring." Mrs. Primm managed to give him a proud smile through her pain.

"Yes. The nursing program is the first step in becoming a doctor." He gently began wrapping gauze around the two pieces of thin board Lealia had retrieved from the kitchen. Not ideal, but it would do.

"And you and Lealia found each other?"

His fingers slowed. "Found?" He turned his full attention to evenly wrapping the gauze. He had felt Lealia stiffen behind him.

"She's perfect for you, Milton. Sweet girl. Pretty too, and spirited enough to keep you from being so serious." Mrs. Primm's words started to slur from the medication. Enough that Milton thought she must have forgotten that Lealia was there. "I just learned she used to be a member of Shiloh. While we were at the 6th Avenue church."

His mind went to their friendship, two church kids playing together. He could remember his disappointment on the Sundays he was unable to attend church because his father had kept them up all night with his carrying-on. He remembered missing Lealia. A part of his heart would miss her now. She would be heading to Howard in November.

He finished the wrapping while Mrs. Primm drifted off to sleep. Thankfully, he was saved from answering any more questions about Lealia. Especially since he had no answers.

When the three of them returned downstairs, Lealia looked exhausted.

Milton reached for her hat. "I will come back in a few days. I need to talk to Dr. Briggs about putting plaster on your wife's arm."

"I'll see if I can help Mrs. Rafferty prepare a few meals to bring over." Lealia accepted her hat, understanding Milton's message loud and clear. *Time to go.*

Mr. Primm grew quiet, and it took a moment for Milton to realize that he was crying. "I never saw a thing like that night. Sometimes when I close my eyes, I still see them people lying out there, cold and dead."

Milton gripped Mr. Primm's shoulder. "I know." No matter how much he tried to get it out of his mind, he had the same trouble as Mr. Primm. Milton had also seen it all firsthand. He swallowed.

Mr. Primm wiped his tears. "Thank you for coming over and for the cleaning."

Milton patted Mr. Primm's shoulder. "It's our pleasure to help."

They started back home, not speaking. Then the silence was broken by Lealia's soft sobs. His heart weighed in his chest too. They would visit many more people and would have to see their pain and grief from the same event that injured so many.

He reached over and took Lealia's hand. Her fingers closed around his, and she gave his hand a squeeze.

Lealia started to look forward to doing visitations.

They had started with the Primms, since they were the closest. Milton, with a bit of his searching eyes returning, watched her the whole time. They had tidied the house, and he'd applied a splint to Mrs. Primm's fractured arm. Lealia watched Milton in action, remembering how careful and knowledgeable he had always been. Throughout the visit, she wished she had gotten reacquainted with him while they were in class together.

But she hadn't seen him then. Her only focus was her schoolwork and getting to Howard.

They had returned to the house, Lealia's head unable to bear more. The next morning she expected him to go on his visits without her and was surprised to find him at her door, waiting to help her down the stairs.

The subsequent visits grew substantially more difficult. It was hard to hear the injured try to make sense of what had happened in the church. There were even a few who still didn't know there hadn't been a fire. She watched Milton gently break the news to them as he had to her. She watched their tears flow as they learned that some of their fellow church members had died.

As troubling as those visits were, she was becoming increasingly concerned about Milton. He was steady and careful when he met with the injured, but Lealia noticed, on more than one occasion, that he was sweating and flushed when they left. And when she touched his arm to console him, she felt him trembling. When she mentioned it, he said he was tired and continued on.

She did not want to press the issue, but her concern grew. He had gotten worse since she first noticed how his attention would drift and his eyes would lose focus. She wondered if his mother had noticed. How could she not? But they were so busy with the visitations, and Lealia had been too tired to ask her when they returned home at the end of the day.

The work, however, seemed to help steady him. They ended each day of visits at the parsonage, to Lealia's relief, to give Reverend Walker an update. On the second day, Lealia told him that many of the injured could not prepare food for themselves. When they came back the next day, Reverend Walker told them he had made arrangements with some of the church's women and there were meals waiting in the office for Milton and Lealia to take to people.

Lealia and Milton collected the meals, and Mr. Hamilton, a Shiloh member she vaguely remembered, met them in front of the church and transported them to Holly's Inn, a boardinghouse for women owned by a Negro woman. The whole ride he talked about how she and Milton were "two rascals" when they were younger. Lealia's heart warmed to see Milton smile a little.

Holly met them at the front door with a smile. "Good morning, Mr. Rafferty. Is that Lealia Bevard?"

Lealia smiled. *Another person I don't remember but who knows me.* "Yes, ma'am."

"What you doin' in town? I thought your family moved to Tuskegee," Holly said, rubbing her hands on her apron.

"We did. I was in town for the Baptist Convention," Lealia said.

"Oh, that was something terrible." Holly shook her head.

Milton lifted the containers of food off the back of the wagon. "We have meals."

"They will be appreciated." Holly led them inside. "Mr. Rafferty, it's not my policy to let men upstairs unless it's the doctor."

Milton gave Lealia a worried look and shook his head slightly at her while Holly closed the door.

"But will you allow him to carry the baskets to the top of the stairs?" Lealia asked. "They are quite heavy. I will do the deliveries once I go up." Even though it had been almost two weeks since the stampede, her head and ankle still gave her trouble when she exerted herself too much.

Holly took a basket from Milton as if it were made of paper. "Come, Mr. Rafferty."

When Milton passed Lealia, he gave her a wide-eyed stare and flicked his eyes to Holly, who was already halfway up the stairs.

Lealia covered her mouth to keep from laughing.

Once the baskets were upstairs, Milton passed Lealia his little notebook and she made her rounds. There were six women who were recovering at the inn. Lealia took notes on each and put bowls of food into their hands. Several of them cried with gratitude. They did not have family in town and had no one to care for them. She assured them that Reverend Walker was making arrangements to care for them until they could recover well enough to go home.

She was, however, surprised when she knocked on the last door and Rodah opened it.

"Rodah!" Lealia cried.

"Hi, Lealia," Rodah said, smiling. Her arm was in a sling, and she looked exhausted. "What are you doing here?"

"Milton and I are visiting everyone who was injured to see if they need anything."

Rodah hobbled back to her bed. "'Milton'?" Despite the pain evident on her face, she gave Lealia a smile, her eyebrows lifted.

Lealia cleared her throat. "I mean, Mr. Rafferty. How are you?"

Rodah sighed. "Better than I was when I first got here. Dr. Briggs came around to see me last week but has not been back."

Lealia made a note next to Rodah's name in Milton's book. "I'll ask him to come soon."

When she looked up, Rodah was watching her. "Is there anything else?" Lealia asked.

"Weren't you hurt?" Rodah asked.

Lealia showed Rodah her ankle. Milton had helped her wrap a bandage around it to keep it stable. It showed just above the top of her boot. "My ankle and my head."

"But you're already better?"

"Not completely, but I wasn't injured as badly as others. I thought I could help while I waited. . ."

Rodah's eyes went wide. "You were meeting with the Education Board. How did it go?"

Lealia put on her best smile even though a weight settled between her shoulders. "They were going to grant me a scholarship to Howard. I'm not sure they'll still give it to me after all this."

"I've been mighty worried about the church." Rodah leaned back against the wall behind her bed and sighed. "I was in the middle of sorting the donations that came in from the convention from all the boards. Now that I am not there, Reverend Massey—" She broke off, a look of disgust on her face.

"Mrs. Rafferty has the same dislike of him."

"He—" She looked as if she was trying to find the right words. "He cannot handle the donations. Especially not now."

"Why not now?" An idea crystallized in the back of Lealia's mind.

"Because there will be a lot of money. The Baptist Convention already brought in more banknotes than I've ever seen in one place. Reverend Massey can help, but he lacks the time and skills to handle a large volume of donations. He has his own business to run."

Lealia moved to sit next to her. "Rodah, what if I helped with the donations? If I did your job until you returned?"

Rodah's face lit up. "That would be beyond perfect! You said you were good with sums."

"And I did bookkeeping while I was at Tuskegee. I can ask Mr. Washington to write me a letter of recommendation."

"Please do." Rodah grasped her hand. "The donations to the Baptist Convention help so many people. If those donations aren't dispersed, people like you will be hurt."

Lealia sucked in a breath. She hadn't considered that. If she helped with the donations, maybe the process of her scholarship might be sped up. She could get back on track with her goals. "I'll speak to Reverend Walker today."

"Thank you, Lealia. Give my thanks to Milton." Rodah said his name in a singsong voice as she grinned at Lealia.

Lealia stood, trying to hide the blush on her face. "I will. I'll let you know how it goes with Reverend Walker."

When she went back down the stairs, Holly and Milton were having a lively chat. She did not miss how Milton watched her every step.

She stood taller when she reached the bottom of the stairs. "All done."

Holly shook their hands. "You doin' good work here." She walked them outside.

The boardinghouse was located close to downtown, walking distance from the train station. An ideal spot. Lealia studied the businesses around the inn, and a burned-out structure caught her eye. "What was in that building?"

Holly gave her head a sad shake. "It was a dry goods store owned by a Negro. Burned down last month. Some say people did not like having a Negro business on that side of the street."

"Oh." Milton studied it. "And they never rebuilt?"

"No, the owner is waiting on the insurance to pay out."

Lealia remembered the newspaper article. "Stokes' Dry Goods?"

Holly looked at her with surprise. "Yes."

"I read about it in the paper when I got here," Lealia said.

"My mother told me about him," Milton added, a quizzical expression on his face. "She said he was very kind and helped her through a hard time."

"He was kind," Holly said. "Helped me out a few times as well."

Lealia looked at the building again. If this had happened in Tuskegee, Mr. Washington would have organized the students and they would have had the repairs done by now.

Holly gave her head a sad shake. "I hope he can rebuild. It would be a great loss to the Negroes in Birmingham if he doesn't."

As they made their way from Holly's, Milton and Lealia talked about the new developments downtown. Neither of them had been in Birmingham in years. It seemed like so many new buildings and businesses had sprung up out of the ground. They took turns pointing out the different additions. When they walked past a bakery, Milton's steps slowed, and Lealia couldn't fault him. The most wonderful buttery scent filled the air outside the shop. They peered through the window and saw a tall Negro woman behind the counter.

"Wow," Milton said. He turned to Lealia and grinned with a joy that she hadn't seen in his eyes since the stampede. "We should go inside."

Lealia's stomach grumbled as she surveyed the goods the shop had laid out. Cookies, cakes, bread. . .it all looked delicious.

Milton stepped up to the counter. "How much for the cookies?"

The woman behind the counter smiled. "For you and your sweetheart, three for a penny."

Lealia blushed and focused on the cookies. Her face heated even hotter when Milton, with seemingly no embarrassment, did not correct the woman and asked Lealia what kind she wanted.

"The chocolate chip."

He turned back to the woman. "Three chocolate chip cookies, please."

The woman wrapped three cookies in paper. "You two are quite the talk of town."

Lealia looked up. "You know who we are?"

The woman smiled. "The two Tuskegee angels."

That made Milton blush. "We're only helping, like anyone would do."

"Not everyone would, but it is appreciated." She handed Milton the cookies, but when he tried to give her his payment, she refused. "Take them with my thanks."

Lealia shook her head. "No, we can pay. You need to keep your business going."

The woman gave her a small smile. "Not when Mr. Rafferty carried my younger sister from the church himself."

Milton lowered his arm, closing his hand around the coins. "I only did what I should."

"You know, people told me you were trouble. Especially when you arrived back with Mr. Washington. I'm glad I didn't believe them."

Lealia watched the struggle on Milton's face, but he only said, "Thank you."

Lealia waited until they had reached a less populated area of downtown and eaten two of the cookies before she turned to Milton. "What happened to you at Shiloh?"

His steps slowed almost to a stop. "It's a long story."

"We have time," she said.

He faced her, and she had to force herself to stand still under his searching gaze. She understood though. He was looking for any indication that he should keep this story to himself.

He let out a sigh. "Do you remember the 6th Avenue location at all?"

"Yes."

"Do you know what happened to it?"

"It burned down."

Milton looked off into the distance. "My father was there the night it burned."

Lealia gasped. "Is he the one who burned it down?"

Milton whipped his attention back to her, so much anger in his eyes that she took a step away. "No. I never said he burned it down. I said he was there when it did. But everyone at Shiloh believes he did it."

Before she could speak, he started walking again. She tried to catch up, but he was going too fast. "Milton!" she called. "You know I can only walk so fast on this ankle."

He immediately stopped. When she caught up to him, most of the anger was gone from his face. "Sorry. I forgot."

Standing in front of him, she wanted to put her arms around him and settle him. Instead, she grasped his hand. "I shouldn't have asked about it."

He lowered his head. "I expected you to ask me about it sooner than this."

"It's hard to believe they would treat you so cruelly."

"That's because you are their beloved daughter, and I am their troublesome son." Milton spoke with so much venom that Lealia covered her mouth.

Then his whole posture sank, his shoulders slumping. "Forgive me. You don't deserve my ire."

She reached out and placed her hand on his cheek. "You are not their troublesome son now."

For a brief second, he closed his eyes and pressed his cheek into the palm of her hand. "No matter how much they dislike me and my family, I cannot ignore their pain. I will not treat them as they treated me and my mother."

"That is because you're an honorable man."

Milton startled, and to her surprise, tears slipped from his eyes. "Thank you," he said, his voice husky.

She stepped closer and wiped the tears from his face. He looked into her eyes, and the whole world melted away. She swallowed at the evident pain in his deep, rich eyes. "I am so sorry, Milton."

More tears. "For years they've slandered our family name. Shunned my mother. And for nothing. My father was not the arsonist. He did plenty of bad things, but not that."

"Oh, Milton."

He sniffled. "I was supposed to—" He stopped and took a step back.

He swiped the rest of the tears from his cheeks and straightened his shoulders. "We should go."

They walked in silence until the church came into view, but it was as if Milton were not there. He was lost in his past.

"Milton, can I get your opinion on something?"

He put on a forced smile. "Yes, sure."

She told him about Rodah and the donations. He listened, his eyes flicking between her and the church.

Then he gave her a real smile. "I think that's a great idea. You already know bookkeeping, and they're probably looking for as much help as they can get. Mom told me that with so many of the Shiloh members out of commission, the day-to-day tasks at the church are not getting done."

"All right. I'll speak to Reverend Walker today."

"Good." He gave her a wry look. "Besides, you can barely carry the baskets anyway."

She popped him on the arm. "Hey! That's not nice."

He broke out in a laugh. "Holly had to carry your basket."

"Stop it! I tried my best."

That only made him laugh more. She gave him a push and walked away from him, but he closed the distance easily with his long strides. "Lealia! Come back. I'm joking."

Although she was smiling, she kept marching forward as fast as her ankle allowed.

When he caught up, he grasped her shoulders, still grinning. Then he sobered a little. "I do think it will be a great idea for you to help if Reverend Walker agrees."

She looked into his eyes, and once again, everything slowed. His smile vanished, and his gaze traveled around her face. She felt hot beneath her hat.

Just as his gaze reached her lips, someone called to them. Milton hastily stepped back. Reverend Walker was striding toward them. "Glad I caught you. I was on my way home, but I wanted an update on your visits."

Lealia told him about the women in the boardinghouse and what Rodah had suggested.

Reverend Walker rubbed his chin. "And you did bookkeeping at Tuskegee?"

"Yes," Lealia said. She didn't have to elaborate. Milton jumped in and told Reverend Walker all about her work for the Children's House at Tuskegee.

"If you feel recovered enough to help, I would greatly appreciate it," Reverend Walker said.

"I can start tomorrow, if you like. Of course," Lealia added, "it would only be temporary."

"Of course. Rodah will recover, and I expect that working as a church clerk will not replace your dreams of attending Howard. See you tomorrow."

After they watched Reverend Walker go into the parsonage, Lealia grinned at Milton.

He shook her hand with vigor. "You did it!"

Although she was happy, the motion made her eyes swim. "Ouch," she said.

Milton immediately let go. "I'm sorry. I forgot again. Let's go home. It's been a long day."

Again, he called his house *their* home. Why correct him?

CHAPTER ELEVEN

I have to get out.

Milton fought, but he was still trapped. All around him were people with flat, lifeless eyes. So many people.

Help! He screamed, but no sound came. He fought harder. Then he realized he was the one to help. To move the living and the dead.

He jolted awake and sat up, his breathing ragged. Another nightmare. Sweat ran down his face and chest. His pillow was drenched. He swiped his trembling hand over his face. The images of the nightmare appeared each time he blinked. He gripped fistfuls of the sheets, and the trembling increased. He fought to breathe, fought to stop the tremors, but they grew stronger. He groaned. *I am at home in my bed*, he told himself.

But nothing changed. He still shivered.

A soft knock sounded on his door. "Milton?"

Lealia.

He squeezed his eyes tight. Had he been yelling? He took gulp after gulp of air, but it still felt as if he were underwater.

"Milton? Are you all right?" The doorknob twisted, and he was never so happy that he had started locking it after the first episode. After his mother nearly found him doubled over, gasping for air.

He pressed his lips together, trying to be as quiet as he could. If he remained silent, Lealia would return to her room.

After he sat there for longer than he could tally, he heard her soft steps retreat down the hall and her door close. He exhaled, lying back on the bed, exhausted from sitting with his muscles tightened.

He had to get this under control. It was easier when he was out and about, helping and checking on people. But at night, he had no control. The tightness in his chest would not abate in the darkness. He knew he wasn't trapped anymore. Not surrounded by the dead. But that did nothing to soothe his emotions.

He rose and washed, tore the sheets from his bed, and dressed.

The smell of breakfast greeted him when he came down the stairs. His mother met him at the kitchen door and planted a kiss on his cheek. "Good morning."

"Morning," he replied and got himself a glass of water.

He took the water out to the dining room table and sat. How was he going to get through the day this exhausted?

He closed his eyes. "Milton." Lealia's voice was so soft, he nearly missed it.

He sat back and opened his eyes. "Morning."

She stood beside the table, eyeing him with sadness.

He sighed. She'd heard everything. "Lealia—"

She held up a hand and glanced in the direction of the kitchen. "We can talk later."

They finished breakfast and headed out to Shiloh.

Halfway there, Lealia spoke. "Do I have to ask, or are you gonna tell me?"

"Nothing to tell." He kept his eyes straight ahead.

She grasped his arm and pulled him to a stop. "Milton, you were screaming for help at the top of your lungs. I'm surprised your mother didn't hear."

He swallowed. "I had a nightmare about being trapped in the church." His voice rose loud enough that people walking along the same road turned and looked at them. *Great. Now it will get around that the junior Rafferty is yelling at women.*

"I only wanted to offer my help." Lealia didn't appear to be angry at his tone. Just sad. "I have nightmares too, Milton. I was trapped under a bench."

He sighed and dropped his head, deflated. "Then you understand. No need to press this."

When he glanced up at her, she looked as if she was very much going to press this. Instead, she pursed her lips and started walking.

She only knows about the nightmares, not the tremors. I can handle this. All he had to do was keep his focus on helping the injured. Most of them were recovering, some even able to make tea for him while he visited. He also had another task to keep him occupied. He needed to start looking for Mr. Stokes. He hadn't had the heart to tell his mother about Evan. About seeing another young man searching for a father.

Milton had written down the names of all the injured. Or he believed he had. There was so much chaos that night. Some of the injured could have been removed before he wrote their names down. He hadn't been to the hospitals yet. Mr. Stokes might be there.

At least Mr. Stokes didn't abandon Evan. He sighed.

"Hey." Lealia bumped him with her shoulder. "Are you listening?"

He turned to her and found her giving him a pointed gaze. "Sorry. I was lost in thought."

"I know. I've been talking for five minutes, and you haven't responded."

He faced her, and she promptly looked down at his shoes. He frowned. Since they'd had that conversation after agriculture class, he noticed that if he gave her his whole attention, she often found anything but his face to focus on. "Why do you do that?"

She tipped her head up but barely lifted her eyes to his. "Do what?"

"What you just did. Demand my attention and then look away."

Now she glared into his eyes. "I do not demand."

Milton laughed. "Oh yes you do."

She huffed and started walking, her posture broadcasting her discomfort.

He grasped her arm to slow her steps. "Lealia. I've upset you. Tell me what's the matter."

She turned to face him, a frown on her face. A frown that put the cutest little wrinkle in her nose. "Do you understand how unnerving your gaze is?"

He reared back. "What?"

Her eyes lowered. . .again. "It's as if you can read my thoughts."

He chuckled a little, stepped closer, and leaned down to her eye level. He gave her an overexaggerated quizzical look. "If I could, what would I see?"

Her lips parted a little, and the most beautiful blush bloomed on her cheeks and all the way up to the tips of her ears.

Oh. His face heated, and he stepped back. *What was she thinking about him?* "Not that you have to tell me," he said with a cough. He started walking, and she followed in silence.

They met Reverend Walker on the grass in front of the church. "Good morning. You two are here just in time."

Milton took a step toward the parsonage. "I was thinking of visiting the hospital today."

"Wait." Reverend Walker gestured to the church building. "We have to go inside today, children."

Lealia paled, and beads of sweat formed on Milton's forehead. "We do?" he asked, his voice tight in his throat.

"Well, you do, Miss Bevard," Reverend Walker said. "The clerk's office is in there."

Milton watched Lealia. How would she react? But he should have known. She straightened to her full height, masking her fear, and took Reverend Walker's arm. They walked to the foot of the stairs together. Milton looked up at the front door of the church.

Lealia turned to him, unspoken understanding in her eyes. She took two steps up. "You can head to the hospital, like you said." His heart warmed. She was giving him a way out. But how would it look if she could go inside and he could not? He curled his fingers into a fist as he felt the first hint of a tremor.

If Lealia can go up the stairs, I can too. But his feet stayed rooted to the ground. Gathering all his resolve, as he had the night of the stampede, he followed them.

The inside of the church was eerily quiet. The same way it was once the stampede stopped. His breath quickened. Reverend Walker and Lealia were far enough ahead of him to not notice him wiping the sweat from his brow.

To his relief, Reverend Walker deviated to the right of the sanctuary doors to a hallway that ran down the side of the church. "The clerk's office is this way, but I need to get the keys from my office first."

The reverend's office was significantly bigger than the one where they had met Evan. The large windows gave him a view of the city.

The clerk's office might have the same view. He sighed in relief. Lealia wouldn't feel trapped in an office like this.

"Miss Bevard, I will get the extra key from Reverend Massey when he shows up," Reverend Walker said as he retrieved his keys from the top drawer of his desk.

"I heard my name."

They all turned to find Reverend Massey standing in the doorway.

"Reverend Massey, good morning. You are just in time to meet our new clerk, Lealia Bevard." Reverend Walker motioned to Lealia. "She studied bookkeeping during her time at Tuskegee, and she's a daughter of this church." He patted Milton's shoulder. "This is Milton Rafferty. His mother attends Shiloh, so I guess that makes him a son of the church."

Milton jolted so hard that Lealia gave him a questioning stare. He was not the church's son. Far from it.

"Good morning, Reverend Massey." Lealia's greeting gave Milton enough time to collect himself. From where he was standing, Reverend Walker missed Reverend Massey's expression, but Milton did not. The man smiled very much like a wolf who was staring at a lamb he was ready to devour.

"Miss Bevard, good to see you again."

Milton gave her a quizzical look. She had not mentioned that she knew Reverend Massey. Lealia must have seen the question on Milton's mind, because she said, "Reverend Massey was on the Education Board scholarship committee." She took a step closer to Milton.

Milton turned his body to shield her. "No need to introduce me, Reverend Walker. I met Reverend Massey at my house a few days ago." Milton made sure to convey in his tone that he had not enjoyed the meeting.

"Well, let's go down to the clerk's office," Reverend Walker said.

Milton would have to get more information from his mother about this man if Lealia was going to be working with him.

It took everything in Lealia's power not to follow Milton out of the church.

She wanted to help, but she did not want to work with Reverend Massey. She remembered Mrs. Rafferty's reaction to him when he came to the house. And from what she knew of the woman, Mrs. Rafferty did not make miscalculations in her assessment of people.

She reluctantly followed Reverends Walker and Massey to the clerk's office, which was a short distance from Reverend Walker's office. Milton gave her one more questioning look before he left, as if he was asking her if she would be okay. She gave him a slight nod, and he disappeared down the hall.

But when she took in the room in front of her, all her worry about Reverend Massey disappeared.

The office was a mess.

There were piles of papers and letters covering the desk. Ledger books sat open on chairs and on the edge of bookcase shelves.

Reverend Walker saw her looking around. "Rodah normally keeps this place neat as a pin. We miss her deeply. Reverend Massey has been trying to help out."

It did not escape Lealia's notice that Reverend Massey bristled at the "trying" part.

Lealia smiled at Reverend Walker, the memory of the Children's House records in her mind. "I've seen worse."

Reverend Massey cleared his throat. "Let me show you where everything is."

Lealia laughed before she could help herself. "You know where everything is in all this?" She motioned to the room. "Let me sort it all out, and if I have questions, I'll ask."

Reverend Walker laughed. "Good point. We'll leave you to it."

The sorting alone took most of the morning. After she'd cleared a space on the desk, she put all the unopened letters on it. Next, she gathered the ledger books, taking a quick look inside to determine what department of the church each one was for. Then she dealt with all the other papers, from notes to memos. She sorted them into normal church business in one pile and notes concerning the stampede in another.

The ones concerning the stampede were heartbreaking. There were notes informing Reverend Walker about the injured. Pleas from members who had taken people in and now needed assistance to care for them. Notes asking the Reverend to send Dr. Briggs to them. In the end, she decided that Milton should get those. If there were any injuries he couldn't handle, he could inform Dr. Briggs.

Then she moved on to the letters. Those she found fell into categories as well. The majority of them were correspondence concerning the Baptist Convention. Her heart grew heavier with each one she read. They were so full of hope and excitement for an event that had ended in disaster. She remembered her own excitement in coming here. None of them had known how heartbreakingly it would end.

She opened each one, making a quick note for Reverend Walker about the contents. When she lifted a letter from the Education Board from the pile, her hands slowed. Two weeks had gone by since the stampede. Since she had sat in front of Reverend Massey and the rest of the Board. Her life had changed so much that it felt as if that meeting and everything before it was a dream.

She opened the letter with her heart in her throat. Yes, some of the board members were injured, but most of them were not. They might be able to keep their promise to give Lealia her scholarship next month.

As she skimmed the letter, however, her hopes sank. It was addressed to Reverend Walker and was about the Board's scholarship fund. From the first words, she knew that something had gone wrong. The next paragraph seized her heart:

> *Although a thorough search has been made, the missing funds have not been located. We cannot determine if the shortage is an administrative or misappropriation error. We will keep you informed, but as of this moment, we feel uncomfortable offering scholarships to more than two students.*

Lealia's head swam. Only two students. She had been one of only two students? That made the scholarship all the more precious. She made a note in the ledger, her vision swimming with tears.

If she had read this letter before the stampede, she would have been overjoyed. Maybe even thought she deserved the scholarship. She would have certainly crowed over her classmates at Tuskegee.

Now all her plans felt like they were made of the silk threads of a spider's web. Beautiful but fragile. Her head began to pound with urgency, and she couldn't stop her tears. A prickle of shame ran through her thoughts. She had been so sure. So confident that everything would occur exactly the way she wanted and that there was nothing to stop her.

She remembered the moment before rescue came. The moment she was waiting to die and all her plans meant nothing. The tears rolled faster down her cheeks. It was as if all her determination was gone in that moment, the helplessness of being trapped robbing it from her.

She wiped her eyes. Crying would only increase the pain growing in her head. If she let this line of thinking consume her thoughts, she would not finish the task of organizing the office. As she picked up the next letter, she thought of Milton. If she did achieve her goals of getting to Howard, how would she adjust to not being near him? They had been on campus together, but she had not known him then. She was much closer to him now. Definitely friends. They could have been more.

When he asked about reading her thoughts that morning, she had been thinking about what it would be like if she wrapped her arms around him and held him until his nightmares stopped. If she took care of him the way he was caring for everyone else. If they could be more than friends.

How foolish that thinking was. She would be gone, and Milton would go back to Tuskegee. That dream did not fit into her future life at Howard.

Milton went around to the hospital and found that almost all the patients from the stampede had gone home. Only one remained, an older woman, Mrs. Jones, who had been caught in the undertow of the surge and was trampled. He asked if he could speak to her. Maybe she saw Mr. Stokes at some point during the night.

When he reached her bedside, her eyes grew wide. "Milton Rafferty?"

He pushed a smile to his lips, but dread kept it dim. Someone from Shiloh. "Yes."

She did not return his smile. "I thought I must have been mistaken when I saw you and the Bevard girl come in the church the night of the disaster. I thought you had run away."

"No. I'm studying to be a doctor at Tuskegee." He did not have to tell her that, but it felt good to. Judging by her tone and the sour look on her face, she probably had been gossiping about him.

Her next question confirmed it. "Did you go to Tuskegee to be with your father?"

"No," he said. "I am helping Reverend Walker with the injured. Do you know Mr. Alfred Stokes?"

"Yes. He owns the dry goods store." She frowned. "Or at least he did."

"Did you see him the night of the disaster?" Milton pulled out his notebook.

"I did." Her expression turned thoughtful. "Not that I was trying to hear, but I saw him having words with someone behind the church. The insurance man."

Several people had already told Milton that Mr. Stokes was waiting for the payout from his insurance to reopen the store. If they were discussing the delayed payout, that would explain the disagreement. "Did you see him after that?"

Mrs. Jones, visibly growing more tired, shook her head.

"Thank you." If nothing else, he could tell Evan that his father had gone to the church. "I will be back to check on you soon."

She quirked an eyebrow. "You will?"

He clenched his jaw. "Yes, I will."

He left the hospital, wanting to grumble. Mrs. Jones was clearly a busybody and wanted gossip about his family. But it had been a small price to pay to know that Mr. Stokes had not abandoned his son. Where was he now? The hospital was the last place the injured had been taken en masse. Mr. Stokes was not anywhere where the living had been—

The thought stopped him cold. *If Mr. Stokes is not with the living, maybe he is with the dead.*

Reluctantly, Milton changed directions.

For some reason, the idea of going to the morgue was easier than the idea of going into the church's sanctuary. In his second year of school, Milton's class had gone to a mortuary one town over. Before they went in, his teacher stood outside the door and said, "This will either make you a better nurse, or break you."

Half the class broke and left the nursing program.

Milton would have broken if he hadn't focused on the fact that every corpse in the room was made in God's image. They could never be disgusting. Every person deserved the same dignity in death as they'd deserved in life. It had not been easy, but he made it through.

Now he could step inside a mortuary because a grieving son was looking for his father. Milton prayed he would not find the man inside.

He headed to Vaughn's Funeral Services first. Vaughn's was the closest to the church, and Milton thought it was as good a place as any to start.

The familiar smell of embalming fluid wafted to his nose when he entered the front door. An older and very tired-looking Negro man glanced up from a desk. He had a dark beard set against his dark skin. His hair was thick around the crown of his head, but the top was bald.

"Good afternoon, young man," the man said as he rose to his feet. "How can I help you?"

"Are you Mr. Vaughn, the mortician?"

"That I am." He tried to smile, but it seemed his lips had no energy to complete the action.

"My name is Milton Rafferty. I am assisting Reverend Walker with the victims of the stampede."

Mr. Vaughn shook his head. "I have never seen anything like that in all my life, and I see dead people almost every day."

"Yes, it was horrific," Milton said. He suppressed a shudder. *Not here. Not now.*

Mr. Vaughn gave him a softening look. "Were you there?"

Milton nodded. "Inside. I managed to escape with some bruising."

"God bless you." Mr. Vaughn shook Milton's hand. "Have a seat."

"I was wondering if you could help me." Milton took a seat in front of the desk, and Mr. Vaughn went back to his chair. "I'm looking for a possible victim of the stampede. Maybe someone who has not been identified yet."

Mr. Vaughn rubbed his beard. "I have a few of them here. No family has come and claimed them. I didn't rightly know what to do with their bodies. I was thinking of reaching out to the reverend to arrange for burial."

"I will speak with him later." Milton opened his notebook. "The man's name is Alfred Stokes—"

Mr. Vaughn bolted from his seat. "Dear God, that's his name."

"I'm not sure I understand," Milton said, rising also.

"There's a man in the vault I thought I recognized. It has been a long week, and in my exhaustion, I could not recall his name. I shopped at his dry goods store!"

Sorrow coiled in Milton's chest. Evan's father was gone. "So he's here?"

"Yes." Mr. Vaughn drew out the word.

Milton frowned. "Yes, but. . ."

"Alfred Stokes does not have injuries consistent with a stampede." Mr. Vaughn smoothed a hand over his bald head. "Come look." He took a step and then stopped. "Uh. . ."

"I'm a nursing student at Tuskegee. We did a class at a mortuary last year."

Mr. Vaughn eyed him. "Are you now? I thought I had heard that from somebody."

Milton sighed. *More gossip.*

They went into the morgue. It was lined with corpses on tables, each one covered with a sheet. "There are three unidentified bodies here and more at the other mortuaries around the city," Mr. Vaughn said as he moved to a table near the rear of the room. He stopped in front of it and looked up at Milton. "You sure?"

"Yes, sir. I saw the dead from the church while I was helping that night."

"All right then." He pulled the sheet back to expose the man's face and chest. The man was older, maybe forty, thick beard. He had a scar behind his ear, and it looked as if his nose had been broken at some point in his life. Milton saw the resemblance to Evan immediately.

More notably, there was a bullet hole just above his heart. Milton sucked in a breath. "He was shot?"

Mr. Vaughn nodded and covered the man back up. "Took the bullet out myself."

"But how?"

Mr. Vaughn gawked at him. "With a gun."

"Sorry. That's not what I meant. I meant, how did he get in the churchyard with a gaping bullet hole in his chest? There was very little blood at the scene."

"Mr. Stokes was covered in it." Mr. Vaughn led Milton back to the vestibule. "Don't know how, but he came to me with the other bodies from the church."

"But I was there that night. I would have noticed him."

"You bet you would. With all that blood, he woulda looked like a ghoul." Mr. Vaughn sat down at his desk. "All I can tell you is that he was brought here that night. But there was so much disorder, he could have walked in himself and I don't know if I would have noticed."

"Thank you, Mr. Vaughn. This will give his son some peace. I'll tell him to come down."

"I'll have Mr. Stokes all ready when the younger Mr. Stokes comes."

Milton stood on the front step of the mortuary for a long moment before he turned in the direction of the church. How did Mr. Stokes get shot? And how did he get among the dead at the church?

In a flash, his memory produced the clear image of the man with the bloody shirt at the end of the row.

Mr. Stokes had been there. Milton had seen him.

CHAPTER TWELVE

To Lealia's relief, after Reverend Walker popped his head in the door to check on her when he came in, she saw no one else for most of the morning. No Reverend Massey.

By early afternoon, she had the office in working order. The mail was sorted, and she had delivered the pertinent letters to Reverend Walker. He told her he would return them after he responded to them, since they were normally filed in the little closet in her office.

Now she had to figure out what to do with all the banknotes. Reverend Walker had left shortly after she delivered the letters, and she'd forgotten to ask him about them.

Some of the letters were from Baptist churches that had heard about the disaster. Many of them included banknotes. She recorded the amounts and then searched the office. Surely there was a lockbox here. The bookkeeping office at Tuskegee had one that held payments from students, and the bookkeeper deposited them once a week.

After searching the bookshelves, she began looking around the rest of the room. She came to what looked like a simple wood panel, but it had a handle on the outside. She pulled it, and it opened to reveal a small closet. Maybe the lockbox was inside.

The closet was dark. She couldn't tell from where she stood how deep the closet was or what was inside. Based on the size of the opening, it wasn't big. Dread hovered like a shadow just over her shoulder. A tiny, dark space like the space under the pew.

She stepped away from the door. The church had electric lighting. Maybe there was a light switch. Searching the walls around the doorframe, she found nothing. She checked the office for a candle but didn't find one.

That meant there was probably a single bulb with a pull string inside the closet. How else was anyone supposed to see? She leaned in the door, stretching her hand up where she expected the string to be. The closet was deeper than she expected.

Nothing.

She took a half step inside, still reaching, her heart hammering in her throat. Her fingers found nothing but empty air. She stretched farther, keeping one foot outside the door and putting her weight on one ankle. She had forgotten that it was her injured one until it buckled and she pitched forward. Unable to see, she put her hands out to brace herself. Instead of falling to the floor, she crashed into something else.

She let out a half scream and then clamped her mouth shut when she realized her hands rested on a bookcase. *The back wall.*

Something tinged rhythmically above her head. It took her a second to realize she must have hit the pull string when she fell and it was hitting against the bulb. She focused on the sound and not the panic rising in her throat. The darkness seemed to be getting deeper every second she stayed in the closet. She caught the string and turned the light on.

The room was so small that her being in it filled it. Shelves lined the walls. It looked like a catchall closet. There was a mop and broom, a toolbox, some table linens. Covering one wall were boxes labeled with the names of the different departments in the church. There was even a blanket and pillow. On the shelf next to the door sat the lockbox. She sighed. That meant she would have to come in this tiny, dark room every day. *But I can leave the light on.*

Her ankle throbbed with a note of protest, and she left the room and sat at her desk. She lifted her skirt and studied her ankle. It didn't look swollen. *Milton won't be happy if I injure it again.* Satisfied her ankle was all right, she went to the closet door and closed it.

If her parents could see her now, they probably wouldn't recognize her. A few years ago, after a lot of rain, the drop door to the attic had swollen and stuck, so her father and brother had hoisted Lealia up through the tiny attic window. She was the only one small enough to get through. In the darkness and heat, she had unscrewed the hinges on the door so Papa and Nathan could push it back toward her. She had been in several other tight spaces, since she was the littlest person in the house. She could never do any of those things now. Not after being trapped under all those people. Even thinking of it made her shiver.

She marched to the desk. Now that she had located the lockbox, she needed the key.

She opened the second drawer as the office door opened. She stood up straight, bracing herself in case it was Reverend Massey. But instead, a very frazzled-looking Milton walked through the door.

She glanced at the clock on the wall. It was only one o'clock. "What are you doing here?"

Milton rubbed his face and closed the door behind him. "I need to talk to you. You're the smartest person I know."

His words knocked out most of the chill she had felt only a moment ago. "Okay," she said slowly, sitting.

Milton sat in the chair on the other side of the desk. He ran his hand over his face. "It may be a little disturbing to hear."

She swallowed. The last thing she needed was to hear something disturbing after her encounter in the closet. But Milton had such a desperate look on his face. . . She braced herself, nodding for him to continue. Maybe he needed to talk about his nightmares.

He let out a breath. "Two days ago, a young man named Evan Stokes came to see Reverend Walker. He was looking for his father among the injured."

"Mr. Alfred Stokes, the owner of the dry goods store that burned down?"

"Yes." Milton's shoulders drooped. She wanted to hold his hand. "Mr. Stokes was not on any of my injured lists. I asked around, and only one person had any information on him. She said that he was at the church the night of the stampede."

"Could he be somewhere else? Traveling?"

Milton shook his head. "We asked Evan that when we talked to him."

"So where is he?" Dread made her fingertips cold, knowing what was coming next.

"I found him," Milton said, wringing his hands. "Mr. Stokes. I found him."

"He's dead." She didn't bother asking. She already knew the answer. Milton's demeanor said Mr. Stokes was dead. Another one dead from the stampede. Her heart constricted with sadness.

"That's not the most disturbing part." He sat forward in the chair. "He was taken from the church to the mortuary with a bullet in his chest."

The breath she was holding whooshed out. "What?"

"I asked Mr. Vaughn about it, and he said everything was chaotic that night but that he was sure Mr. Stokes was brought in with the others."

"But no one was shot at the church. Not that you know of, right?"

"Right. I remember thinking as I carried people out how little blood there was, but then I remembered. I saw a man lying in the church with blood all down the front of his shirt."

Lealia's shoulders drooped. "I can't offer much assistance, since I was trapped and unconscious most of the time. My clearest memories happened before the stampede started." An image of her and Milton sitting on the bench across the street came to mind. *We had no idea what was about to happen.*

"I know. Maybe you can help me figure out how he got there."

Lealia frowned. "If everything was as chaotic as you said it was after the stampede, then he could have come there on his own to get help and no one noticed."

"I thought about that. But I saw the wound. He would not have gotten far without dropping."

Of course he'd seen the wound. The stampede hadn't changed Milton's unflappable constitution. Or at least it hadn't driven it completely away. "Or without someone else seeing him bleeding," Lealia added.

Milton stood from the chair and started to pace. "Correct. So how did he get there?"

"Given what we know, there is only one way he could have." Lealia spoke slowly, not wanting to admit what they were both thinking. "Someone carried him there."

Milton ran his hand down his face. "And that bullet hole says someone murdered him."

This episode lasted longer than usual.

He had gone through dinner thinking about Mr. Stokes, trying to make sense of what he had seen. Even Mr. Vaughn saw that Mr. Stokes' presence among the church dead was strange. Even stranger was the fact that he hadn't heard a gunshot. He thought of the eerie quiet after the stampede. It had transformed the sanctuary into both a hospital and a morgue in minutes. A gunshot would not have gone unnoticed.

Besides, the police were on hand that night. They of all people would have noticed someone bleeding.

Mom noticed his silence, and he tried to come up with a reason. Lealia, to her credit, must have known what was on his mind and redirected his mother's attention by telling her about her work and her search for the church's lockbox. Milton's mind was occupied by his own mystery, but he didn't miss the note of terror in Lealia's voice when she mentioned that the lockbox was in a dark closet.

He had gone to bed exhausted and, just before dawn, woke up with his breath stuck in his throat. The nightmare had shifted, and now Mr. Stokes' gray face was among the others. The trembling started. He wrapped his arms around himself, stomach pitching. The house around him was dark and quiet. He was unsure if he had yelled out, but he knew he could not scream now. That would bring Lealia to his door.

Am I going to wake to this every day for the rest of my life? Before he could stop himself, he groaned. He had studied for years how to care for the injured. Now he was being haunted by the memory of them. And this had happened at Shiloh, the place that had already hurt him and his mother.

The trembling slowed, leaving him feeling wrung out. He thought of what Lealia had said when she first went down the stairs after her injury. That a month ago, she was an active, healthy woman. A month ago, he was studying, going to class, treating other students in the school's nursing unit. Now he was barely hiding his tremors. One slip, and his mother and Lealia would see.

Realizing that sleep was useless, he rose and got dressed then slipped out of his room and went downstairs. His mother had not awakened yet. He grabbed his coat and went out the back door. The night had cooled from the warmth of the day before. He took in a deep breath, his eyes on the lightening sky. It was bright enough to see the yard around him and Mom's attempt at a garden.

From behind him, the door opened. He turned slowly, ready for his mother's questioning.

Lealia stood at the door. Her hair was down, pulled away from her face with a ribbon. She hugged herself in the cool air. "I heard you come out."

Shame locked his words in his throat. She'd heard him *before* he came out.

She crossed the distance to stand next to him, her eyes on Mom's garden. "That is one sad garden."

Much to his surprise, Milton laughed.

She went inside the little fence his mother had erected around the plants. "Go get the garden tools."

He shook his head. "I'm the last person you want touching plants."

Her laughter rang through the yard. "You can't be all that bad."

"You have no idea," he said with a grumble. Nevertheless, he retrieved the tools.

Lealia was clearing the weeds when he returned. She laughed at the worried look he had on his face. "Come on. I'll show you what to do."

And she did. Pointing out what were weeds and what were plants. Showing him how to better position the tomato plants around the stakes. All the while, she explained what she was doing. In a matter of about fifteen minutes, the garden looked much better. They even found a few tomatoes to harvest.

"You're really good at this," Milton said as he placed the tomatoes in a bowl he'd gotten from the kitchen.

She looked up at him, the early morning sun making her face glow. "I should be. I've been helping my father in the fields for as long as I can remember."

"Will you miss it when you go to Howard?" He knew it was a difficult question for her, but he needed to know if she would miss the garden. Because if she did, she might miss him too.

Her face completely shut down. "I can always start a garden

wherever I live." She stepped away, but he touched her arm.

"I didn't mean to upset you."

She glanced up at him, struggle in her eyes. He understood. She wasn't where she wanted to be any more than he was. She looked down at the bowl of tomatoes. "I may have to go back home anyway. Reverend Walker told me that all the church's boards are committing their resources to caring for the injured." She let out a sigh and brushed her hair from her face, leaving a smudge of soil on her cheek. "As they should. The injured need the funds more than I do."

His hand seemed to move with a mind of its own. He cupped her cheek and used his thumb to brush the dirt away. "There will be more donations and more funds. Who knows, Reverend Walker may be able to give you something for working at the church."

She looked up, a flicker of hope in her eyes. "Very true." She gave him a little smile.

His heart thudded hard in his rib cage. Her face was just inches from his. Close enough. . .

Her eyes flicked down to his lips, and heat scorched up his spine. He leaned closer, and she did not move away.

Their lips touched with the softest whisper, her lips like silk against his. Her face was warm under his palm, and tendrils of her hair brushed his fingers.

She pulled away a little. "Milton," she murmured against his mouth. He kissed her again, threading his fingers around the back of her neck and tugging her forward. She let out a little sigh. Even though Lealia was not the first girl he'd kissed, in the rising sun, surrounded by the sounds of the world awakening, she might as well have been the only girl he'd ever kissed.

But he'd held his eyes closed too long. Even with Lealia's soft lips against his, the memories filled the dark space. His closed eyes gave his mind the perfect backdrop to play images of the stampede at Shiloh. The injured and the screams. He kept kissing her to forget. To not see. He pulled her closer.

Suddenly Lealia moved away, her eyes wide with surprise. Then that surprise shifted to anger. She shoved him in the chest, hard. "How dare you?"

His words stuck in his throat. This was a mistake. He should have taken her back inside. Not stood here in this magical light with her. "I—"

"If you're going to give a girl a kiss, you should at least be present for it."

Shame hit him like a lightning bolt. "You're right. I am sorry."

She put her hands on her hips. "You should be. No girl wants her first kiss to be like that." Her lips trembled as she spoke.

First kiss? He couldn't corral his words enough to get them to come out of his mouth. He had given her her first kiss? His pulse hammered in his ears.

She pushed past him. "The next time you kiss me, do better." She was through the garden's gate before he could say any more.

He heard the back door open but didn't move from where he stood. His emotions were in such a tangle. The tremors. Lealia, who would be gone as soon as the Education Board sent her scholarship money. The injured. Shiloh. Mr. Stokes and his own father.

All the world seemed to be closing in to drown him.

No, he thought. *I cannot drown.*

Lealia's emotions swirled like a storm.

Milton had kissed her.

She had heard him tossing and turning in his bed in the predawn. Heard his ragged breathing. The same as the other night, she had gone to his door. But just like that night, he eventually quieted. Her heart had felt heavy for him even though she was probably having the same nightmares.

She was surprised he hadn't mentioned hearing her scream in her sleep since that time he had come and woken her up. Her nightmares had seemed extra vivid last night, the closet and the space under the pew blending together. She should have expected that being in the small closet would affect her that way.

But then, she had gone out into the garden, and Milton, those lovely, searching eyes looking into hers, his strong hand on his cheek, had kissed her. She could have melted into a puddle at how wonderful it was. However, she was alarmed at how urgent his kiss became. It was as though he was there in the garden with her and then all of a sudden he wasn't. As though he had gone somewhere much more troubling.

It took all her self-control to not blush straight through breakfast with Milton sitting across from her. Her first kiss.

She had tried to avoid walking to the church with him by attempting to leave before he did. "I can go alone," she had said.

He shook his head and lowered his voice so his mother couldn't hear. "I need to talk to Reverend Walker about Mr. Stokes."

The sun lit the bright blue skies as they set off from the house in silence. When they reached the stairs to the church, they both stopped. Yesterday they had gone in with Reverend Walker. It had been easy, as if he was an embodiment of God's peace. Without him, Lealia's knees wobbled.

"We need to talk to him about Mr. Stokes," Milton said.

Is that how he does it? Focuses on everyone else's needs and happiness to get over his fear? With only a look of agreement passing between them, they raced up the stairs, inside and up to the reverend's office. The quiet told her that Reverend Walker had not arrived yet. As they went down the hall, Lealia heard a thump in her office.

She turned to Milton. "Why don't you check Reverend Walker's office. I think I heard someone in mine. Might be him. He usually puts the mail on my desk before I arrive."

Milton nodded and went ahead, his footsteps loud in the quiet hall.

When she reached her office, the door stood slightly ajar. Odd. She pushed the door open to find Reverend Massey behind her desk, riffling through the papers on it.

He looked up in surprise, and if Lealia had seen what she thought, that was an expression of guilt on his face.

She put on her best smile. "Good morning, Reverend Massey. Is there something I can help you find?"

He stepped back. "Good morning, Miss Bevard. I was just...um..." he blubbered.

"You have undone all my hard work," she said scoldingly, keeping her tone lighter than the caution she felt in her chest.

"I thought a letter had come for me." He moved from behind her desk with two quick steps. She noticed that one of her drawers stood open.

"I put the letters away." She picked up the ledger she used to track the mail and thumbed through the pages. "No, no letter for you."

"Oh, very well." He bolted so fast from the room that he nearly bowled over Milton, who was coming in the door. He gave Milton a hasty "Good morning" and was gone.

Milton watched him go, frowning. "What was that all about?"

Lealia went to her desk, eyeing the mess Reverend Massey had made. "I don't know. He said he was looking for a letter."

"Reverend Walker is not in his office," Milton said.

"What do you want to do?"

Milton thought for a moment. "I think we should go tell Evan. He deserves what little peace he can get in knowing what happened to his father."

Lealia exhaled. "I agree."

"Then he can work with Mr. Vaughn about making burial arrangements."

Lealia tidied up her desk, honestly not wanting to go with Milton on this errand. But she also disliked the idea of him handling it alone. His nighttime struggles had seemed to lessen, but she couldn't pin down what exactly was causing them. More than likely it was because his experience of the stampede was different from hers. She had only been trapped half an hour. He helped with the injured almost all night.

As she closed the drawer Reverend Massey had opened, she saw a glint of metal buried in the pens and pencils. She reached in and pulled out a ring of keys. "Ah!" she said with excitement.

"What's that?"

Lealia went to the financial ledger where she had put all the banknotes. "Hopefully, the key to the lockbox." She went to the closet, thankful she'd left the light on.

Milton followed her. When he stood in the doorway, he took in a deep, shaking breath. "This is a tiny room."

"Yes, and it was dark when I first came in here." She tried one of the keys on the ring without success. The same with the second. When she tried the third key, she heard a click. "Got it."

The lockbox was nearly full, and she had to stuff the new banknotes inside. "I'll have to ask Reverend Walker about making a deposit soon."

She closed the box and locked it. Milton moved to the side, reaching for the pull string for the light.

She stopped him with her hand on his chest. "No!"

He snatched his hand back from the string.

She let out a nervous laugh. "Sorry. I'd like to leave the light on."

He looked down at her, those searching brown eyes darkened by the limited light in the closet. "I understand," he said quietly but did not move away. He was inches from her. "Lealia."

"Hmm?"

"This morning. In the garden."

Her face grew hot. "Yes?"

"You were right. I was not present. Forgive me."

She swallowed and dropped her gaze to his chest. "I forgive you."

He moved a little closer. "Although this is a perfect opportunity to make it up to you, I am still not fully present. I keep thinking about Evan."

She swallowed. "Yes, of course."

He didn't speak for a moment. Then he said, "I would like to make it up to you, when I am present."

She couldn't hide her blush nor did she break her gaze. "And you will try your best to do better than the last kiss?"

He leaned back, a mock look of outrage on his face. "It was that bad? Then I must make it up to you."

Unable to stand that close to him any longer, she pushed past him and out the door. "We should go." She took a deep breath as she heard him close the door behind him.

They left the office with Lealia desperately trying not to think about the second kiss she would get from Milton.

CHAPTER THIRTEEN

The address Evan had given them was located on the opposite side of Birmingham from Milton's house. They passed the bakery and Holly's boardinghouse on the way. Milton would have suggested they visit the injured there, but he didn't want to keep Lealia away from her work any longer than necessary.

Honestly, he needed some time away from her to clear his head.

Why on earth had he kissed her? She was certainly lovely as she stood in the garden with her hair and her guard down. She was in her element. Even thinking about how beautiful she'd looked made his heart thump faster.

Then he remembered why he was outside in the first place. The tremors. They had pushed him out of the house and caused him to forget himself with Lealia. As much as he wanted to kiss her again in some kind of apology for the first one, he could not. Even when she was standing in the closet looking as if she wanted him to kiss her. *Not until I can get my tremors under control.*

They walked to the front door of the Stokes' house, and Milton knocked on the door. A minute later, Evan appeared. He gave them a hopeful look, and his gaze lingered on Lealia for a second longer. Milton shifted. "Mr. Rafferty," Evan said.

"Evan, this is Miss Lealia Bevard." Milton kept his face neutral. "May we come in?"

"Um, yes." They stepped into a very neat room with high-quality decor, better than any furniture his mother had at home. Milton fought to hide his surprise. Then again, Mr. Stokes seemed to have done well with his dry goods store.

"Do ya'll want to sit down?" Evan motioned to two armchairs. Milton was struck at how young Evan was to be all alone in the world. He seemed to be a few years younger than Lealia and him, maybe nineteen. "I have a little food if you are hungry."

"No thank you," Lealia said, taking one of the seats.

Milton took the other, fortifying himself. *I'll have to break bad news to patients just like this when I become a doctor.* He swallowed. "Evan, you mentioned an aunt in Richmond. Do you have any other family local?" If Evan broke down, whom could they fetch to care for him?

Evan shook his head. "No. Just her and my da. My ma died a few months after I was born."

Milton took a deep breath. "There is no easy way to tell you this—" he began, and tears immediately sprang to Evan's eyes.

"He is no more?"

Milton nodded. "He—his remains are at Vaughn's Funeral Services."

Evan stood, hands fisted. He stared at the wall and began to pace. His tears fell freely now, but he kept his lips pursed.

Milton rose from his chair and stood in front of Evan, forcing him to stop his movement. The pain in the young man's eyes sliced through Milton's core. The loss of a father. Milton understood that pain even though he and Evan had lost their fathers in different ways. He put his hand on Evan's shoulder and for all the world wanted to tell him that it was going to be all right. But it was never going to be all right.

Evan broke, and Milton did the only thing he knew to do. He put his arms around him and let him cry. From the corner of his eye, he could see that Lealia was crying too.

Evan's sobs slowed. "What am I going to do without him?"

"I wish we could have given you different news," Milton said as Evan stepped back.

Lealia was standing now, with a glass of water in her hand. Milton hadn't even noticed her going to the kitchen to get it. Evan took the glass from Lealia, and Milton guided him to a seat.

Evan took a drink of the water. "I suspected he was gone, since he was at the church the night of the stampede and had not come home."

Milton and Lealia exchanged a glance.

Evan caught it. "What?"

Lealia sat next to Evan on the sofa and took his hand. "There is more."

Milton sat on Evan's other side, and Evan looked from Lealia to Milton with dread on his face. "More?"

"Mr. Vaughn said that your father's injuries were inconsistent with being trapped in the stampede."

Evan frowned. "That's a fancy word. What do you mean 'inconsistent'?"

On the other side of Evan, Lealia gave Milton an encouraging look, and he thanked God she was there. He couldn't make it through this without her. "Your father died of a gunshot wound."

Evan sat back, his eyes wide and round. "Gunshot?"

"Yes," Milton said.

"But how?" he asked, his voice breaking.

Milton remembered Mr. Vaughn's response when Milton had posed the same question. *With a gun.* But he knew that was not what Evan was asking. "Mr. Vaughn said that your father was brought in with the deceased from Shiloh. He said there was a good bit of confusion, but he is sure that your father was brought to him that night."

Milton didn't think Evan could look more horrified, but he did. "Someone shot him at the church?"

Lealia spoke then. "Both Milton and I were there that night. There were no gunshots before the service."

"I was helping after," Milton said, "and—" In that moment, the room closed in. His collar was too tight. He swallowed hard and closed his eyes but not before seeing Lealia's alarmed expression.

"Milton was helping move the injured, so he saw more than I did."

Milton fought to open his eyes, but he could feel the tremors starting in his hands. *Not now.*

"So someone shot my father? But who?"

Milton dragged in a breath, trying to speak. Again, Lealia saved him. "We think you should go to the police after you go to Mr. Vaughn's. They will probably want to know if your father had an argument or disagreement with anyone recently."

Evan scowled. "Only that fool insurance man."

Milton only half heard Evan's answer. It was overshadowed by his pulse thundering in his ears. His thoughts went along the same pattern:

the injured, the dead, their cries, the tightness... Milton shuddered hard and popped out of his seat. "We should go."

Lealia's jaw dropped. Evan stood and shook Milton's hand. "Thank you for finding him."

It took all his fortitude to keep his hand from shaking. "You're welcome. Let us know if we can provide any more assistance."

Lealia had to rush to give her condolences to Evan before Milton bolted from the house. The world seemed to be narrowing around him. His heart pounded, and it was too hot. He was halfway to the next block before he registered that Lealia was calling him.

She caught up and grabbed him by his shoulder. "Milton! Slow down."

He stopped but didn't turn. He couldn't face her.

"What was that?" she asked, stepping in front of him.

"What was what?"

She put her hands on her hips. "You practically ran from the house. What's going on?"

Milton ran several answers to give her through his head. All of them would be a lie.

Her expression softened. "Is this about your father?"

Her question sent his emotions even more off-kilter. "My father?"

"I know he left the family. Is that why you were so upset in there?"

Milton swallowed, gratefully following the direction she had turned the conversation. "I understand how he feels."

"What happened with your father?"

He clenched his jaw. He wanted to talk about his father less than he wanted to talk about his tremors. It was clear, however, from the look on Lealia's face that she wasn't going to walk away without an answer. *Can I share this pain with you?* His heart wanted to.

"My father left when I was twenty." He wrung his hands.

"Before you came to Tuskegee? Have you seen him since?"

Milton shook his head. "He left and never looked back."

Lealia took his hand and squeezed it. "This must be difficult for you, but you did a good thing locating Mr. Stokes."

Milton nodded. It was a good thing for Evan to know that although his father had left, it wasn't because he wanted to.

Lealia arrived at the breakfast table before Milton.

She had gone to bed very worried about him after their visit to the Stokes' house yesterday. Thankfully, she had not been awakened by him in the night. Or she had slept soundly enough not to hear him.

When she reached the table, Mrs. Rafferty was sitting, her head resting on one hand, a cup of tea in the other. She looked up, and Lealia saw she had tears in her eyes.

Lealia rushed to her side. "Are you all right?"

"Yes, dear." Mrs. Rafferty gave her a watery smile. "My heart is broken for Evan Stokes. Milton told me last night."

Lealia sat next to Mrs. Rafferty. "He was quite upset when Milton and I gave him the news."

Mrs. Rafferty shook her head. "Mr. Stokes was the nicest man. Why would someone kill him?"

"Someone should contact the authorities." Lealia grasped Mrs. Rafferty's hand.

Mrs. Rafferty let out a sharp laugh. "Not in this town. The authorities don't care about Negro crimes. Why do you think they still haven't identified the arsonist who burned Mr. Stokes' store down?"

Mrs. Rafferty's words stung. Even though the Negroes were fighting to be recognized as equal citizens, it was hard to get recognition or help with their problems. That was a part of the challenge Mr. Washington faced. Getting the whites to be invested in the issues of the Negro community.

Milton came down the stairs looking haggard. He tried to smile, but his exhaustion made it seem like a grimace.

"Oh, Son." Mrs. Rafferty rose and hugged him. "Are you all right?"

"Yes, just tired." Milton sat at the table.

Mrs. Rafferty put her hands on her hips. "I think you should stay home and rest."

Milton jolted. "No, I have visitations to do. Most everyone is feeling better, but there are a few that are still injured."

"They will survive one day without you," Mrs. Rafferty said.

Lealia watched Milton, understanding dawning. Staying inside made him panic. It might be good for him to stay and rest, but she knew he would not. He would be wound tight, trying to appear stable for his mother's sake.

"Reverend Walker asked me yesterday to deposit some of the donations coming in from the other churches, and I hoped Milton would show me where the bank is," Lealia said. "Reverend Walker would have done it, but he is traveling to the North for a few days. Several churches invited him to come and accept donations in person."

Milton's posture deflated with relief. He faced Lealia and mouthed *thank you.*

Mrs. Rafferty shook her finger. "To the bank and straight back here."

"Yes, Mom," Lealia said, making Milton laugh.

After breakfast and many promises that they would return to the house as soon as they were done at the bank, they set out for the church.

"I know Mom said for us to hurry home, but I was thinking we could go talk to Evan again," Milton said once they reached the outskirts of downtown. A wagon rode past a little too close to the curb, and Milton grasped Lealia's hand, pulling her back.

"Why?"

"He may know who might want to hurt his father."

They started walking again, but Milton did not release her hand. "But what if he doesn't wish to pursue anything? Your mother told me how the authorities here ignore Negro crimes."

Milton was silent for a moment. When the church came into view, he said, "You know, no one can locate the delegates who started the fight."

"What?" Lealia said, facing him.

"One of the other members told me. They know it was one of the Baltimore delegates who started the fight, but now he's disappeared." Milton shook his head. "Two people will get away with hurting others without consequences."

She pressed her hand to his face. "But what about how it hurts you?"

He closed his eyes, brushing his cheek against her hand. "It helps more than it hurts. I cannot sit in the house. Mom would see. . ." His words trailed off.

"You could go back to Tuskegee."

His jaw worked under her palm, and something flashed in his eyes. It was gone before she could decipher it, but it looked like sadness. "I could, but I've already started the process of helping here, and I want to stay until it is finished."

Lealia did not believe Milton would lie to her, but his words felt like. . .well, maybe not a lie. . .but more like he was purposefully not saying the whole truth. She let it go.

When they reached the front door, they found a note from Reverend Walker that his wife would unlock the kitchen door for them each day until he returned. As they reached the hallway leading to the offices, Lealia's mind went to the last time she had come to the church. Reverend Massey was going through her desk. Although he'd said he was looking for a letter, she struggled to believe him. *He searched the desk drawers.*

In the office, she took the keys from the pocket of her dress. She hadn't wanted to misplace them or leave them unsecured. "Can you get an envelope from my desk?" She went to the closet door and stopped.

The light was out.

She tipped her head and frowned. She hadn't turned that light out.

Milton came and stood beside her with the envelope in his hand. "Here you go. There's a letter on your desk from Reverend Walker."

"The light is out."

Milton opened the closet. "The light—" Realization dawned in his eyes. "I thought you left it on." He stepped in and grabbed the pull cord.

"I thought I did too." Frowning, she stepped inside and opened the lockbox. She took the banknotes out and put them in the envelope Milton handed her. She closed the box, and after Milton had stepped out, she closed the door, leaving the light on.

She went to the desk for the letter from Reverend Walker. "I should read this before I go." She lifted it and found it was already open. She turned. "Milton, did you open this?"

He glanced over her shoulder, standing near enough to make her flush. "No, I didn't touch it."

She opened the letter and read it.

Miss Bevard,

The people of Atlanta have been extremely generous. Please see that the enclosed $100 banknote goes to Mr. Rafferty to meet any needs he encounters on his visitations.

Reverend Walker

Lealia laid the letter on the desk in front of her. She turned to Milton. "There's supposed to be a one-hundred-dollar banknote in here."

His eyes widened. "One hundred dollars."

"Yes, and it's not here."

She and Milton scoured the whole office looking for the note but couldn't find it. "Maybe Reverend Walker changed his mind and took the banknote with him," Milton suggested.

"Then why leave the letter?"

Milton eyed her and the open envelope. "You think—"

"But who?" she asked before he could finish. With all that was going on in the church with the injured, who would take the money that had been given to help them?

⁂

The trees along the church swayed in the October breeze. Milton stuffed his hands in his pockets. *Soon I'll need a proper coat.* Lealia had put her hat on today as the colder temperature had made itself known in the mornings. She was quiet most of the walk. He could tell she had something on her mind. His tremors had been bad this morning, and he was too tired to carry on a conversation.

He needed to clear his mind because in the darkness after the tremors, an idea had come to him. They had only briefly talked to Evan when they had notified him about his father. They needed to ask again if he knew something that would lead to his father's killer. Milton didn't understand his drive to find out who killed Mr. Stokes. Maybe it was his addled brain or the fact that Mr. Stokes had been kind to his mother.

Whatever the reason, a crime had been committed, and the perpetrator was still out there. He told Lealia his thoughts about Evan, and she nodded.

"I agree. You should go there first."

They walked a little farther, and then Lealia said, "While we're sharing our thoughts, I think someone stole that banknote."

"We cannot be sure of that." Milton said. "Reverend Walker could have forgotten to put it in the letter."

"Maybe," she said, then stopped walking. Her attention was trained in the direction of the church. He looked too.

Reverend Massey was walking up the front stairs. Lealia grabbed Milton's arm and pulled him closer to some shrubs nearby as she watched. "I wouldn't speak evil of anyone, but I think Reverend Massey stole the banknote."

Milton widened his eyes. "What?"

"I caught him in my office rummaging through my desk. When I asked him what he was searching for, he concocted a story about looking for a letter."

"You don't know for sure that he took it. What can we do?"

"Confront him." Lealia started walking toward the church.

"No, Lealia," Milton called out, but it was too late. She was already marching ahead with that confident stride he had seen at Tuskegee.

Reverend Massey spotted them coming up the street and waited until they reached the church. "Good morning. The door is locked."

"Reverend Walker is still in Atlanta, and he normally unlocks the front door."

"I see." Reverend Massey turned to Milton. "So, you are still here."

He did not put it as a question, and Milton felt his hackles rise. "I am."

"I think it's interesting that you are helping the members of this church." Massey smirked. "You must have incredible compassion to stick around."

"Compassion is important." *Especially for reverends who might be stealing.* Milton spoke through his teeth. "People are in need. It would be heartless to not help."

"Help the people who hate you?"

Lealia's grasp on Milton's arm tightened. "No one hates Milton."

"They absolutely hate him and his family, since they believe his father was the one who burned down the 6th Avenue church."

"My father did not burn down the 6th Avenue church," Milton said. A vein pulsed in his head. *Now I see why no one likes him.*

Reverend Massey raised his hands. "Not saying he did, but it doesn't matter what I think."

"You're right, your opinion matters little." Milton clenched his fists, his anger starting to gather in a haze around his vision.

"More than one person has told me to keep an eye on you because you'll probably start stealing from the church. I'm starting to believe them, the way you're always here. Maybe you're a danger to the church like your father."

Milton froze. As much as he believed this man would lie, Milton knew that what he said about Shiloh members hating him was true. He remembered the glares. The words whispered behind hands when he had walked into the convention. A convention he didn't even want to attend. One that now sent him into a panic every morning. After all he'd done, he was still being blamed for something that didn't happen.

Milton stood tall, concentrating his gaze on Reverend Massey. "Where were you the night of the stampede? I remember seeing you around, but you weren't on the stage with the other clergy."

Reverend Massey took a step back. "I didn't sit on the stage."

Milton gave him a once-over. Saw how his hand nervously twitched at his side and the way he kept licking his lips as if they were parched. "I was here until dawn helping with the injured, and I don't remember seeing you. Did you help?"

"I am not going to stand here and be questioned by someone with a father like yours."

"My father has nothing to do with the fact that you're entertaining lies when your own actions will not stand up to scrutiny. You cannot account for your whereabouts on the night of the stampede. Maybe we should wonder if you are a danger to the church."

Reverend Massey narrowed his eyes. "Watch how you talk, boy. Your tongue might get you in more trouble than you can handle."

Milton stepped a little closer. He had not suffered every night with nightmares and terrors for this man to question his motives. "Are you threatening me?"

Lealia rushed to stand at his side. "Milton, you said we were going to visit Evan today." She tugged him away from Reverend Massey but not before Milton saw a look of alarm cross the man's face.

When they were a block away, Milton pulled Lealia to a stop. "Are you sure you want to leave him unattended in the church if you think he's the thief?"

"He doesn't know that he can get inside through the kitchen," she said. "He's still trying to go in the front door."

That made Milton laugh. "Very true."

CHAPTER FOURTEEN

Evan warmly welcomed them into his house.

"How are you holding up?" Lealia asked after refusing refreshment.

"I miss my pa," he said, leading them to the same chairs they had sat in before. "The house is so quiet without him."

"Is there anything we can do to help?" Lealia asked.

He smiled sadly. "You've helped enough. If it weren't for you two, I would have never known he was gone." Tears formed in his eyes, and he wiped them with his sleeve. "Now if I only knew who killed him and why."

"You have no ideas?" Milton asked.

Evan shook his head. "My Pa was well liked, and people loved his store. No one I know would have wanted to hurt him."

Lealia exchanged a look with Milton. "Did you go to the authorities?"

"I did," he said. "They said the case would be cold by now. Especially since his body was found at the church."

"As far as we know, they didn't interview anyone at the church," Lealia said. Tuskegee didn't teach investigative techniques, but it did teach logic. It made no sense not to talk to people who were at the church that night.

"I don't expect much from them. If it is what they consider a Negro affair, they will do nothing." Tears flowed down Evan's cheeks. "I lost my father and our only source of income. I would reopen the store, but I have no idea how to get the insurance payout from Reverend Massey."

Lealia and Milton sat forward at the same time. "Reverend Massey?" Milton asked.

"Yes, he owns the company who insured the store," he said. "Pa went to see him a few days before—" Evan swallowed. "Before the convention."

"Did he mention what they talked about?" Milton asked.

Evan chuckled. "You bet. Pa was fumin' when he got back. Said that Reverend Massey told him that there was some special thing that the state insurance board needed to do and it was out of Reverend Massey's hands."

"You are sure there was an arsonist?" Lealia asked.

"Some of the shops around Pa's store did not appreciate Pa being there. . .if you know what I mean," Evan said.

Lealia frowned. Reverend Massey was the "fool insurance man" Evan had mentioned the day the they told him about his father. The day Milton's tremors made them leave.

Evan frowned. "It's not the first time someone has had words with Reverend Massey. He's been slow with his payouts before. He got into an argument at church with the doctor."

Milton shifted beside her. "Dr. Briggs?"

"Yes," Evan said. "I couldn't hear all they said, but it happened right at church in front of a lot of people. Someone told me later that it was over insurance money."

Alarm grew in Lealia's mind. "Did Dr. Briggs ever get his payout?"

Evan shook his head. "Not according to the church gossips, but I don't believe that. How could Reverend Massey just not pay out the money? That is what my pa believed as well. That's why he went so long before confronting him."

Lealia could see Milton's mind working. She was almost certain it was going in the same direction as hers. Reverend Massey was a thief. A wolf in sheep's clothing. "He's been helping out around the church," she said. "Maybe I can ask him about it."

"Yes, I saw him in town, but I was unable to speak to him for long." The heavy sadness in Evan's expression lifted a little. "I had thought he was all bad, but he showed me a one-hundred-dollar banknote and said once he went to the bank he would come and give me fifty dollars of it to help with my expenses."

Lealia fought the urge to gasp and felt Milton stiffen beside her. It was hard to ignore the coincidence that Reverend Massey showed

Evan the same amount that was missing from the church.

Lealia rose. "If I see Reverend Massey, I'll mention that you need to meet with him."

"Thank you," Evan said.

They left the house, and as soon as they were far enough away, Milton asked, "What are the chances that Reverend Massey just happened to have a banknote in the same amount as the one missing from your desk?"

"Exactly what I was thinking," Lealia said. "If Reverend Massey does give Evan the money, it is going to help those injured in the stampede like Reverend Walker wanted."

"He wanted the whole amount to go to the needy," Milton said, anger in his voice.

Lealia sighed. "And why the delay in the insurance payout? Why is it taking so long?"

"Maybe there was some problem with the banks," Milton mused.

Lealia huffed. "If this situation was a bookkeeping ledger, it would have too many debts and not enough credits. Too many things not adding up."

"I agree," Milton said. "We need more answers. I think I will pay Dr. Briggs a visit."

Without discussing it, they turned in the direction of the house. Lealia's mind filled with so many questions. Not just about Mr. Stokes and Evan and Reverend Massey but about Milton and her future.

She was most concerned about Milton. She stopped him at the front door. "I want to check on the garden first. The chill is beginning, and anything left out there should be harvested."

He didn't resist and followed her around the side of the house.

She was right. There were a few more tomatoes and a few squash to be picked. As they worked, she watched Milton. He was clearly lost in his own thoughts. She wanted him to talk about whatever was bothering him.

"You know, what Reverend Massey said about the members of Shiloh judging you is true."

He stopped, looking up at her with despair in his eyes. "They've talked to you too?"

She nodded, relaying her conversation with the woman at the church the night of the stampede. Milton hung his head as she talked.

"I didn't believe it then, Milton. I refuse to believe it now."

He let out a sad laugh. "You know, I disliked you when I first met you."

"Really?"

He nodded. "You were Shiloh's beloved daughter. I couldn't stand that they treated you so well and me so bad."

Lealia looked out over the field next to the house. "What did happen with your father and the fire?"

"Like I said," Milton said, his words sharper, "he did not set the fire."

"I know." She touched him softly on the shoulder. "But why does everyone think he did?"

"Because he was found at the church when it burned." Milton dropped his head. "He was drunk, like he always was. It also didn't help his case that he left town."

Lealia stepped closer. "I am sorry. I wondered if maybe he had died and that was why he wasn't here."

"He could be dead," Milton said. Unlike Evan, Milton would probably never know if his father died unless some kind person notified him.

She put a hand on his arm. "I'm certain that the people of Shiloh don't think you're like your father."

"I doubt it," he said quietly. "And now—" He snapped his mouth shut.

"If you can change your dislike of me, they can change their dislike of you. Unless you still think I'm off-putting." She hoped to make him smile.

It worked. "No, I do not."

She poked him in the ribs. "So you like me now?"

He was still smiling, but his expression turned serious in a blink. "I did kiss you."

Warmth flowed over her skin. "You did."

"May I kiss you again?"

"Are you here with me right now?" She felt the danger and the thrill in his request. She would eventually leave Birmingham, and she could not go back to Tuskegee. He would return, finish school, and go where his dreams took him. How could there be any future for them?

She had little time to think as he leaned closer. When he got close enough for her to feel his warm breath on the cooling air, the back door opened. "Milton? Lealia? Are you two out here?" Mrs. Rafferty called.

"She has terrible timing," Milton muttered.

Lealia laughed. Mrs. Rafferty had great timing. She was saving them from making things worse.

Dr. Briggs' office was located very near Shiloh, just on the edge of downtown. As Milton made his way down the street, he stopped every few feet and stared in awe at the beautifully built homes there. The neighborhood was new. Well, new in the past four years. It had not been there when Milton had left for Tuskegee. Mom had told him that Birmingham was growing, but he hadn't imagined it growing this fast. Or this nice.

The houses lining the street were made of brick. They were the same size as the lecture buildings on Tuskegee and could probably hold several classes at once. Trees framed manicured lawns, and some of the houses had flower beds surrounding the windows. Very different from his small wood-frame home.

This neighborhood was home to the more affluent Negro professionals in Birmingham. Mr. Stokes' house, although not as grand as these homes, was located on the far side. Milton took in each one, wishing he could show his classmates. This was what hard work could do.

Dr. Briggs' house was no less grand than the others. A trail of vine gave it a cozy look. Milton took it all in as he crossed the small stone porch to the door. *Dr. Briggs must do very well.* He should. He was one of the few doctors in the area that accepted Negro patients. If this neighborhood was any indication, a good number of his patients could afford to pay his fees.

Milton used the heavy brass door knocker and waited. In a few minutes, a graceful, stately woman opened the door. She was nearly as tall as Milton and wore a day dress that probably cost more than all his clothing combined. "Good afternoon, are you here to see the doctor?"

"Yes," Milton said.

"I am Mrs. Briggs. Please come in." She motioned him inside.

If the outside of the house made him stare, the inside took his breath away. *This house looks like the inside of the Carnegie Library.* The walls had dark, rich wood paneling. A large sofa filled one room, and as Mrs. Briggs led him to the back of the house, he saw a dining room with a polished table that looked as if it could seat eight.

"My husband is expecting a patient soon, but we will see if he can squeeze you in," she said, her voice soft and cultured. *I wonder if Mrs. Briggs is just as educated as her husband.* "What ails you?"

The question, spoken in her soft voice, disarmed him. It broke through the barrier he had built to contain his pain. Pain that rushed to the surface of his mind and was almost out of his mouth before he could stop it. He swallowed it back down. "I am not here to speak to him about my health. It's an entirely other matter."

Mrs. Briggs studied him. "Oh, I thought you were unwell. Shall I announce you?" She stopped at a closed door.

"My name is Milton Rafferty."

Mrs. Briggs brightened. "Oh, Mr. Rafferty. Graham has told me about you. He said you have done an excellent job with the injured from the stampede. Said you've been a great help."

Milton adjusted his jacket, the praise feeling foreign. "I'm only doing what I can."

"Sounds like you have done more than you are giving yourself credit for." She tapped on the door and then opened it. "My dear, you have a visitor."

Dr. Briggs looked up and gave Milton the same warm, welcoming smile as his wife. "Mr. Rafferty. What brings you by? Is Lealia well?"

"She is."

"Oh, yes. Your lady friend. I understand she was hurt in the stampede," Mrs. Briggs said.

"She's not—" Milton cleared his throat, unable to stop the heat building in his cheeks. "She is a fellow student at Tuskegee. She is doing much better, thanks to Dr. Briggs."

"Glad to hear that. I will bring in some refreshments," she said.

"Thank you, Violet." Dr. Briggs motioned for Milton to sit. "What can I do for you?"

Milton sat, taking in the room. It was as nice as the rest of the house. It was half the size of the entire first floor of his home. Bookcases lined the walls, and the large window in the room faced a beautiful garden with a stone bench.

"There's something I want to speak to you about." Milton swallowed. "Something personal."

"About your injuries."

"I only had minor injuries." *Minor in body.* Milton forced himself to be still and not shudder.

"No, about your other injuries. The ones that keep you from resting. I noticed it the last time I attended Lealia."

"How—" Milton started, then snapped his mouth shut. "I am all right."

Dr. Briggs steepled his hands. "You seem that way on the surface. However, you were inside the church. You helped with the injured and the dead if I understand it correctly. How are you handling that?"

Dr. Briggs' voice was mild but firm. He spoke evenly, but his words were like an assault on Milton's mind, each landing like a hard punch. "I—" The room grew hot. "I—was helping."

"I know, which warrants my asking if you are okay. I saw the injured and the dead after. You witnessed—"

The room closed in a blink, and Dr. Briggs faded away. He was inside the church again. The bodies. He fought hard to keep himself under control. Used all his concentration to keep the images at bay. He squeezed his eyes closed and instantly regretted it. The people trapped at the door appeared, as if his eyes were open and he was staring at them. He stood, and the whole room swayed and tears sprang to his eyes.

Then strong hands were pushing him down. Through his fog, he heard Dr. Briggs say, "Sit. Put your head between your knees, and breathe."

He obeyed, but he still felt as if he were being pressed against the wall in the church.

"Milton! Focus on my voice," Dr. Briggs said. He seemed so far away. As though his voice were coming from another room.

A moan escaped his lips, and his chest hitched, his tears flowing faster. *I have to get out.* All his thoughts were in a jumble, the need to escape disrupting them even more. *I cannot breathe.* He heard himself whimper, "God, please."

"Milton!" Dr. Briggs gripped his shoulder hard. "Find your way back. God is here with you."

God. . . In his mind, he saw himself in the sanctuary that night, nearing his breaking point and feeling strength pour into him. Over and over again he had thought he had no more to give but then found a little more. Enough to help one more person. Again and again. *God.*

The panic in his mind burst, and with it came a flood of tears. Milton sobbed. Deep, heavy sobs. Grief, pain, and fear flowed out, and once it started, he could not stop it. As each emotion presented itself, Milton let it fall away, like his tears. In the swirl of his emotions, Lealia appeared. His feelings for her. How things could never be between them. How she would leave too.

His father appeared next. His angry face when he left them that night. Milton had thought his father's actions hadn't affected him, but now he saw how deeply that night had wounded him. The intensity of the pain. He wrapped his arms around his knees, rocking, and cried more.

He could not tell how long he wept. Somehow, he had ended up on the floor. Dr. Briggs' hand stayed on his shoulder, grounding him. Once his tears slowed, he lifted his head.

"Take your time," Dr. Briggs said. A cool glass of water was pressed into his hand, followed by a handkerchief in his other.

Milton drank the water, shame and distress replacing all the emotions he had just cried out. Why had this happened in front of Dr. Briggs? Although he was relieved that it had not happened in front of his mother or Lealia.

He looked up to find both Dr. and Mrs. Briggs standing over him. Dr. Briggs gave him a kind smile. "Are you ready to get up?"

Milton nodded, not trusting himself to speak.

Dr. Briggs helped him into the chair, and Mrs. Briggs patted him softly on the shoulder before she left and closed the door. Once Milton was settled, Dr. Briggs leaned against his desk, facing Milton. "Son, how long has this been happening? Tell me all."

"Since the stampede." Milton sniffled and wiped his face with the handkerchief. "Every morning since the stampede, but never this bad."

Dr. Briggs exhaled. "I wish you had told me."

Milton wiped his face again. "I did not know how to tell anyone."

"I understand. Are you having nightmares?"

Although he'd thought he couldn't cry anymore, the tears started again. "Yes. I wake up drenched in sweat and unable to stop shaking."

"You have a panic disorder," Dr. Briggs said. "It's a normal reaction when someone has been through something like you have."

"How is this normal?" Milton's voice was raspy.

"Because the human mind needs order. It needs to make sense of things. When something like the stampede happens to a person, there is no sense in it. This disorders the thoughts and causes panic even while you are sleeping." Dr. Briggs put his hand on Milton's shoulder again. "It's not normal to watch people die and be unable to help them."

Milton dropped his head. "It was horrible. I was so worried about my mother, Lealia, my classmates, the people around me."

"These are normal feelings to have. You care about them."

"How do I stop it?" Milton asked. A flicker of hope touched him. Maybe he could be free.

"This is a good start. Crying and talking about it," Dr. Briggs said.

"But whenever I think about it—" Milton shuddered and swallowed. "When I think about it, the episodes start."

"That's because you're trying to stop it instead of letting it happen. You're fighting against the natural relief of letting it out. That makes it worse." Dr. Briggs stooped in front of him. "Look at me."

Milton did and saw only kindness and compassion in the man's eyes.

"It took strength to do what you did, but now it is time for you to heal."

"But I still have things to do to help Reverend Walker."

"You can still help, but go slowly. Treat your mind the same way you would treat Lealia's ankle." Dr. Briggs stood. "She can move on it, but with care. Treat your mind the same. You also need to rest. Try doing some calisthenics or other activity before bed. Something to tire you out so you can sleep."

Milton swallowed. "Thank you, Dr. Briggs."

"You are welcome." He moved back to his seat. "Stay as long as you need."

Although the offer was kindly made, Milton found he could not bear the embarrassment of staying any longer than a few more minutes. He thanked Dr. and Mrs. Briggs profusely and left. He got halfway to the church and realized he had not asked Dr. Briggs about Reverend Massey. He would have to go back later when he got over his embarrassment.

Lealia paced the floor. She had come in early, greeted Reverend Walker, and gone straight into her office and closed the door behind her. She needed to think and did not want Reverend Massey to interrupt her. Milton had gone to Dr. Briggs to ask about the payout. Lealia suspected what he would discover: Reverend Massey was committing insurance fraud.

Added to that, he was stealing from the church. That was harder to consider. That a man who was supposed to spread the gospel would steal from the very church he was supposed to serve. She remembered Mrs. Rafferty saying Reverend Massey was sent by the Baptist Board to Shiloh from another church.

Her eyes widened. If he had been, there would be letters. If she had learned anything about the Baptist leadership, it was that everything was documented by letters. Letters that were possibly in her office.

In the closet. She shuddered as she walked to the door. If the answers were there, she would have to go in. She opened the door, propped it open, and studied the labels on the outsides of the boxes. Since she didn't know when Massey arrived, she would check the letters less than three months old. She ran her finger along each box until she found one marked Church Letters. She pulled it out of its place and carried it to her desk.

The box contained general correspondence. Would a letter about Massey come to the general church address? She skimmed three months' worth of letters and found nothing. She returned the box to its place on the shelf and kept searching. *I am not completely sure what I am looking for.* As she searched through the second row of boxes, she found one marked Pastoral Mail. This was it. She took the box and rushed to her desk.

She thumbed through the letters, and her heart skipped a beat when she found the first one addressed to Baptist headquarters. It was from Reverend Walker to the Baptist board. *I called Milton nosy. Guess I'm the nosy one.* She set the top letters aside, took the pertinent letter out of the box, and started reading.

She felt her eyes grow wider with each word. The letter was Reverend Walker's pointed disagreement that Shiloh was the best place to send Reverend Massey. As she read, she respected Reverend Walker even more. He felt that he was being punished by having to accept a reverend into the church who had known issues. He went on to rebuke the Baptist leadership for not letting him choose his own associate clergy.

The paragraph that surprised her most was how Reverend Walker felt that he should not have to babysit Reverend Massey, watching his every move. Lealia pressed her hand to her mouth. *What did Reverend Massey do?* She searched through more letters but didn't find any additional ones about Massey. Maybe there was another box she could search. As she put the letters back one by one, Massey's name jumped out of one of them.

It was from Reverend Walker to a Mr. Gilbert. Lealia peeked up at the door to make sure no one was there, then read the letter.

> *Dear Mr. Gilbert,*
>
> *I am heartbroken to hear of your dealings with Reverend Massey and Massey Insurance Company. I had hoped that you and Reverend Massey could resolve this issue together. Let me assure you, the church is in no way connected to Massey Insurance Company and therefore cannot provide any remuneration for your loss. I do not have access to the funds collected by Massey Insurance Company. Furthermore, the church does not have the funds to help you with such a large amount.*
>
> *I am sorry that this situation has had a negative impact on you and your business, but unfortunately, I cannot assist.*

Lealia sat holding the letter, mind working. Reverend Massey had not paid Mr. Gilbert. Not paid Mr. Stokes, and possibly Dr. Briggs. How was he still in business? She returned the letters to the file box and set it in its place in the closet. She checked the other file boxes once more for other letters that might give her more information but didn't find any more.

If Reverend Massey was having financial troubles, they could be bad enough to compel him to steal. She would have to ask Reverend Walker about the one-hundred-dollar banknote eventually. He might have kept it and deposited it himself. She didn't want to accuse Reverend Massey of anything if he wasn't guilty.

If he was stealing from the church during the time of their greatest need, however, he was truly a monster and not worthy to be a reverend.

CHAPTER FIFTEEN

Milton forced himself to walk to Dr. Briggs' house again. As he did, he remembered Lealia's face when he'd told her that he and Dr. Briggs had talked about something other than Reverend Massey. To his relief, she had teased him for forgetting and had not asked what they had actually talked about.

Then she'd told him about the letter. Massey had possibly swindled three people, maybe more. Getting answers ranked more important than his embarrassment, and he set out for Dr. Briggs' as soon as he finished breakfast.

He didn't want to face the man and his wife again so soon after he had fallen apart. He had followed Dr. Briggs' advice and asked Lealia early in the evening to help him in the garden. She happily agreed, and they had worked over an hour expanding the garden, removing rocks, and prepping the soil in case Mom wanted to plant in the spring. He had gone to bed near exhausted and had slept a little better.

As soon as he woke, however, the tremors started. He'd immediately done what Dr. Briggs told him to do. *Focus on something.* He could hear his mother moving around downstairs. He made himself think about how much he loved her. How he could see pride in her eyes when she looked at him. He squeezed his eyes tighter and thought of Lealia in the garden, a big, floppy hat on her head, laughing at his ineptitude with plants. He thought of the Primms, who had completely recovered and resumed their normal lives.

It was hard to concentrate on those things, but the panic passed.

At least if Dr. Briggs asks me how I'm doing, I can give him some sort of positive report.

Mrs. Briggs opened the door, and a look of concern colored her face. "Milton, are you all right?"

He dropped his head, feeling sheepish. "Yes. Yesterday I came to speak to Dr. Briggs about something but never got to ask."

She nodded knowingly. "Come on in."

Dr. Briggs gave Milton the same cautious greeting his wife had. "Is all well?"

Milton actually smiled. "Yes, sir. I never got to ask you what I came for yesterday."

"Right. I forgot you came to talk to me." He motioned to the same chair Milton had sat in the day before. "Ask away."

Interestingly enough, being in Dr. Briggs' office this time didn't cause his panic to rise. It did the opposite. Even though Milton had sobbed like a baby the day before, he felt peace as he took the chair. *Maybe one day I will feel that peace when I go to Shiloh.*

"I have something I want to ask you about. Something personal."

Dr. Briggs sat back, frowning a little. "Very well."

"I was speaking to Mr. Stokes' son, Evan, about his father's death."

"It's very sad. Mr. Stokes was a good man, who helped anyone he could in the community. It's hard to believe that someone would kill him like that." Dr. Briggs shook his head.

"I asked Evan who would want to hurt his father, and he told me that the only person his father had a disagreement with was Reverend Massey."

Dr. Briggs stiffened. "Is that so?"

"Yes," Milton continued. "Evan told me that his father had argued with Reverend Massey about his insurance payout and accused Reverend Massey of stealing his money."

Dr. Briggs let out a heavy sigh. "I had hoped that the rumors I heard about Massey being his insurer were untrue. I had hoped that Mr. Stokes would be able to reopen his store. I guess it doesn't matter now."

"Evan told me that you had a disagreement with Reverend Massey as well. Is that true?"

Dr. Briggs eyed him. "To what end are these questions?"

"Lealia and I have been helping Reverend Walker." Milton chose his words carefully. "Actually, Lealia more than I, but there have been some strange things happening round the church. Reverend Massey always seems to be nearby when they do."

"You are trying to ascertain if Reverend Massey is behind these strange occurrences?" Dr. Briggs asked.

"Yes."

"Do they involve money?"

Milton squirmed. "Yes."

Dr. Briggs rubbed his forehead. "I will tell you this, but please only relay it to those who need to know. You can tell Lealia."

"I understand."

"Last year, I had a small fire in my examination room. A candle fell over and scorched the wall." Dr. Briggs seemed to age as he spoke. "I had my office and home covered by Massey's insurance company at the time. I filed the claim, but Massey never paid it out."

"What?"

"The disagreement you spoke about was me confronting Massey about it. Based on his response, I gave up on getting the payout. He kept saying he filed an arson report with the state insurance commission and was waiting for a reply, but I didn't believe him. I paid for the repairs myself and canceled my coverage with Massey."

"He told Evan something similar. I'll be sure that it goes no further than it needs to."

Dr. Briggs smiled. "I'm not concerned. You are kind of an outsider in the Shiloh community."

"You could say that," Milton said wryly.

"Reverend Massey is a bit of an outsider too, though he tried to ingratiate himself with the church members." Dr. Briggs shook his head. "You know Shiloh. Very picky about who they claim as theirs."

"My mother told me he came from another church." Milton was careful not to mention the letter Lealia found in her office. He nearly smiled as he remembered how she had told him about her being "nosy."

"He was sent from a church in Pell City," Dr. Briggs said. "There was some scandal there, but I am afraid I don't know any more than that."

Dr. Briggs stood. "But my wife might." He went to the door and called her.

She came in with a smile on her face. "Yes, dear?"

"Milton is asking about Reverend Massey."

Mrs. Briggs' smile immediately fell. "What about him?"

"Do you know why he came to Shiloh?" Milton asked. "What happened at the church in Pell City?"

Mrs. Briggs looked from Milton to her husband and back. "What was told to me was told in confidence."

Milton sighed. "I understand."

"But," Mrs. Briggs said, "I can tell you that there was money missing at the church and the clerk in Pell City believed Reverend Massey took it."

Milton's jaw dropped.

"The person who relayed it to me said they could not prove it, because they didn't catch him in the act, but they were fairly certain it was Reverend Massey."

"Milton says there are some odd things happening at Shiloh," Dr. Briggs said.

Mrs. Briggs stood taller and adjusted the apron she was wearing. "I do not make it a habit of speaking ill of anyone, but I do not like that man. He is—" She looked up at the ceiling. "Slippery. He came into a ladies' meeting one time, trying hard to sell his insurance. Thankfully, all the ladies knew about our experience with him, and he got no new clients."

Milton stood. "Thank you for confiding in me. I trust you will not share that I was asking about him."

Dr. Briggs patted him on the shoulder. "You have our assurances."

Mrs. Briggs' bright smile returned. "I was planning to send a note around inviting you, your mother, and your Lealia around for dinner. When do you leave for Tuskegee?"

My Lealia. "I'm unsure. I agreed to stay until all the injured were recovered. The only person left is Mrs. Jones at the hospital."

Dr. Briggs shook his head. "That is a prickly one." His tone told Milton that Mrs. Jones had tested his bedside manner to the limit.

"Yes, she is," Milton said with a laugh.

"Send me a note and let me know when you all are free," Mrs. Briggs said. "Also, keep us posted about Reverend Massey."

"I will."

Milton left, and on his walk back to the church for Lealia, he realized he had more questions than answers. No one would say outright that Reverend Massey was stealing, even though everyone they had talked to suggested that he had.

Lealia watched Milton come down the street from the church foyer window. He was different. She could not say how, but he seemed lighter. He had made little noise this morning when he woke. What had happened to him at Dr. Briggs' house? She prayed that he had talked to the doctor about his trembling. She thought he must have, since he had gone all the way there yesterday and not asked about Reverend Massey.

She walked down the hall to the offices, the church quiet around her. There was another note on the door from Reverend Walker informing her that he would be out of town again to collect more donations. Her skin chilled as she read the last line of the note:

Reverend Massey also has a key to the front door.

Lealia let out a deep sigh. Her peace, however, was restored when she found both her office and the Reverend Walker's office locked. *Maybe the key to the front door is the only one he has.*

There was a new batch of letters and notes on her desk, and she went to work. She wanted to be done before Milton returned so she could listen to what he had to say. She might be able to find out why he seemed less tense than usual. On the walk to the church, he had been laughing about a particularly difficult instructor at Tuskegee. She laughed too, but the more they talked, the more the memories of Tuskegee turned bittersweet. Regardless of what happened to her next, and she could not say what that would be at the moment, she would miss Tuskegee.

Once she was done opening the letters, she had another pile of banknotes on her desk. The Baptist churches were sending in whatever little donations they had to help the victims. Lealia had watched with pride yesterday as Reverend Walker met with several people, some Shiloh members and some not, and told her to take notes on how much he would give them from the donations. It had made her feel good to know that she was helping even though she probably was not helping herself. Reverend Walker had told her that all incoming funds would go to the injured. That meant none were going to the Education Board fund. That was as it should be, but she prayed that some of the donations would not be needed for the injured and would go into the scholarship fund.

She made notes to the ledgers. Normally, she would take the banknotes and put them directly into the lockbox, but first she needed to count how much they already had in it. Reverend Walker had told her that when the box reached $500 to make another deposit. With the money that had come in today, she was pretty certain she would have over that amount.

She went to the closet door. When she reached it, she stopped short. The light was out.

She was sure she'd left the light on when she was here yesterday. Reverend Walker had not returned from his trip. So who turned the light out again? Her hand trembled. First the missing banknote, now this. She reached in, fingers grasping for the light. The pull chain brushed against her fingers, and she stretched farther for it.

Suddenly, someone shoved her from behind. She let out a cry as she fell forward in the room, her shoulder striking a shelf.

But before she could right herself, the door slammed shut and she heard the key turn in the lock with a click.

She screamed, and her knees buckled.

She rushed to the door and pounded on it. "Help! Someone, help!"

But the door did not open.

She pounded harder, tears springing to her eyes. *Oh, God.* She screamed again for help, her fists stinging with each strike on the door.

No answer.

Her breath caught painfully in her throat, and she stumbled backward. *Turn the light on*, she commanded herself, but she couldn't get her balance enough to reach for it.

She heard herself whimpering. Like the night of the stampede, the air seemed to thicken and the oxygen in it decrease. She panted, sweating heavily now. Her mind flashed images of the underside of the bench, the wood floor, the small space. . .

"Please," she whispered.

The door swung open. "Lealia!"

Milton.

She shot out the door, throwing her arms around his neck and nearly knocking him over.

He held her tight, and she cried into his shoulder.

"What happened?"

"Someone pushed—" She swallowed hard. "The door. Locked." She gasped for air.

Milton carefully led her to her desk and into her seat. "Hey," he said, softly. "Look at me. You're safe."

She glanced up at him. He was a little out of breath. He must have run to get to her.

She sobbed and leaned forward on his shoulder. "So scared."

"I know," he murmured against her temple. "I heard you screaming all the way down the hall."

Is this how he feels when his panic episodes happen? If so, she never wanted him to experience that again. She didn't want to experience it again herself.

He pulled back. "Did you see who pushed you?"

She closed her eyes, remembering the strong hands that pushed her. "No."

Milton looked at the door. "They could still be in the building."

"There was no one here when I arrived, not even Reverend Walker." The level of terror jumped several notches in her throat. Someone had followed her into the building without her knowing. "Whoever they are, they have a key to the closet."

"Not anymore," Milton said, opening his hand. A key rested in his palm. "It was still in the lock."

She shuddered. "We'll have to ask Reverend Walker who all has a copy of the closet key."

Milton nodded. "I think I should check the church. Close your office door and lock it."

Her first instinct was to grab Milton and not let him go. He was right though. The person could still be in the church, waiting to do more mischief.

She watched him go and then locked her office door as he instructed. Her stomach in knots, she put her ear to the door, listening. She could hear Milton's footsteps getting fainter and fainter. Even though he was only gone for a few minutes, it felt like an hour.

She heard footsteps approaching, and then someone tapped on the door. "Lealia, it's me."

She straightened up and opened it.

"There's no one in the building, but the front door was ajar." He held her hand.

"Someone was here, Milton. I didn't lock myself in the closet."

"You gave me a fright." He sighed. "Do you need me to put the banknotes in the lockbox?"

"Yes, please." She walked to her desk on wobbly legs. "I don't think I can go back—" Her words died in her throat.

The letters and banknotes she had left on her desk were gone.

"Lealia, are you all right?"

"The banknotes," she said, her voice trembling. "The banknotes are gone."

Milton looked down at the desk. "Are you sure?'

"They were right there." She tapped the place where the notes had been. "I've had a stressful few weeks, but I'm sure."

They stood there, Lealia too afraid to speak. To put words to what she knew Milton was thinking.

There was a thief in the church. A thief with a key.

No matter how much he and Mom tried to console her, Lealia kept crying.

"Reverend Walker is going to think I stole the money," she said, pressing Milton's handkerchief to her eyes.

Milton moved to sit beside her on the couch. "I doubt he'll believe that."

"Why not?" Her expression turned angry. "It makes perfect sense. Money began going missing as soon as I started working at the church."

Mrs. Rafferty brought her a cup of tea. "You're assuming that money hasn't gone missing before?"

Milton jumped on that idea. "Very true. If Reverend Massey got put out of his last church for suspected theft, that doesn't mean he stopped stealing."

"It's more than that." Lealia exhaled, and her shoulders sank. "I was hoping that some of that money could go into the Education Board's scholarship fund."

The room grew still, and Milton understood her distress. If there was no money in the fund, there was no money for her scholarship. "Maybe the Education Board already has the money," Mom said.

Lealia closed her eyes and sighed. "Maybe."

"If it makes you feel better, the church will probably accuse me of stealing before they accuse you," Milton said.

The comment was supposed to lighten her mood, but a look of horror crossed both her and his mother's face.

"Milton!" Lealia cried.

"Milton Abner Rafferty, do not say something like that again," Mom said, swatting him on the leg.

Lealia's expression, however, turned quizzical. "Your middle name is Abner?" He could tell she was trying hard not to smile. "Like Abner in the Bible?"

"Yes, like in the Bible." If his middle name made her feel better, then he had done his job.

Lealia giggled. "You've done better than me. I don't even have a middle name."

Mom smiled. "After some praying, I picked that name. It means 'father of light.'"

Lealia tipped her head. "Then I will not laugh at it."

The conversation moved on, but his own words stuck in his mind. He would probably be accused of stealing. Reverend Massey had hinted that people already thought he was up to something devious at the church. Lealia was their sweet daughter. He would take the blame before she did. That thought stayed with him all through dinner. *I should go back to Tuskegee before—* He snapped himself out of that thought. He would not leave his mother there to deal with the gossip again. He would stay until the situation was resolved.

Lealia rose. "I'm going to check the garden before it gets too dark out."

Mom yawned. "I think I'm going to turn in early. I've gotten spoiled being at home nursing you." She smiled at Lealia. "Being back at work is wearing me out."

Milton stood too. He wasn't going to miss a chance to be in the garden with Lealia. "I'll go with you."

The October air was cooling quickly, so they put on their coats. Lealia stepped out and inhaled. "Not much time left before the first frost. We should harvest as much as we can before I—" She stopped.

"Before you. . . ?"

She turned to face him. "Before I leave." There was such turmoil in her eyes. *Not for me. She cannot be conflicted about me.*

"You think that will be soon?"

She shrugged. "All the local Education Board members have recovered. Donations are coming in. I cannot see why not."

Milton reached out and took her hand. It was already cool. He laced his fingers in hers. "They promised you a scholarship. I doubt they'll go back on their word."

"I don't believe they will either." She stared out over the fields. "Would it be wrong if I am not sure anymore what I want to do?"

Milton's eyebrows shot up. "Yes."

She turned to face him. "Why?" Her voice squeaked.

"Because that is the one thing you've always been sure about," he said. "You going to Howard like your brother."

She pursed her lips and looked away.

"No." He used his finger to turn her chin. "You are going to Howard to become a lawyer. Nothing changes that."

"Everything that has happened changes that, Milton. You have to see." She swallowed hard. "When I was trapped under the bench, I gave up. I was waiting to die."

"Stop. Don't talk that way." He tugged her closer and grasped her other hand. "You did not die."

"But it made me wonder about everything." She held his gaze.

Made you wonder about me? His heart wanted to hope, but he knew that he was definitely a downgrade from going to Howard. He was poor, had not even completed his studies, and had absolutely nothing to offer her but a questionable reputation. "Let me help you be sure.

The Education Board will give you the money any day now, and you'll be at Howard in no time."

She sighed.

"Lealia, I need you to go to Howard and be okay." *I need you to be okay because I love you.* The thought came unbidden, but it didn't surprise him. He would be a fool indeed if he didn't realize he had fallen for her and fallen hard. That was why he had kissed her and cared for her, made sure she had everything she needed while she was here. Some of his actions came from kindness, but most of them were from love. A hopeless love going nowhere.

She looked up at him, a beam of the setting sun across her face. "What?"

He swallowed. She could not give up her dreams. "I need you to go to Howard and leave all this pain in Birmingham. I need the stampede not to break you."

Her eyes widened, and he realized what he was implying. The stampede had broken him. It had shattered everything he thought he knew about himself. It had shown him that in some ways, he was as weak as his father. Dr. Briggs had said what he had done required strength. Maybe, but he did not feel strong now.

She released his hand and touched his face. "But what about you?" She spoke so softly a breeze would have carried the sound of her voice away.

"I will go back to Tuskegee."

"You know that's not what I am asking. What about you being broken? I hear you struggling every morning, Milton. I saw you at Evan's house."

He sighed. Hearing her talk about his episodes was easier since he broke down in Dr. Briggs' office. "I will recover. I need time."

They stood there, side by side, until the sun set. As much as he hated to go in, Lealia's fingers, which were still laced in his, were growing cold.

He led her inside, leaving all the things he wanted to say unsaid.

CHAPTER SIXTEEN

To her great surprise, Milton did not rise from the table after they finished breakfast.

"Are you all right to go to the church by yourself today?" he asked.

"Yes." She kept her voice from showing the shiver of fear she felt from the thought of staying in the church alone after being locked in the closet. "You are not going with me?"

"I'll come by later," he said. "The house needs a few repairs, and I'm going with Mom to pick up a few things she needs."

"All right," she said.

"I'll come by the church this afternoon." He gave her a searching gaze. "Unless you need me to go with you now."

He seemed more relaxed. More rested. Perhaps that was what he needed, rest. "I'll be fine."

"Besides, Mom and I haven't spent much time together with all that's been going on. Once I go back—"

"Of course." Lealia didn't want to think about what he was going to say. "I should be fine."

On her walk to the church, she steeled her nerves to talk to Reverend Walker about the missing money. She should not delay, especially now that two sets of donations were missing. She took off her coat and hat and hung them in her office. There was some unopened mail on her desk. She picked it all up, not wanting to take another chance, and took it to the lockbox.

But this time, she dragged a chair to the door with her. Someone would have to move the chair to shut her in, and the sound of the chair moving would give her a warning. After securing the letters in the lockbox, she took the chair back to her desk. She had just settled it into place when the office door opened. She held her breath.

Reverend Walker came through the door. “Good morning. I thought I heard you moving around in here.” He held up some envelopes, grinning at her. “Miss Bevard, did you deposit these letters as well as the banknotes?”

Lealia frowned. “No, I did not.”

“These were in the church’s mailbox this morning with a note from the bank. It said they were left at their branch yesterday. I figured you had made a deposit and took the letters in accidentally.”

She crossed the room, and he handed her the letters. She tried to hide her surprise.

These were the letters that accompanied the banknotes that had disappeared off her desk the day before. “Uh—I—”

Reverend Walker gave her a compassionate look. “Is this work too much for you?”

She blinked. “No. I—” She couldn’t bring herself to tell him. Besides, her mind was working. If the letters turned up at a bank, maybe she could recover the banknotes. She laughed nervously. “I guess I can be a little absent minded.”

“Think no more about it. I am so thankful to have you filling in for Rodah.” Reverend Walker patted her shoulder. “Sorry to rush out, but I must meet with a member who has fallen ill.”

Lealia nodded.

Once he was gone, she flipped through the envelopes and saw that it wasn’t only letters. In between two of the envelopes was a deposit receipt from Gaines Savings Bank. She scowled at it. How did that get in with these letters? Reverend Walker must have truly been in a hurry, because he had not even noticed the bank’s name was different from the name of the bank the church used. Lealia grabbed her things, stuffed the letters in her coat pocket, and rushed down the stairs.

She made it back to the Rafferty house in record time. Milton opened the door with surprise. “Lealia. What are you doing here? What’s the matter?”

She did her best, although nearly out of breath, to explain what happened. “Can you take me to the Gaines bank?”

"Yes, I can, but why?"

"Just come on. I'll explain on the way."

He retrieved his coat, and they started down the street. She watched a troubled look cross his face as she recounted her conversation with Reverend Walker.

"What's your plan?" he asked her.

"I suspect that Gaines Bank is Reverend Massey's bank. I want to see what they have to say about this."

"Lealia," his said, his voice chiding, "don't you think you need to speak with Reverend Walker about this first?"

"I just can't bring myself to tell him about the stolen money yet. This could be a chance to recover it before he's any the wiser."

"And if you recover the money, it may go to the Education Board fund for your scholarship."

She turned to face him and plastered a smile on her face to hide how his words stung. *He's probably thinking I'm in a rush to get out of here.* "You make me sound so mercenary."

He laughed. "That was not my intention."

"It's the right thing to do. Just as much as it is the right thing to do to figure out who killed Mr. Stokes."

Milton sobered. "You're right."

Gaines Bank was one of the smaller ones in the city. It shared a floor with a lawyer's office. The clerk at the teller window looked up and smiled when she and Milton approached. "If it isn't the two angels of Tuskegee. Lots of people talking about you two."

Lealia felt herself blush, and Milton shifted beside her, his discomfort evident. "All good, I hope?"

The clerk nodded with vigor. "Oh yes. You two have helped so many of the injured during the aftermath. People are saying Mr. Washington left his best two students here. How can I help you?"

Lealia held up the envelopes, unsure out how to handle the situation.

The clerk laughed. "I thought it was odd that Reverend Massey didn't separate the letters from the banknotes."

Lealia forced a smile to cover her distress. "Reverend Massey—" She tried to think of something to say.

Milton jumped in. "Everyone at the church is working really hard right now."

"Reverend Massey must be worn to a frazzle, because he deposited the church money here. I mentioned that I thought they kept their accounts over at Woodley's."

She and Milton had deposited the first batch of banknotes at Woodley's Bank, which was how Lealia knew the church didn't have accounts at Gaines. "So then, did he take the notes to Woodley's to deposit them?"

"Actually, he deposited them here. He said he had another errand to run and that he would come back and move the deposit later. You can save him a trip."

Lealia fought to keep her composure. "Yes," she said, smiling brightly. "I will take it over to Woodley's today."

The clerk checked the ledger and issued the notes to her. "Here you go."

"Thank you," Milton said.

"You keep up the good work." The clerk extended his hand across the desk. "Especially you, Mr. Rafferty. You saved a little girl and her mother. My sister and niece."

Lealia remembered seeing Milton fighting through the crowd that night to get to the woman with the child in her arms.

Milton slowly took his hand. "Glad I was there to help." His voice came out rough.

They left the bank, Lealia feeling like a weight had lifted from her shoulders. She grasped Milton's hand. "See? What we are doing is making a difference."

He smiled at her. "Yes, it is."

They continued walking in the direction of Woodley's. Lealia stole a glance at Milton. "I saw you save the woman and the little girl that night."

Milton looked down at her. "It's so hard to hear people thank me for what I did."

"Why?" She took his hand and gave it a squeeze.

"Because I feel I only did what anyone else would have done."

"That is untrue. Reverend Massey wasn't helping." She was unable to keep the acid from her tone.

He shook his head. "We don't know that for sure. Maybe he was helping."

"We both know he wasn't," she huffed. "He isn't like you. He would have thought of himself first. That's one of the things I love about you. You're always looking for ways to care for others."

Milton studied her with his curious stare.

"What?" she said, laughing.

"Nothing."

They made the deposit at Woodley's, and Milton walked her back to the church. It was not until she was sitting at her desk that she realized what she had said.

That's one of the things I love about you. . .

She had not meant to say that. However, since she had, it forced her to acknowledge the truth. She was in love with Milton. She had started to like him just before the stampede, but now she had grown to love him.

She let out a groan. *And I carelessly told him.*

Regardless of her feelings, a relationship with Milton was impossible. They would soon be in two different states.

Maybe he didn't hear her say she loved him. But then she remembered his expression after she had. *He heard me.* Her heart sank a little. *He heard me and did not respond.*

Milton's tremors only lasted a short time this morning. It was still a struggle to right his thoughts, but he did. He dressed and set himself to do the repairs on his mother's house. He had heard her leave for work and determined to surprise her that night when she got home. Lealia would be leaving for the church soon, and he would escort her there and come back and get to work.

A knock sounded on the front door. Milton opened it to see Dr. Briggs standing on the porch. "Good morning, Milton."

"Good morning. Come in."

"Actually, I was wondering if you wanted to come out."

Milton frowned and noticed Dr. Briggs' carriage standing at the curbside. "Do you need my help?"

"No. I think I may be able to help you." He lowered his voice. "I have thought about what you told me about Reverend Massey, and I think I know someone you could get some answers from. The location is on the way to one of my visits. Get your coat."

Milton raced up the stairs to his room and grabbed his coat off the hook in his closet. Lealia ran down the hall. "Is something wrong?"

"No. Dr. Briggs is outside. He says he can take me to someone who can give me answers about Reverend Massey's insurance company."

"I'm going with you." She bolted back to her room.

"No," he said, but it was useless. She returned with her coat and hat before he could finish putting on his.

They raced down the stairs. Dr. Briggs laughed when they both shot out the door. "You two really are inseparable. Let's be on our way."

After they climbed into the front seat of the carriage, Lealia in the middle, they set off. Dr. Briggs steered them to the far side of Birmingham, past Shiloh and Holly's Boardinghouse. "Where are we going?" Milton asked.

"To the office of the state deputy insurance commissioner." Dr. Briggs looked over at Milton. "Who is also the local fire marshal."

"You think he can tell us something?"

"When you left my house the other day, I started thinking. If Reverend Massey hasn't made any payouts, how can he still be in business? Then I remembered that there was a way to check into anyone selling insurance in the state just like you can look up a doctor."

"Do you think he'll answer our questions?" Lealia asked.

"If not, you will be of great use to Mr. Rafferty," Dr. Briggs glanced at her. "All insurance records have to be filed in that office."

Lealia turned to Milton, a wicked little grin on her face. She narrowed her eyes. "I get to be nosy."

The state offices were located in a brick office building. Dr. Briggs dropped them off in front of the door. "I have to go attend a patient nearby. I should be done with my visit in roughly half an hour."

Milton helped Lealia down from the carriage. "We'll be ready to go when you return."

They went inside and found three offices on the ground floor. They located the door with a painted sign that read State Insurance, knocked, and heard a sharp, "Come in."

They stepped inside an office, but it was hard to tell how large it was, because it was packed with overflowing bookcases.

Lealia leaned in close and whispered, "This resembles the clerk's office the first day I started."

Milton stifled a chuckle.

A large reading table sat on one side of the room. A harried-looking man sat at a desk just inside the door. He was so frazzled that his blond hair stood straight up on his head. "Can I help you?"

"My name is Milton Rafferty, and this is Lealia Bevard. We were wondering if we could ask you some questions."

The man stood and extended his hand. "My name is Vernon McDowell." He motioned to the table. "We can sit over there. Do you have questions about insurance?"

"Yes," Milton said.

Mr. McDowell had to move some of the files in order for them to have a clear space. "Sorry about this being so untidy. I am the only person here, and my work does not allow me time to file."

Lealia beamed. "I'm studying bookkeeping at Tuskegee and am helping Shiloh, as the church clerk was injured in the disaster. Perhaps I could help you the few minutes I am here."

Mr. McDowell looked at her with surprise. "You would do that? I heard so many good things about Mr. Washington and his school."

Lealia stood. "Just tell me where things are supposed to go."

Mr. McDowell breathed a sigh of relief. "If you can gather the files and sort them in alphabetical order, that would help so much."

Lealia kept grinning, and when Mr. McDowell turned back to Milton, she mouthed *nosy*.

It took all of Milton's self-control not to laugh. "I am helping someone who lost a loved one at the Shiloh stampede."

Mr. McDowell took on a sympathetic look. "Horrible. I read about it in the paper. Eighty people dead."

Milton swallowed. *Focus.* "More than that, sir."

"Hard to believe that no one could calm the crowd."

"I was inside. As was Miss Bevard. Men tried, but there was too much chaos." Milton tried to push the images to the back of his mind.

"I am sorry to hear that," Mr. McDowell said. "Are you asking about a life insurance policy of one of the deceased? You might do better to ask the company who insured them."

"It's not a life insurance policy. It's a business policy," Milton said. "The business burned down, and the deceased was waiting for an investigation. His son is in dire straits now that his father is gone. He is a young man and grieving."

Mr. McDowell nodded. "What are the names of the business owner and his insurer?"

"Mr. Alfred Stokes and Massey Insurance."

Mr. McDowell huffed. "Him again."

Lealia stopped sorting. "You have had problems with Reverend Massey before?"

"Many problems." He pointed at a section of the bookcase that held thick folders. "Those are his problems. Everything from missing records to incomplete reports."

"He is still allowed to operate?" Milton asked.

"He wouldn't be if I could catch him." Mr. McDowell rose and started to pace. "Every time I go to audit his records, he manages to elude me."

"But he is at Shiloh Baptist Church every Sunday," Lealia said with surprise.

"Yes, I know, but there is only one of me. What else do you want to know?"

Milton told him about the arson and investigation. "His son told us that Reverend Massey was waiting on your investigation into the fire before he could make the payout."

"Is that so?" Mr. McDowell walked over to his files on Massey's insurance company. "I could be wrong, but Mr. Massey never filed a request for investigation. Let's see." He took one of the fat folders off the shelf and began flipping through the pages. After a few moments, he shook his head. "No, he never filed for an investigation."

"What about Dr. Graham Briggs?"

Mr. McDowell flipped through the pages, but Milton already knew the answer.

"No. No Dr. Briggs either."

Lealia spoke up. "What about a Mr. Gilbert?" Milton did not know who Mr. Gilbert was, but Lealia's question got the same response. Mr.

McDowell shook his head.

Milton and Lealia stared at each other.

"One more question sir," Lealia said. "Why would Reverend Massey not be able to pay out the claim?"

"Because he's broke," Mr. McDowell said with a sour laugh. "He is completely insolvent. I believe he has committed fraud by taking in payments without any way to cover losses." Mr. McDowell tapped the folder. "Every paper in this folder is a complaint filed against him."

"That means he's breaking the law?"

Mr. McDowell ruffled his hair. "I believe so. I cannot tell you for sure, because he hasn't submitted to an audit in a long time."

Milton glanced at the clock on the wall. The half hour was almost up. "Is there any way you can start the investigation into the fire at Mr. Stokes' store?"

"I can, but I am unsure what good it will do. If Mr. Massey is insolvent, as I believe he is, there will be no money for the young son." Mr. McDowell tapped the file again. "I will talk to the son. If he can provide enough information, maybe it will help me to resolve this."

"We'll speak to Evan and arrange a meeting between you."

"I wish I could get you two to pin Mr. Massey down in one place, because I have a lot of questions for him," Mr. McDowell said, his tone angry. "I would probably arrest him first and then ask the questions."

Lealia looked surprised. "You can arrest him?"

Mr. McDowell's tone lightened. "Another reason I have no time for filing. I am also the city's fire marshal."

They left the office after thanking Mr. McDowell and promising to send word once they spoke to Evan. Dr. Briggs drove up as soon as they stepped outside. They climbed into the carriage, Milton's thoughts swirling. Too bad they couldn't pin Reverend Massey down for Mr. McDowell.

Dr. Briggs pulled away from the office. "Did you get some answers?"

Milton recounted the information they had gotten from Mr. McDowell.

Dr. Briggs shook his head. "I knew Reverend Massey lied about submitting a request for an investigation into the Stokes fire. That means Evan will never get the money from his father's store."

"But he may learn who actually started the fire. That may help," Lealia said.

"I will go to Evan's house soon." Milton looked at Dr. Briggs. "Thank you."

"Glad I could help."

From her window, Lealia could see Milton walking toward the hospital. She sighed. Since she had set foot in Birmingham, little had gone as she had planned. She had gotten the scholarship but not when she wanted. Now it was even further delayed. She had gotten injured and had to stay longer, but she had found something useful to do. She had only expected to spend a few days with Milton but now. . .

She stopped herself. That line of thinking would come to a painful end.

There was, however, another just as perturbing topic her mind worked on. Reverend Massey. She hadn't mentioned the theft and the deposit at Gaines to Reverend Walker. Should she? Reverend Walker knew there was a problem with Reverend Massey when he arrived. He would probably believe her.

The problem was that things were the same as they were when Reverend Massey left Pell City: There was no hard proof. If confronted, Reverend Massey could say he was distracted and deposited the money in the wrong bank. Or that he had intended to give Evan the entire one-hundred-dollar banknote. Then what?

It would look like she was telling tales against him. Until she had hard evidence, Reverend Walker would probably not take action. If he could. Reverend Massey was a Baptist Board appointee. What if Reverend Walker could not remove Reverend Massey without the Board's approval? And all the insurance delays were equally troubling. Mr. Stokes, and now Evan, needed the money to rebuild. If they'd paid their premiums along with all of Reverend Massey's other customers, the money should be there.

Her door opened, and Reverend Walker stepped in, smiling wide. He was holding a letter. "Good news."

Lealia smiled back at him. She could use good news with how dark her thoughts were. "Judging from your smile, it must be very good."

"The Baptist Convention Board has decided to send all the funds they raised during the convention here." He handed her the letter.

Lealia's heart soared. "That is wonderful news."

"The donation will be enough to cover the medical bills of the injured and the funeral expenses, and there will be enough to replenish the Education Board fund," he said. "The letter suggests it will be a substantial amount. A representative from the board, Reverend Parker from Montgomery, will be delivering it."

Lealia's smile slipped a little. That meant her scholarship was probably on the way. "That is very generous of them."

"Yes. They said that there is no greater need than what happened here. Reverend Parker will be coming to give the presentation on Sunday at church. I'm planning to have our first service since the stampede this Sunday, and I would like for you to be there."

Lealia's mouth went dry. "Inside the sanctuary?"

Reverend Walker held her gaze. "If you can."

She looked down at the papers on her desk. Could she? She had grown so used to walking past the sanctuary doors when she came in for work. As if there were nothing behind those doors. But to go inside. . . She swallowed, hard. "I do not think I can."

Reverend Walker nodded. "I understand."

"Do you think your members will come?"

"I pray so. We need to come together, pray, and start to move forward."

Move forward. "What does that even look like now?"

Reverend Walker raised his eyebrows. "What does what look like now?"

"Moving forward." She heard the quiver in her voice. "So much has happened. People's whole lives have changed. How does one move forward when the direction is not clear?"

Reverend Walker moved and sat in front of her desk. "Are you talking about the members of Shiloh. . .or yourself?"

Confusion lay heavy on her mind. "Myself, I guess," she said in a small voice.

"I did not think your direction was unclear. You will get the scholarship and go to Howard."

She opened her mouth to speak but then closed it.

"Child," Reverend Walker said gently, "I have complete confidence that you will find your way."

She looked up. "You have more confidence in me than I do."

He chuckled. "Maybe. You forget I watched you and Milton dive into the chaos after the stampede and figure out what to do."

"People needed help."

"And you two figured out what to do," he repeated. "And you've done it well."

Lealia looked at the work on her desk. "All I did was some bookkeeping."

"You have done more than that. You've visited the injured and taken them food. You made sure Milton was informed about the victims' needs. You've freed me up to go out and do visitations and funerals. You did all this for the least of these, and God is pleased."

Lealia's chest heaved, her tears flowing. "I do not know what comes next."

Reverend Walker handed her a handkerchief. "You'll know when the time comes. I'm sure of it."

CHAPTER SEVENTEEN

The next morning, Milton found a note from Mom. It read that Reverend Walker had sent word that there was not much work on Lealia's desk and that he would be traveling, so she wasn't needed at the church. Milton, trying to heed Dr. Briggs' advice of giving his mind a rest, decided it would be good to do the repairs he'd promised his mother. It would give him a moment to put Shiloh out of his mind.

As Milton prepared to get started, Lealia rolled her sleeves up to help.

She smiled at Milton. "Remember, I got a good Tuskegee education too."

They patched the torn screen door, fixed the leg of the table beside the couch, and repaired the banister, all the while talking and laughing. Lealia braved the cold, and they installed a better fence around the garden. After that, they prepared dinner. Culinary arts was another skill they had learned at Tuskegee.

Mom came to the supper table, beaming.

"What am I going to do when you two leave?"

She said it in passing, but the force of it struck Milton hard. He would have to go back in a few days. It was nearing November. If he did not return soon, he would miss the whole fall term. He was sure he could make up his studies over winter break if he worked hard. Then again, after all he had been through in the past two months, he was unsure if it was wise to push himself so hard.

The night passed as it normally did, but the tremors weren't as severe. Actually, Milton was better. He still didn't have the courage to tell his mother, but in his room, he stopped fighting against the tremors.

He accepted that his mind was, as Dr. Briggs said, disordered, and let his emotions flow through him instead of fighting.

This morning he had let himself cry when he awakened. He cried for the dead. For the waste of losing a loved one over something as trivial as a fight. After the last of the darkness from his nightmare passed, he lay there thinking of his life. Events of his childhood and the past days filtered through his mind.

His thoughts stopped on Lealia telling him that she loved him. Well. . .not quite that she loved him, but that his care for others was one of the things she loved about him. He had wanted to respond but couldn't find the words to say. It wouldn't be a lie to tell her that he loved her too. It would, however, be wrong.

After breakfast, Milton walked Lealia to the church and then decided to go check on Mrs. Jones before he went to Evan's house. When he arrived at the hospital, however, the nursing staff told him that Mrs. Jones had been discharged. He should have been happy with the news. She was the last of the badly injured. Rodah still had her arm in a sling, but she didn't need his and Lealia's visits anymore.

He could go back to Tuskegee now. He pushed the thought away and went to the church.

Reverend Walker met him in the hallway. "Good morning, Milton."

"I was just coming to see you. Mrs. Jones was released from the hospital today."

Reverend Walker smiled. "Praise the Lord."

Milton shifted. "That means everyone has recovered." His heart sat like a stone in his chest.

"Well done. I could not have cared for the injured as well as I did without your help."

"Thank you, sir," Milton said, taking a step backward. "I guess that means I am done here."

Reverend Walker nodded. "Yes, but if you have the time, I have another task for you."

Although Milton knew he was only delaying the inevitable, he said, "Yes, sir."

"All of the unclaimed items are sitting in a room downstairs." Reverend Walker sighed. "I thought by now people would have come looking for their things, but they have not."

"I would be glad to help."

"Great. I asked Reverend Massey to take care of it, but he has not gotten around to it." Reverend Walker went to the door. "I would like to have our first service since the stampede this Sunday and would like that room cleaned out."

"Oh." Milton nearly tripped as he followed the reverend down the hall.

"I think it's time," Reverend Walker said. "Time for us to worship together and ask God's healing for our church. Also, I have some news to announce."

Milton swallowed the lump in his throat. He did not envy Reverend Walker this task. If the members of Shiloh had gone through half what he had, coming back to church would be hard.

Reverend Walker put his hand on Milton's shoulder. "I would like you and Miss Bevard to be in attendance."

Milton jumped like Reverend Walker had struck him. "In the sanctuary?"

Reverend Walker studied him. "Yes."

"I will do it if you think it will encourage the members." Milton's mouth was dry.

"Come with me."

Reverend Walker led Milton up a flight of stairs. When they got to the top, there was a door directly across from the stairwell. Reverend Walker went to the door and opened it, and Milton saw that it led to the balcony above the sanctuary.

Milton gasped, not an ounce of anxiety in his heart.

From this view, the sanctuary was beautiful. Calm, as if peace radiated from the walls. The sun shone through the stained-glass window, making the pews below seem as if they were inside a kaleidoscope.

"I come up here to pray sometimes," Reverend Walker said from beside him. "To pray for my members. Miss Bevard. You."

Milton stared at him.

"I heard all the stories about you," Reverend Walker said. "But that is not the young man I saw that night. Whatever others may think about you, I saw the truth about you then and since. You have been a great help to this church. . ." He smiled. "Whether they appreciate it or not."

Milton looked down into the sanctuary. "Why did God let this happen in His own church?"

"Hmm." Reverend Walker took in a deep breath. "I have asked Him that question many times myself. The only answer I can give you is that man has free will."

Milton frowned. "I don't understand," he said. "No one would choose this."

"Those two delegates who were fighting, they chose to fight," Reverend Walker said. "The woman in the choir who yelled and confused everyone chose to do that. That night was a combination of people's choices."

"I understand that, but why didn't God help us?"

Reverend Walker looked at Milton with surprise. "He did." He touched a finger to Milton's chest. "Through you. Through your choice. Your free will."

Milton peered down at the sanctuary again. "I don't think I can go in there yet."

"And that is your choice," Reverend Walker said. "It won't be easy for any of us. I only wanted you to know that you have done enough."

Milton blinked, surprised by the tears smarting in his eyes. "Thank you" was all he could manage to say.

Reverend Walker went back down the stairs. *His choice.* Milton wished he felt as free in his choices as Reverend Walker supposed. If he were free, he would marry Lealia, return to Tuskegee, finish his studies, and collect his mother once he became a doctor. Or marry Lealia and go with her to Howard to finish his studies. Howard had a medical school. He could go back to Tuskegee, but would his panic disorder allow him to finish? What would happen if he awakened in the middle of the night, screaming, surrounded by his classmates?

He had moved to close the door to the balcony when voices drifted up to him.

"That's what you said before," an angry man said.

"I only need a little more time."

Reverend Massey.

"I have no more time to give you. You've been stringing this along for months. Where is my money?" Milton took a step closer to the door.

Milton was grave on the walk to Evan's house.

He told Lealia about the conversation he overheard in the sanctuary. "Massey said he was about to come into some money. I shudder to think he might have meant the donation that is coming."

Dread and frustration filled Lealia's chest. "And we still cannot prove anything. He could be talking about the donation. But we cannot go to Reverend Walker and say we think he's planning to steal the donation like he tried to steal the banknotes."

As uncomfortable as she was about talking to Reverend Walker, she wanted to be free of the weight of it. Especially if Reverend Walker could stop Reverend Massey from hurting someone else.

Milton agreed but then said, "There is something we can do. We can set up the meeting between Evan and Mr. McDowell."

The wind had picked up as they walked, and the sky threatened rain. They walked at a quick pace through town, Lealia's thoughts moving as fast as her feet. Reverend Walker had said she would figure out what to do next. She prayed that was true. Evan needed the money to reopen his father's store and have his livelihood returned. But what if it was better to leave this alone? Mr. McDowell had said he was sure that Reverend Massey's company was broke. Evan would not get any money out of him. Was it wrong to give him hope?

"I don't know if this is the right thing to do," Milton said, bringing her back from her musings.

She smiled. How many times since the stampede had their minds worked exactly the same? "Me neither."

"But all I can think is that if Massey took Mr. Stokes' money for insurance, how many more people has he swindled? We already know about Dr. Briggs and Mr. Gilbert. What if there are more?"

"True." She took his hand and squeezed it. "Arranging this meeting between Evan and Mr. McDowell may do something to help."

"Yes," he said. "Even if this remains unresolved when I go back to Tuskegee, at least I will know it's still moving forward."

Lealia kept her eyes ahead. This bubble that she and Milton had lived in all these weeks was very close to popping. It would burst, and they would be heading in different directions. She did not release his hand. She would enjoy every remaining moment she had with him.

Evan opened the door, his expression haggard. "Hello," he said as he invited them in.

Milton and Lealia exchanged a look and went inside. Milton patted Evan's shoulder as he passed.

"It is good to see you," Evan said. He motioned for them to sit and then sank into the chair across from them. "I was thinking of coming to the church to see you, and here you are."

Lealia's heart ached for him. He was alone in the world now. "We have some information to share." She watched the range of emotions, from hope to despair, cross Evan's face as Milton told him what they'd learned.

"So I'm never getting that payout?"

Milton shook his head. "Sadly, I don't think so. At least they're going to try to find out who burned your father's store down. The person will be brought to justice."

Evan scoffed. "Justice. I'll believe it when I see it. It will never happen."

Lealia reached over and took his hand. "That doesn't mean we shouldn't try."

Evan nodded. "You're right. I will meet with Mr. McDowell whenever it is convenient for him."

"I know this is hard, but we're here to help."

"Thank you." Evan gave them a weak smile. "I wish I could go back to Tuskegee with you. There's nothing here for me now."

Milton smiled. "You can. I can talk to Mr. Washington when I return. What will you do with the house?"

"The lease is in my father's name, so I will have to move when it runs out. Maybe sooner." He rubbed his chin. "I just thought of going to Tuskegee recently. Pa was really impressed with Mr. Washington."

"Are you going to school here?"

Evan shook his head. "I learned to read in Sunday school at Shiloh but not much more. There aren't many schools for Negro children around, and the ones that are here are full. Pa needed help at the shop, so I worked there since I was young."

"You should consider attending Tuskegee," Lealia added. "It's a great school."

She felt Milton turn his gaze on her. *I just know he has that watchful look on his face.*

"I'm not too old?" Evan asked. "I heard that students start at Tuskegee at fourteen."

"No," Milton said. "I first came to Tuskegee when I was twenty-one, and I'm twenty-five now."

"As a matter of fact, we have a classmate who just arrived, Boone, who is nearly thirty," Lealia said, giving Evan an encouraging smile.

"I have to make some sort of decision about my life." Evan exhaled. "My goal was to work in the store with my father. Now that he is gone and I do not have the money to reopen. . ."

"If you need to talk to us, we are glad to listen," Milton said.

A gust of wind rattled the window. Evan looked at it. "You two should probably go before this rain starts."

They stood. "We will be back once we talk to Mr. McDowell again," Milton said. "Be well, Evan."

"Thank you."

Evan was right about the rain. It seemed closer, and the air was charged with it. They were walking fast, but then Milton slowed a bit. "If Tuskegee is a great school, why do you want to leave it?"

Lealia rounded on him. "I don't know!" Angry tears formed, and she fought to keep them in. "I don't know anything anymore."

He grabbed her arm. "Forgive me. I didn't mean to upset you. I just thought maybe you'd changed—"

She put a finger to his lips. "Do not say it. Please."

He slowly reached up and lightly grasped her wrist, moving her hand to his cheek. "Okay."

The first fat drops of rain fell to the ground, and they took off at a run.

Lealia and Milton had decided that morning that after they spoke with

Evan, Milton would go back to Mr. McDowell's office and schedule the meeting with Evan, and she would go to the church. As she went down the hallway, she could hear Reverend Walker and Reverend Massey talking animatedly. She quieted her footsteps.

"She is young," Reverend Massey was saying. "Do you trust her with handling a $5,000 banknote?"

Lealia put her hand over her mouth. Was this the large donation Reverend Walker had told them about?

"She only has to transport it to the bank," Reverend Walker said. "I am sure Milton would accompany her. It's that simple."

"I am the head of the finance committee. I should be handling it."

"You've never handled deposits before. As the church's clerk, Rodah handled them, and that doesn't change. Lealia is the acting church clerk."

Lealia soundlessly rushed to her office. Although being nosy helped sometimes, it had its limits. It did, however, warm her to hear Reverend Walker stand up for her.

She went to work on the new pile of letters on the desk. The top letter was unopened and had a note clipped to it in Reverend Walker's hand. *For you.*

Lealia lifted the letter. It was addressed to her from Mr. Washington.

Before she could open it, Reverend Massey strode in the door. He still seemed angry as he looked around the room. "Mr. Rafferty is not here?"

"Good morning to you too." She knew it was probably not wise to provoke him, but the words were out of her mouth before she could think about it. *I don't like you any more than you like me.* The conversation in Reverend Walker's office proved it.

"I don't have time to play with you today, girl."

Lealia let the jab pass. "Milton is clearly not here."

She watched Reverend Massey's eyes drift to the closet door. She smiled sweetly at him. Maybe he was angry enough to loosen his tongue. "I am glad you stopped by. I wanted to ask you why you took the letters and banknotes from my desk."

He opened his mouth to say something, but she saw his expression change before he spoke. "I am not sure what you mean."

"The clerk at Gaines sent the letters you left at the bank back with a note." She stood, bracing her fingers on the desk. "I don't understand why you deposited them there and not at Woodley's."

"You are new here, so I can see how you'd be confused." His words were tight.

"Well," she said, her own anger rising, "you should know that I went over to Gaines."

"Yes, I am aware that you moved the deposit to Woodley's," he said with a sneer. "I thank you for your helpfulness."

"I also know you have been dishonest in your business dealings—"

"Whatever you think you know, you know nothing!" His face contorted from the controlled, almost unbothered, expression to pure rage. She took a step away.

That seemed to snap him back into himself. He looked behind him at the door and lowered his voice. "You will keep your mouth shut, or I will make your scholarship money disappear. Don't say a word to your little boyfriend."

She gasped.

He smiled, and it was cold and dark. "You know so much, do you? You also know I am on the Education Board. All I have to do is tell them that funds have gone missing under your watch, and your scholarship is gone."

"You would lie and blame me?"

His lip curled. "I have done worse."

Footsteps sounded in the hall, and he turned. "Nice talking to you, Miss Bevard." He left as quickly as he had come.

Reverend Walker appeared in the doorway a moment later. He looked around the room. "Oh, I thought I heard Reverend Massey in here."

Lealia swallowed. "He left."

"If he comes back, let him know I would like to speak to him."

Lealia prayed Reverend Massey would never come back.

CHAPTER EIGHTEEN

The church bells sent Milton into a panic episode. For the first time since the stampede, he had slept most of the night. He had awakened with a jolt, disoriented, and the tightness had started in his chest. He got up and splashed some water on his face. To his relief, the episode passed more quickly than any of the others.

But then the church bells had started ringing. Reverend Walker and the rest of the members of Shiloh were preparing to go to church for the first time since the event. To walk into the sanctuary. . .

His breath caught, and he was shaking hard. He let out a little moan as he leaned over.

There was a soft knock on his door. "Milton?" Lealia asked quietly.

He clamped his mouth shut.

"Milton," she said in the same soft voice but with more force behind it. "I know you can hear me. Say something."

And she says she does not demand. "Something." The joke came to his lips so easily, he found himself chuckling. He heard her laughing too. Then she went back down the hall.

He dressed and went downstairs for breakfast, and all his good feeling evaporated. Mom was dressed for church.

He swallowed.

"We are serving refreshments after church today, and I want to be there early." She moved to stand next to him. "I'll be back as soon as service is over. Why don't you and Lealia have a nice, leisurely breakfast?"

He breathed a sigh of relief. She understood and was not going to try and convince him to go. "I think that's a good idea."

"What's a good idea?" Lealia asked, coming into the living room.

She noticed Mom's clothing. "You're going to church."

"I am." Mom moved to Lealia and hugged her then Milton. "Love you both."

Milton watched her go, grateful for her understanding.

He went into the kitchen and found that his mother had made more food than the two of them could eat. He took on the duties of preparing plates, and Lealia sat down at the table. They talked little as they ate. Milton suspected her mind was on the same topic as his: the church service. If he had been stronger, he would have accepted Reverend Walker's invitation. He chastised himself. This had nothing to do with strength. Lealia was strong, and she could not do it.

Lealia spoke, surprising him. "Reverend Massey threatened to take away my scholarship if I said anything about the money he deposited at Gaines."

Milton's anger flared. "What?"

She nodded. "He told me not to tell anyone about it. Not even you. He must not know you went with me to Gaines."

"Why didn't you tell me this before?"

She looked away from his gaze, and this time he let her. "Because I was afraid. I knew I needed to tell you. And there's more."

Milton grasped her hand, hoping it gave her courage. "More?"

"When I went in yesterday, I heard him and Reverend Walker having tense words about who was going to deposit the donation."

"I am assuming Massey wanted to do it."

"He did." She paused. "Milton, the donation is five thousand dollars."

Milton drew in a sharp breath. "That much?"

Lealia nodded. "I think that Reverend Massey is going to try and steal it."

"We don't know that for sure."

"And that's the problem," she said, her voice rising. "We don't know, but we know he has tried before. Should we just let him try again?"

He looked at her, at the anger flashing in her eyes. *My word, she is beautiful when she's angry.* "What do you think we should do?"

"Steal it first."

Milton jolted. "What?"

Her expression changed to one of amusement. "I mean, move the lockbox to somewhere he can't find it. Just temporarily."

"We could put it in Reverend Walker's office." Reverend Massey had a key to the front door and to Lealia's office, but Milton was certain he did not have a key to Reverend Walker's office.

"The representative from the Baptist Board is presenting the donation today. If we hurry, we can go back to the church and talk to Reverend Walker afterward."

"How will we explain why we want him to move the box?"

"That won't be hard, since he already doesn't trust Massey. Now, if we hurry, we can talk to him before the service starts."

They practically ran to the church. Mr. Hamilton met them at the door. "Hello, you two rascals."

"Not rascals anymore," Milton said.

Mr. Hamilton laughed. "The way you two just ran in here, I would say that you are definitely up to something."

"Has service started?" Lealia asked.

"Not yet." Mr. Hamilton linked his arm in Lealia's. "You two are guests of honor. Let me get you good seats."

Lealia politely protested, but Mr. Hamilton ushered her inside. She looked back at Milton with pure desperation on her face before Mr. Hamilton led her through the double door. *If I didn't follow, she would understand. She would forgive me.* Knowing her, she would probably leave as soon as Mr. Hamilton's attention went elsewhere.

Still, he could not let her go in alone. He gritted his teeth and entered the building.

Mr. Hamilton had seated Lealia near the front, next to Milton's mother. In the same section he had sat in that night. With wooden steps, Milton made his way to them, already feeling warm. Both Lealia and his mother looked up at him with surprise.

Mom smiled, although he could see the worry behind it. "Milton, you came?"

Lealia scowled at him. "Why did you come in here? I'll be all right."

"I—" His vision burred. He blinked fast, not wanting to keep his eyes closed too long. "I'll be fine."

"No." Lealia stood, attracting the attention of the people sitting around him. She grabbed his hand. It was already clammy.

"What is going on?" Mrs. Rafferty said. She spoke in a whisper, but the sanctuary's ceiling carried her words up and over the congregation.

The sanctuary stilled. Like that night. Just like that night.

Milton's throat closed, and his vision started to narrow. Lealia was dragging him to the side door at the front of the sanctuary. The same route— He let out a moan.

He stumbled along behind her, catching whispers of the people around them. Lealia's hand tightened around his, and he let himself be led like a child.

His mind registered the hallway, Lealia's office. His knees buckled.

And then there were hands, guiding him to the floor. "Milton."

Dr. Briggs?

"Listen to my voice, Milton." Dr. Briggs seemed very close. *Am I hallucinating?*

Then he heard Lealia crying.

He focused on that sound. She had gotten him out of the sanctuary. He imagined how it had looked, her dragging him down the hall.

His breathing started to even out, his mind clearing. He lifted his head to find he was sitting on the floor, leaning against Lealia. Dr. and Mrs. Briggs and Reverends Walker and Massey were standing in front of him. Lealia had tears running down her face. Reverends Walker and Massey wore expressions of surprise.

Dr. Briggs' face was calm. "Better?"

He looked at them all, his stomach churning. No, he was not better. He had just had an episode in front of everyone. All of Shiloh saw him. They had to have.

A second later, his mother bolted through the door. "Milton!" She stopped when she saw him on the floor. "What happened?" She dropped to her knees in front of him and grasped his face.

"Milton has a panic disorder," Dr. Briggs said calmly. Milton was glad the man spoke, because he could not get his voice to work.

"Oh, Milton." She hugged him. "I was so worried."

He closed his eyes and tried to focus on his mother, her love. He failed.

All he felt was absolute shame.

He had broken in front of everyone. Shiloh would never stop talking about him.

Lealia sat in Reverend Walker's office, sniffling. Her heart ached for Milton. After listening to him struggle every morning, she knew how hard he'd tried to hide his affliction. She could see the shame in his eyes when he'd looked up at the people gathered around him. And his mother. . . Lealia pressed her hand to her face. She did not even get a chance to console him, as Dr. and Mrs. Briggs had rushed them all out of the room so he and his mother could be alone.

Reverend Walker paced the floor behind the chair. She could tell he wanted to ask her questions. She didn't know if she could give him answers. Thankfully, Reverend Massey had left. She didn't want Milton to have to face him.

After a few minutes, Reverend Walker spoke. "I have to go, Lealia. Service will be starting soon, and I have to deal with another unexpected thing."

She turned in her seat. "What unexpected thing?"

"The Baptist representative, Reverend Parker, arrived, and the donation—" He paused, looking at the door. "The donation is not as large as we first thought. Only half."

Lealia's eyes grew wide. "Did he say why?"

"He said that once they got a report from me that the injured had fully recovered, they decided to give us less and send the balance to their originally intended departments."

Lealia gave him a watery smile. "It is still a good amount." Still enough for Reverend Massey to try to steal.

Reverend Walker smiled. "You're right, Lealia. I need to look at the bright side." His expression turned more concerned. "What are you and Milton doing here? I thought you were not ready to attend today."

Lealia told him about their plan to move the lockbox. Reverend Walker nodded. "That is good thinking, but Reverend Parker still has the banknote. I told him to keep it in his bag. He will be joining me and my wife for dinner at the parsonage tonight. Come by about six o'clock, and we will come over here and lock it up."

"I was going to ask Milton to accompany me to the bank, but he will likely need to rest after today. Can we leave the lockbox in your office for the night? It's a lot of money to lose."

An expression crossed Reverend Walker's face that suggested he understood what she was implying. "Yes, that's a good idea."

"It'll make me feel better."

"We should go. I would like to look in on Milton before I start the service."

They walked down the hall together, and Reverend Walker knocked on the door of Lealia's office before he pushed it open.

Milton was sitting in a chair. He looked exhausted and a little gray. Dr. Briggs stood at his side, his mother behind him, tears in her eyes. Milton barely raised his eyes to her. *Oh, Milton. I am so sorry.*

"I just wanted to check on you before I went down and started the service." Reverend Walker studied Milton.

"I am better, sir," Milton said, his voice hoarse.

Reverend Walker went to Milton and put his hand on his shoulder. "If you need to talk to me, I will be here tomorrow."

Milton nodded.

After Reverend Walker left, Mrs. Rafferty turned to Lealia. "Let's take him home."

"I have my carriage," Dr. Briggs offered.

"I would rather walk," Milton said, slowly rising to his feet.

Lealia took his hand, Mrs. Rafferty took the other, and they left the office. Milton's steps were surer now, but he still kept his head low. As they reached the end of the hallway, another reverend approached them from another direction. He seemed distressed.

"Do you need some assistance, Reverend?" Lealia asked.

He laughed. "Do I look that lost? I am trying to find my way into the sanctuary before the service starts. I imagine Reverend Walker expects the Baptist representative to be on time."

"Oh, you are Reverend Parker." Lealia gave him a brief smile. "I am the temporary church clerk. Reverend Walker told me about you."

Reverend Parker beamed. "And he told me about you. Good work. I am so happy that part of the donation we give today will go to a deserving young person like you. We have instructed Reverend Massey to disperse the money to you as soon as the banknote is deposited."

Lealia jolted and felt Milton tense beside her. "Thank you," she said.

"The sanctuary is right through that door."

When he opened it, Milton shuddered.

Lealia looked up and past him to Mrs. Rafferty, who wore an expression as if she was about to scold them both. "You two have got a lot of explaining to do."

Milton went straight up to his room when they got home, refusing Mom's assistance. He did not want to face her or anyone.

After the episode, he explained to her what had been happening to him over the past weeks. He saw the hurt in her eyes as he did.

Then Lealia and Reverend Walker had come in, looking equally distressed. All he wanted to do was go home. His humiliation was not over though. He didn't miss the whispers of the members of Shiloh as Lealia and Mom led him through the hallways. He was not even out the door before their gossip started. He would never live down his father's reputation, and now he had given himself one to go with it.

He sank onto the bed. How could he show his face to Reverend Walker again? He would tell Lealia to return to the church tonight and go through with their plan. He could not go back.

A soft knock sounded at the door. He was tempted to stay silent, but he said, "Come in."

Mom peeked her head around the door. "I was hoping you were sleeping."

He sighed. "I tried."

She sat on the bed beside him and then asked the same question that Dr. Briggs had. "Why didn't you tell me?"

His shoulders slumped. "I was ashamed."

"Of what?"

He looked at her for a long moment, trying to find the words. "Of what everyone would think of me if they knew I was having these episodes. They would judge me. Like they judged Dad."

"If anyone can judge you after all you did for Shiloh, then they are not worth our concern."

Milton looked at her with surprise. This was the most negative she had ever spoken about Shiloh.

She grasped his shoulders. "You carried person after person, helped person after person, did visitations, and distributed meals. You kept helping until you almost broke your mind. Everyone should be proud of you."

Then he remembered Dr. Briggs' and Reverend Walker's hands on his shoulders. Two men who were proud of him. Two men who had encouraged him even in his brokenness.

"Milton, I love you," she said softly. "The Primms love you. Lealia loves you."

Milton frowned. "She—"

"She will not say it because she is trying to find her own way. But she does. She has been absolutely distraught since we brought you home. The opinions of strangers do not matter."

Milton took Mom's hand in his. "Is that how you survived being at Shiloh all this time?"

"Yes," she said with a chuckle. "I absolutely would not allow them to run all the Raffertys away."

He hugged her, letting the truth of her words sink into his mind.

She pulled back. "Come down for dinner, or Lealia is going to come up."

He laughed. "So bossy."

When he came downstairs, Lealia was sitting on the edge of her seat. She sprang up and into his arms in almost one motion. "Milton, I am so sorry."

He let his arms close around her. She would be gone soon. Reverend Parker said her scholarship would be given to her as soon as the funds could be dispersed. "Don't be sorry. You got me out of there."

She stepped back and gave him a deep scowl. "Why did you come into the sanctuary in the first place? You didn't have to come in."

He missed having her close to him. "I realize that now."

It took half the dinner and Milton bursting out in laughter when she gave him a particularly pointed look for her to stop scowling at him.

Each time he let his guard down, however, he remembered that these might be the last hours he would spend with her.

Lealia helped Mrs. Rafferty clean the dishes after Milton yawned several times in a row. Then his mom shooed him up to bed. Lealia's head felt heavy too, but her mind whirred. Soon she would be gone.

As they finished up, a knock sounded at the door.

"Probably someone checking on Milton." Lealia opened the door and found Mr. Hamilton standing on the porch. "Good evening, Mr. Hamilton. Come in."

"Thank you, but I am just heading home. Reverend Walker wanted me to stop by and tell the two rascals not to come back to the church tonight. He said he will see them tomorrow."

Lealia put her hand on her forehead. "I forgot we were supposed to meet Reverend Walker at the church."

"Reverend said you two were probably worn out from today." Mr. Hamilton peered past Mrs. Rafferty. "Is Junior well?"

"Yes," Mrs. Rafferty said, looking at Lealia. "Mostly tired. We all are."

"When I saw Miss Lealia drag him out of the church, I knew he had had a fright." Mr. Hamilton wiped his face. "I had one too, when I came in to unlock all the doors. I felt the quiet down in my bones."

"I will be sure to tell him you were worried about him," Mrs. Rafferty said.

After Mr. Hamilton had left and Mrs. Rafferty shut the door, Lealia let out a sigh.

"Are you well, dear? There was a lot of excitement today."

Lealia sat on the couch. She had no right to compare her distress to Milton's. He had had an episode in front of the whole church. Her only problem was that she was going to get the scholarship and set out for Howard like she had planned.

She looked at Mrs. Rafferty. "How did you adjust when Mr. Rafferty left?"

"Oh," Mrs. Rafferty said, "I was not expecting that question."

"If I am prying..."

"No, you are not." She sat down next to Lealia and grew thoughtful. "I don't feel like I had to adjust. Milton's father hadn't been the best husband for a while."

"Milton told me he left."

"He did." She chuckled. "If I'm honest, I was glad he did. He was a weight that I did not want to carry. Milton leaving for Tuskegee was harder."

"But how did you know what to do? How did you know it was right to send Milton away?"

"I didn't." She took Lealia's hand. "That's why it's called faith. Sometimes you don't know if something is going to work or if you're going in the right direction. You have to trust that God has a bigger plan for you than where you are right now."

Lealia looked at their hands. "That is what my principal told me as well." It felt like that conversation had happened years ago, not weeks.

"Your principal was right. I sent Milton to Tuskegee because I knew God had a bigger plan for him than his father and Shiloh."

"I think he knows that now."

"I hope he does—and that you do too. Whatever you decide to do next, trust that it is a part of a bigger plan even though you cannot see past this point."

Mrs. Rafferty's words soothed Lealia a bit. When she went up to bed, however, all her confusion returned. Should she go to Howard even though her heart did not want to?

CHAPTER NINETEEN

Milton woke from the nightmare, bolting upright in bed. His heart hammered. The sanctuary had swirled in his dreams. Bodies. Mr. Stokes. He felt bile rise in his throat. He felt like the stampede had happened yesterday. Like the dead and injured were still outside on the lawn.

Then he heard footsteps running up the stairs. His door opened, and Mom flew in. "Milton. Milton, wake up."

He heaved a breath. "I'm awake." His voice sounded as if it were coming from someone else. He heard Mom move across the room to the window and open the curtains. The first tints of dawn brightened the room.

Mom came to stand next to the bed, her eyes full of concern. "I'm all right, Mom," he said, untangling himself from the blankets.

"A nightmare?"

"Yes." He wiped his hand over his face. "As bad as before."

"Maybe because you were in the sanctuary yesterday."

Milton hadn't considered that. "Probably."

"Hello?" Lealia's soft but disembodied voice came from the doorway. "I have water."

Milton laughed. "Thank you."

Mom went to the door and took the glass from Lealia. "Okay. I'm going back to my room now," Lealia said.

"Me too." Mom handed him the glass of water.

When he eventually came downstairs, he noticed that both Lealia and Mom looked less worried. He hadn't realized how much they must have fretted about him every morning after hearing him scream at night.

Milton watched them move around, and it warmed his heart at how close they had gotten. Mom treated Lealia like a daughter.

He shook his head. *Do not entertain that line of thinking. You heard Reverend Parker.* Lealia would be receiving her scholarship soon and would be gone. He should be preparing to do the same. He needed to get back to Tuskegee.

"Reverend Walker said for us to come by for the banknote today," Lealia said. "It's closer to lunch now than breakfast. We should get going."

Mom shook her head. "I hate that Reverend Massey cannot be trusted."

Milton cleared his throat. "I think I am going to check on a train ticket back to Tuskegee."

Mom's face grew solemn. Lealia's face grew sad.

He looked down at his plate. "There is nothing left for me to do here except the meeting with Mr. McDowell and Evan."

Mom swallowed. "Right. When do you want to leave?"

He glanced at Lealia, but she turned away and headed for the stairs. "I should go and get my coat," she said.

Milton sighed. "Maybe by Friday." Lealia probably didn't hear him because she was already upstairs.

When she returned with her coat, he was sure she had been crying. "I am ready when you are," she told him.

The day was dark. The clouds were heavy, and there was no sun. He wondered if the clouds held rain or snow. It was certainly cold enough for snow. As they walked to the church, Milton took in Birmingham with new eyes. Yes, it was a place of great pain, but it was something different now. It was a good city. Growing fast and full of opportunities for Negroes. He could come back here if his mother wished it.

Lealia reached over and took his hand. "You are not listening to me again."

He laughed. "Sorry. What were you saying?"

"I asked if you had decided where you will go after Tuskegee?"

He glanced down at her, and she looked away. He shook his head. That would never change. "I thought I might come back here."

She met his eyes, surprised. "Really?"

"I think my mother would like it." He could see how his future could work here. "Dr. Briggs said there are not enough doctors to treat Negroes in Birmingham. I didn't see a single one when I was doing visitations at the hospitals."

"Dr. Briggs was impressed with your skills. I'm sure he would recommend you to anyone he could not get around to himself."

"Honestly, I don't know where I'm going to go. I have to trust that I'll know what to do when the time comes."

"Your mother told me the same thing last night."

He was just about to ask her what they had talked about when they saw Mr. McDowell standing on the church lawn. He brightened when he saw them approaching.

"That scoundrel has eluded me again." He shook Milton's and then Lealia's hand. "I made the trip all the way down here to talk to him, and Reverend Walker told me he slipped out just before I arrived. Do you know where he could have gone?"

Milton shook his head. "Unfortunately, no."

Mr. McDowell huffed. "Well, since I'm here, I may as well meet with your young friend."

Lealia touched Milton's arm. "I will go inform Reverend Walker and meet you at Evan's house shortly."

Milton nodded. "Mr. McDowell, if you will follow me."

Excitement prickled Milton's spine as they set off for Evan's house. If he and Lealia could manage to prevent Massey from stealing the money, or at least convince Reverend Walker that they were going to try, he could go back to Tuskegee next week.

"After you two left, I took another look at Massey's records." Mr. McDowell glanced at Milton with raised eyebrows. "Found some interesting stuff."

"You did?"

"I confirmed that Mr. Massey has filed more claims than payouts. Every one of the complaints against him read the same. He collects the premiums but does not pay out. One complaint is several years old."

"So Evan, Dr. Briggs, and Mr. Gilbert are not the only ones?"

"Not by a long shot," Mr. McDowell huffed.

The church was quiet but warm. Not with light. The cloudy day made the church feel like the sun was going to set any minute. She could not explain it, but Lealia could almost feel the worship and prayers offered to God the day before, and it had somehow refreshed the building. Refreshed her. As confused as she felt about her future, she understood what Mrs. Rafferty had said. This moment was a part of a bigger plan.

A plan that did not include Milton.

She had nearly burst into tears hearing him talk about his train ticket back to Tuskegee. She had gone upstairs, unable to listen to any more. Also to hide her tears. She would have to say goodbye to him and whatever had bloomed between them. It was not to be.

She reached Reverend Walker's office first. The door was closed, so she knocked. "Reverend Walker?" Odd. Mr. McDowell had said he was here.

She walked down to her office and found it empty too. As she approached her desk, she smiled at the stack of letters. She might as well take care of them now, before heading to Evan's. She quickly sorted them and realized that some of the unopened ones were from the batch Reverend Walker had given her Friday. She separated them quickly and reached the letter addressed to her from Tuskegee. She had never read it. Her hand trembled as she opened the letter.

> *Dear Miss Bevard,*
>
> *I have heard nothing but good things from Reverend Walker about your continued work at Shiloh. He says you are a godsend and a credit to the Tuskegee name.*
>
> *I am very proud of all you have done, but I am not surprised. I was impressed with your work here with the Children's Home.*
>
> *Mrs. Robinson told me of your plans to attend Howard. Reverend Walker told me that the Education Board is preparing a scholarship for you. I know from experience how hard finding tuition money is. Which is why I would like to make you another offer. If you ever need to return to Tuskegee for any reason, a full scholarship will be waiting for you.*
>
> *I look forward to what you are going to accomplish.*
>
> *- Booker T. Washington*

The letter felt like a stone in her hand. A full scholarship for the rest of her studies. She swallowed. She could go back to her parents' house, back to school if she wanted. *Home.*

A rumble of thunder sounded outside. She quickly returned the letter to its envelope. As she did, she noticed that sticking out from under the rest of the letters was a loose sheet of paper. She pulled it out. It was a note from Reverend Walker. He must have put it under the stack of mail before he left.

> *Lealia,*
>
> *I waited as long as I could for you to move the lockbox, but Reverend Massey showed up with a matter I need to attend to. The donation is in the top drawer of my desk. The key is in your top drawer. We will deal with the deposit once I return.*

Dread coiled around her heart. Was Reverend Massey trying to get Reverend Walker out of the building so he could steal the note? She dropped the paper onto her desk, grabbed the key from her drawer, and rushed down the hall. All the while she tried to think of a place she could hide the box in the church. It wasn't heavy. Maybe she could hide it in the balcony.

She burst through the door and rushed to Reverend Walker's desk. The key turned easily, and she saw an envelope sitting on top of his other papers. She glanced in the envelope and breathed a sigh of relief. The banknote was still there. She closed the drawer and locked it. Another rumble of thunder.

She looked up and saw Reverend Massey standing in the doorway with a gun pointed at her.

She gasped and stepped back.

He grinned. "I knew he'd tell you where he put it."

Lealia's hand was trembling badly, but she tried to lighten her tone. "Where he put what?"

"Do not try that with me, girl. Put the banknote on the desk and step away."

Lealia's heart hammered. "This is wrong," she said as she put the banknote down.

"Do not lecture me." He stepped to the desk, staying far enough away from her that she couldn't grab him. He need not worry. She was not taking any chances with the gun.

He snatched up the banknote. "Thank you," he said, waving the gun. "Now to your office for the rest of it."

As they walked, a bead of sweat rolled down her back. "Please, think about what you are doing."

"I know what I am doing," he said, his words cutting. "I'm getting all I can, and no one will ever see me again."

"That money is for church work," she said, reaching her office door.

"This money is for me," he yelled. "Not for your do-gooder boyfriend to hand out. Where is he, by the way?"

She pinned her lips shut. *Too far away to help.*

Reverend Massey laughed. "Oh, I remember. He's probably somewhere shaking and crying. That was an impressive display he put on yesterday for the whole church."

"You are cruel," she said, taking one slow step after another toward the closet.

"Get the box and stop talking."

She stepped inside, grateful that she had left the light on. On a gray day like this, the closet would have been pitch black. Reverend Massey poked her in the back with the gun. "Get the box."

She took it off its shelf and handed it to him with shaking hands. As she did, she felt the keys shift in her pocket. She stilled.

Another boom of thunder sounded like it rumbled across the roof.

Reverend Massey set the box down outside the door. "Since you enjoyed the last time I put you in here so much, I figured you would enjoy it again."

Her eyes grew wide. *He was the one who pushed me in here.* He had done it to distract her so he could steal the money then just like he was doing now.

"Goodbye," Reverend Massey said with glee before he slammed the door shut.

She screamed and pounded on the door.

"Scream all you like. No one will hear you. I'm going to sit here and count my money."

Milton only half listened to the conversation between Mr. McDowell and Evan as he paced the floor. *Where is Lealia?*

She couldn't have gotten lost. Not as much as they had walked the city. She knew the way as well as he did. So why wasn't she here yet?

He pulled back the curtains and examined the sky. Maybe she was trying to wait the storm out. He shook his head. Lealia was more likely to come running all the way here in the rain.

The meeting, what he heard of it, was going well. Mr. McDowell asked Evan about the fire first, and Evan was able to produce all the notes his father had taken before he died. Mr. McDowell said they looked promising.

"This is illegal," Mr. McDowell said after he studied the dry goods store's policy. "He was charging your father for fire and flood insurance, but the policy doesn't include either one. I was already hoping to arrest him just for being annoying, but now I have grounds."

This was good news, but Milton looked out the window again.

He turned back to the two who were now sitting at the small table on the opposite side of the room. "Excuse me, Mr. McDowell," Milton said. "Did you say that Reverend Walker was at the church when you went there earlier?"

"Yes." Mr. McDowell glanced up from his notes. "We talked about Massey for a bit and then he said he was heading out. He said he was just jotting down a note for the clerk."

He left a note for Lealia. Some work she needed to complete for him? Possible, but they were supposed to go there for the banknote. "Did he say anything else?"

"That if I wanted to wait for Reverend Massey I could and that he was expecting him back this afternoon."

Something jolted in Milton. He had thought Massey was gone for the day. "Massey was supposed to come back?"

Mr. McDowell's face grew worried. "Yes. Reverend Walker told me to return later and maybe I could catch him."

Lealia was at the church alone with Massey. Massey, who was probably trying to get to the banknote.

Milton snatched up his coat. "I have to go."

Both Evan and Mr. McDowell looked up in surprise. "Where?" Evan asked.

"To the church." He shoved his arms into his sleeves. "Uh—I need to check on something."

He was out the door before the two of them could say more.

He ran down the street, jacket flapping behind him, the sky thundering above him. *I'm probably overreacting. Dear God, let her be okay.*

He reached the foot of the church stairs and stopped. He bent over, trying to catch his breath. Trying to focus. If Massey was inside with Lealia. . . He bolted up the stairs two at a time. When he reached the top, he pushed the door open.

Inside, the church was dark and quiet. The two large doors to the sanctuary stood open. The chandeliers inside were lit, and the dark sky was framed in the windows. He stood in the foyer for a second, listening and trying to quiet his breathing. The only thing he heard was his pulse hammering in his ears.

CHAPTER TWENTY

She tried to focus on her breathing, but Reverend Massey thumping around her office increased her anxiety. That and the storm raging outside.

The closet, even with the lights on, made her heart hammer. *You are okay.*

Judging from the sounds coming from outside the door, Reverend Massey was looking for the key. She leaned back against the wall, her palms pressed against the shelf.

Reverend Massey's footsteps pounded across the room and stopped outside the door. "Where is the key, Miss Bevard?"

She looked around the closet and saw a broom. She gripped the handle, her palms sweaty. "Open the door, and I will tell you."

He let out a laugh that chilled her. "You can't fool me into letting you out."

"Reverend Walker will return soon." She stared at the door, wishing she could turn the doorknob and—

She covered her mouth to keep from gasping. She had told Milton that she had a good Tuskegee education too. Every building on the campus had been constructed by the students, including doors and their knobs. She knew how to put them in, thanks to her carpentry classes. She also knew how to take them out.

She looked around the room, searching for the toolbox she had seen the first time she had come into the closet. It sat on one of the bottom shelves. She moved quietly, reaching down to open it.

It held a hammer and two screwdrivers.

That's all I need.

When Reverend Massey stormed away from the door again, she reached for one of the screwdrivers, careful not to make any sound when she drew it out.

Breathing heavily, she knelt in front of the door. The ornate doorknob had two exposed screws, one at the top and one at the bottom. She tried the first screwdriver, but it was too big. She quietly pulled out the other one. It was not the right size either, but it was small enough to fit in the screw. She dried her hands on her dress and began working.

Massey and the storm still raged outside the door. "Where is the key?"

The first screw popped out, and she caught it before it hit the floor. "Have you looked in all the drawers? Maybe you should go tear up Reverend Walker's office." As she loosened the second screw, she pressed her hand to the plate, keeping it from falling.

"Do not sass me, girl!"

The cover slid off, exposing the plate around the doorknob. It had two screws as well. It would be trickier now. Once she loosened those two screws, the doorknob would fall from the other side of the door. She notched the screwdriver head in one screw and slowly started turning.

Just as she finished taking out the first screw, she heard a bang from somewhere deep in the church. She stilled. Reverend Massey stopped moving outside the door as well.

It was faint, but Lealia could hear a commotion, maybe footsteps, then, "Lealia!"

She popped up and almost dropped the screwdriver. "Milton!" she screamed, then instantly regretted it. Milton would come, and Massey would point the gun at him.

She heard Reverend Massey let out a frustrated grunt and run from the room. She went to work, quickly twisting the screwdriver, praying the whole time. *Please keep Milton safe.*

She undid the last screw. The doorknob on the inside dropped into her palm, and the other knob fell onto the floor outside the door with a thud. With sweat running into her eyes, she took the screwdriver tip and disengaged the locking mechanism. It clicked, and she flung the door open. Reverend Massey was gone, but she could hear people yelling downstairs. Milton was down there. She picked up her skirts and ran.

His worry heightened. "Lealia!" he bellowed.

His voice bounced around the church.

Then he heard, "Milton!"

He broke into a run across the foyer, the fear in Lealia's voice driving him forward.

Then he heard footsteps running through the sanctuary. Lealia. He had thought she was in her office from the direction her voice came from, but she was here. Relief flooding him, he pivoted and ran toward the double doors of the sanctuary. Milton took three strides in and pulled up short.

It was not Lealia.

It was Reverend Massey.

He held the lockbox in one hand and was running full tilt up the center aisle.

He skidded to a stop when he saw Milton. He studied Milton for a moment and then smiled. "Well, if it isn't the other pest who keeps buzzing around."

"Where is Lealia?" Milton stayed rooted to the spot. His vision was starting to narrow. *God, I could use some of the same help You gave me the night of the stampede.*

"Oh, I made sure she did not hinder my exit."

"Is she—" Milton swallowed. "Hurt?"

Massey reached in his jacket and produced a gun. "You should be worried about yourself. Hands up."

Milton complied, his mind battling. He had to get out of here and find Lealia, but he had to stop Massey if he could.

"I'm walking out this door." Massey's eyes narrowed.

"This is wrong, Massey. You're stealing from a church." Milton tried to keep his voice level, but the walls seemed to be creeping in.

"Why does everyone think I care about that? I'm broke. This money will get me out of town."

"You don't have to do this." Milton calculated how he would get out. His breath quickened. Not just get out to find Lealia, but get out before he broke. The walls were already starting to feel like they were closing in.

"You think I haven't done worse." Massey looked truly amused. "The last person who tried to stop me ended up with a bullet in his chest."

Milton sucked in a breath. "Mr. Stokes."

"Yes, Mr. Stokes," Massey said, his tone snide. "He, like you, would not leave this alone." He waved the gun. "You think I won't kill you too?"

Milton froze. Massey could easily do it. There was nothing between him and Milton. "I only want to know where Lealia is."

Massey laughed, but it sounded more like a snarl. "I locked her away in her little closet."

Oh no. Sweat formed between Milton's shoulders. Lealia was probably panicking right now, and he couldn't get to her. He took a step back. "Let me go to her."

"You're not going anywhere but to the grave." Massey leveled the gun at Milton.

A thump sounded somewhere behind Massey. As if something had fallen to the floor.

Massey turned and looked behind him.

Milton fought for control. His mind produced the images of the stampede. All the horror. But he had to focus on what was happening right now. Massey was distracted. If he could get close enough. . . He took a sliding step forward.

But just as he moved, Massey swung around, his full attention on Milton.

"Stop!" Massey yelled. "I will shoot you dead."

Milton was panting now, his vision swimming. "I'm not letting you pass."

"You can barely hold yourself up. Still scared of being in here?" Massey stepped closer.

He was right. Milton felt like the air was too thick for his lungs. How much longer could he hold up?

The door on the opposite side of the sanctuary flew open. Massey turned, and to Milton's shock and horror, Lealia ran in. Her hair was flying out behind her, and her face was streaked with tears, but she was alive. Milton nearly cried.

Massey swung around, pointing the gun at her. She stopped, her eyes wide.

"Why can't I be done with you two?" Massey was seething now. "I was going to let her live, but now I'm going to kill you both!"

Lealia stumbled and fell backward, her hands stretched behind her to break her fall. She landed, and the pews blocked Milton's view.

Milton heard Massey cock the gun, and everything in him went silent. He had to stop him.

"Stay down!" he screamed at Lealia, and with one more quick prayer, he launched himself at Massey.

When Milton slammed into him, Massey let out an "oof." They both hit the floor hard enough to knock the wind from Milton's lungs. He heard the gun clatter to the floor and Lealia scream. Milton wrapped his arms around Massey and held on.

Where Milton's advantage was youth and strength, Massey's was size. They had landed on their sides, and Milton's right arm was pinned under Massey. The man rolled onto Milton, pressing his arm into Milton's throat. Milton used his legs to push off the floor and shoved Massey enough to free his arm.

Massey rounded on him. "You should not have done that, boy." He drew back and punched Milton in the face. Milton's vision turned to stars. Head swimming, he looked up just in time to see Massey raising his fist for another punch. Milton grabbed Massey's hand as he swung. The force of the punch drove Milton's elbow into the floor, and he cried out.

"Let me go!" Massey said, trying to pull his hand away.

Lealia appeared above them both, holding... Was that the lockbox? Before Milton could scream at her to move, she swung the box with all her might and cracked Massey in the back of the head with it.

Massey yelled and slumped, but the blow did not knock him out. It did, however, give Milton enough time to detangle himself and scramble toward Lealia.

"Go!" he managed to say, but she didn't move.

"I am not leaving you."

Massey crawled in the direction of the gun. "I will kill you both. Just like I did Stokes." Massey was reaching for the gun when Milton heard footsteps running up the aisle behind him. He grabbed Lealia and pushed her between the pews.

"Stop right there, Mr. Massey."

Milton and Lealia turned to see Mr. McDowell rushing down the aisle, gun in hand. Evan stood in the doorway behind him. Massey froze.

Milton gasped, his head still ringing from the punch, and Lealia wrapped both arms around him. "Let's go." She pulled him toward the door.

He looked back just as they reached the door to see Mr. McDowell putting Reverend Massey in handcuffs.

The rain started in earnest once Lealia dragged Milton out of the sanctuary. Evan grabbed Milton's other arm, supporting him as they went through the door. Milton took only a few steps before he collapsed on the floor. Lealia dropped down beside him, fighting against the tears forming in her eyes. Evan looked back, alarm on his face. "I should check to see if Mr. McDowell needs assistance."

"Milton, are you all right?"

"I–I'm okay." He lay on the floor, arms sprawled out. He was breathing heavily. There was blood on the corner of his lip.

"You're bleeding."

"He punched me," Milton said between breaths. "And I hit my elbow." He lifted his head and studied her. "What happened?"

She scooted closer to him, relaying the events in her office as she gently lifted his head off the floor and onto her lap.

His eyes still looked a little glazed, but some of his color was starting to come back. "How did you get out of the closet?"

"I used my good Tuskegee education." She grinned at him.

He frowned. "What?"

"I unscrewed the doorknob and used the screwdriver to disengage the lock."

He stared at her for a moment and then burst into laughter. "You are amazing."

"Thank you."

Mr. McDowell came out of the sanctuary with Mr. Massey, who was in handcuffs. "Will you be all right, Mr. Rafferty? I need to take this one in."

"He stole a large banknote from my desk," Lealia said, "and he was trying to take the lockbox."

Milton sat up and winced. "He told me he killed Mr. Stokes."

"It will be your word against mine, boy," Reverend Massey yelled.

"No, it's actually your word against mine," Mr. McDowell said. "I heard you say you killed Mr. Stokes when I ran into the church."

"I heard you too," Lealia said.

Massey's shoulders deflated. Mr. McDowell searched Massey's pockets and produced the banknote. He handed it to Lealia. "I believe this should be in your care."

"Thank you," she said, her lips quivering. Her tuition money was saved.

"Why did you come?" Milton asked Mr. McDowell.

"The younger Mr. Stokes and I thought it was odd how you left like your coattails were on fire. We decided to follow you. I knew Miss Bevard was here as well. All that talk of murder made me wonder."

The rain started to slow as Mr. McDowell led Reverend Massey down the stairs and in the direction of the police station.

Lealia looked back at the sanctuary. "I need to go and get the lockbox. Will you be okay here?"

Milton nodded. Lealia moved as quickly as she could to get the box. When she carried it out into the foyer, Milton was sitting against the wall, his legs stretched out in front of him. She reached in her pocket, grabbed the keys, and opened the box. As Milton watched, she carefully put the banknote inside.

"Someone should go alert Reverend Walker at the parsonage."

"I'll go," Evan said.

Milton reached for her and pulled her to him. "I was so worried about you."

She snuggled against him. "And I about you. I was afraid you were going to run up to my office and straight into Massey with the gun."

"I thought you were in the sanctuary." Milton tried to put his arm around her and winced.

She moved to the other side, and he chuckled, draping his arm over her shoulders. "We should probably have Dr. Briggs look at that," she said.

Milton nodded. She leaned her head against his, and they sat there, listening to the rain patter on the stairs outside.

After a few minutes, Evan and Reverend Walker rushed through the door. "Thank God you two are all right," the reverend said.

Lealia smiled at him. "Yes, thank God."

As she helped Milton off the floor, being careful with his elbow, they told Reverend Walker all that had happened, including Massey trying to steal the banknotes and what Mr. McDowell had told them about Reverend Massey's business.

"I will send a letter to the Baptist Board first thing tomorrow."

Lealia picked up the lockbox. "You should probably secure this."

Reverend Walker took the box, a grateful look on his face. "Thank you again. Please come over to the parsonage."

As they crossed the lawn, Evan said, "We should probably send for the doctor."

"I can treat him," Lealia said, giving Milton a cheeky grin.

Evan looked surprised. "You can?"

"Yes, with my good Tuskegee education."

Milton laughed. "You can do it all."

Yes, she could.

CHAPTER TWENTY-ONE

Lealia arrived at the church the next day to find Rodah in her office.

"Rodah!"

Rodah rushed to Lealia and hugged her tight. "Hi!"

She could not help the tears that formed in her eyes. "I'm so glad to see you're back to work."

"So glad to be back." She released Lealia. "I figured I should come in and get caught up, since you'll be leaving soon."

Lealia dipped her head to hide her face. *I'm supposed to be happy about this.* She sat in the chair in front of the desk. "Yes. I have my meeting with the Education Board on Friday."

Rodah grinned. "Me too."

"You do?"

"Yes. You inspired me." She sat behind her desk. "I wrote to the Education Board while I was recovering and asked them for a scholarship. I have been paying for my studies on my own, and it is taking forever to finish."

"I understand. Will you change schools?"

Rodah shook her head. "I fear my grades aren't good enough for somewhere like Howard. I'm not as smart as you."

"I think you should try if you want to."

Rodah studied her. "Milton is leaving soon too."

At another time, the mention of Milton's name would have brought color to Lealia's cheeks. Now it only brought sadness to her heart. She pasted a smile on her face. "Yes, he goes back to Tuskegee on Friday."

"Mr. Washington must be extremely proud of you both."

Mr. Washington was proud. She had a letter from him to prove it.

She and Rodah set to work. Lealia showed her everything she had done and told her about the outstanding tasks. When they went to the closet, Lealia lifted the toolbox from the bottom shelf. She showed it to Rodah. "Never, ever take this out of this closet."

Rodah looked confused but only said, "All right."

Once they were done, Rodah walked with her down the hall. "Lealia?"

"Yes?"

"Do you love Milton?"

The question was so unexpected that Lealia nearly stumbled. "Why would you ask that?"

"Because I thought you did, but you're both leaving and going in different directions. I would have thought you two would have gotten married and moved here with Milton's mother."

Lealia sighed. "That is a nice dream, but we have both worked so hard to finish our studies. We cannot give that up now. We and our parents have sacrificed so much to get to the point we are now."

Rodah nodded. "I understand. It's just sad that you two cannot be together."

Lealia inhaled, fighting her tears. "Yes, it is."

The next few days went by in a blur.

He thought his mother was never going to let him out of her sight. Milton couldn't blame her. He had managed to get hurt again, even though it was hardly his fault. Lealia had checked his elbow and said it was a soft tissue injury. Dr. Briggs came to the house and agreed. He put Milton's arm in a sling and gave him some medicine for the pain.

He'd needed it, because he had to go down to the police station and be interviewed.

Lealia never left his side through it all. He still marveled that she had dragged him out of the sanctuary. She could have run, but she didn't. When he asked her about it, she had laughed and said, "Your mother wouldn't have been happy with me if I'd left you there to have another episode."

Laughing, he nudged her with his shoulder. "Seriously, Lealia. You could have been hurt."

She sobered. "I would have been destroyed if something had happened to you."

Her words warmed his heart.

They also made his preparations to return to Tuskegee even harder. He and Mom had gone to the train station to purchase a ticket. As they walked back home, Mom had linked her arm with his. "The next time you come, you'll be ready to become a doctor."

"That's if I pass all my classes. You know how bad I am at agriculture. Too bad Lealia—" He swallowed his words.

"Will you keep in touch with her?"

He heaved a sigh. "If she wishes it."

"I think she wishes for more than that," Mom said, giving him a knowing look.

"I am, however, unable to give her more. I cannot compete with Howard."

Mom stared at him for a moment but said nothing more.

He had expected her to bring the subject up again, but they barely had time to talk. Once word got out of what he had done, well-wishers were knocking on the door all day. Some days their tiny living room was filled to the brim with people. Many of the people he had visited when they were injured came to see him. The Primms. And Rodah, who had completely recovered. Even Mrs. Jones had briefly visited.

Milton was amazed to find that not one person judged him or brought up his father. They only offered their thanks, and some brought him supplies for school. Milton had accepted them all with gratefulness.

During those visits, Lealia kept out of the way, although their visitors were just as grateful to her as they were to him. She had saved the church donations as much as he had. He watched her smile as they thanked her. He would miss that smile.

Reverend Walker visited the day before Milton was scheduled to leave. "I am so proud of you two."

They sat at the table, and Mom made tea. "Thank you," Milton said.

"I thank God in my prayers every day for sending you," Reverend Walker said. "I am going to miss you both. It was nice having two more competent young people around the church."

"You have Rodah back," Mom said.

"I do, but I have grown quite used to having Lealia down the hall from me." He reached for his coat. "Speaking of. . ." He handed her a letter. "The Education Board sent you this."

Milton watched as Lealia opened the letter with shaking fingers. He knew what the letter would say, and Lealia's face confirmed it. "They want to meet with me about my scholarship."

"That is good news," Milton forced himself to say.

She was smiling as she read, but then, when her eyes reached a certain point in the letter, she frowned. "They want to meet with me tomorrow." She glanced up at Milton. "Right before your train leaves."

"Oh." Mom's eyes went from his face to Lealia's. "I guess you will have to say your goodbyes before your meeting then."

Lealia looked down like she was rereading her letter.

He did not want to say goodbye any more than she did.

CHAPTER TWENTY-TWO

It took Milton a little longer to come downstairs the next morning. His train was leaving at ten, and he needed to pack his things. Lealia went down to see if she could help Mrs. Rafferty with anything and realized that Milton's mom just needed company. She went from telling Lealia how proud she was of Milton to crying that he was going back to Tuskegee. Lealia consoled her by reminding her that it would only be a few more months before he returned.

Those words did nothing to comfort Lealia though. This was goodbye for her and Milton. Whatever had been blossoming between them was now dead on the vine. She couldn't give up her scholarship at Howard after she had worked so hard for it, any more than he could change schools and finish his studies when he was so close. They were going in different directions.

She had awakened that morning feeling as if her time in Birmingham had been good. She'd been where she was supposed to be. She had fought against being here in the beginning. She had done everything she could to move her scholarship process forward. However, God had sent her on another route. One that helped Shiloh, gave Evan Stokes some peace, and allowed her to spend some time with Milton. She had not planned it, but it was good.

Milton's footsteps on the stairs made her heart sink. He carried his travel bag in one hand, his coat in the other. He tried to give her a smile, but he looked as forlorn as she felt.

"Good morning," he said, his voice low.

"Good morning." She put on a smile, trying hard to keep from crying.

Mrs. Rafferty moved from the kitchen and peppered Milton with questions. He answered them all with his characteristic patience. All the while, though, he kept glancing over his mother's shoulder at Lealia.

They sat down to the last breakfast they would have together. Lealia forced herself to eat, since Mrs. Rafferty had cooked all of Milton's favorites. Lealia could tell that Milton was also struggling with his emotions. *At least it's not like his struggles before.* As a matter of fact, she had not seen or heard him have an episode in several days. She had actually heard him, after a long day of sitting at the police department, snoring. It had kept her awake, but she didn't care. She was so delighted he was sleeping soundly that she lay in her bed and grinned.

Mrs. Rafferty cleared the table and made a big fuss about making sure Mr. Primm was coming with the wagon, even though they all knew he was. "I will just pop over and see if he's ready." Lealia saw through the ploy, and she was sure Milton did too, but she didn't care. If she was going to break down and cry, she didn't want Mrs. Rafferty to see.

Milton stood in front of her. "Godspeed on your meeting today."

She looked at his chest. It was rising and falling as fast as hers. "Thank you. I hope you have a safe, uneventful trip back to Tuskegee."

He laughed. "Me too. I think I've had enough excitement for a lifetime."

They stood in awkward silence for a moment. "Lealia," he said, his voice a rich rumble in his chest, "I promised to make up for that kiss in the garden. To kiss you when I was not distracted."

She couldn't lift her eyes. "I understand. You're distracted now with—"

She didn't get to finish. He tipped her chin up and kissed her. Soft. Slow. Bittersweet. She put her arms around his shoulders, and just when she leaned in, ready to lose herself in his kiss, he pulled away.

He took in a deep inhale. "Goodbye, Lealia."

"Goodbye, Milton."

He lifted his bag and walked out the door.

She had held her tears in for his sake, not wanting to make their goodbye any harder for him. Now she collapsed on the couch and cried.

Milton arrived at the Primms and found Evan and Dr. Briggs there to see him off as well.

He started with his goodbyes to the Primms. Easier than his goodbye to Lealia. Lord willing, he would be back in Birmingham with them and his mother in a few months.

Mrs. Primm hugged him as tightly as his mother had. "We'll keep an eye on Lealia," she said quietly.

"Thank you." It gave him some comfort that she had someone looking after her until she heard from the Education Board and made her travel plans to Howard.

Mr. Primm gave him a hearty hug but didn't speak.

Milton shook Evan's hand. "Be well, Evan."

"Thanks." Evan said. "This might not be goodbye. I'm thinking of applying to go to Tuskegee. It hurts too much to stay in Birmingham."

"Write to me if you do. My mother will have my address."

Dr. Briggs shook Milton's hand. "I want to tell you that I meant what I said when I first met you. I could use a bright, competent nurse like you. You will be a great doctor."

Milton stood taller. "Thank you, sir."

"I'll have a position for you when you finish school," Dr. Briggs said. "I'll have one for Lealia as well."

Milton's heart twisted. "She's not returning to Birmingham. She is on her way to Howard." *And far away from me.*

"She will do well. My offer still stands for you. The Negro community here could use two doctors. We saw that after the stampede."

"I appreciate it."

"Do not simply appreciate it. Come claim your position next summer after school."

Milton smiled. "Yes, sir."

Milton helped his mother into the front of the wagon and climbed into the back, setting his bag beside him. Mrs. Primm waved until they were out of sight. When they turned the corner to pass Shiloh, Milton's heart heaved. So much pain and so much joy in one place. He had met with Reverend Walker a few days before and had been surprised by the generous gift the church had given him.

"I wish I could give you more," Reverend Walker had said. "I hope you will visit next year, when you have completed your studies."

Milton had promised and walked out the door.

He had come to Shiloh angry and broken. He was leaving it well on the path to healing.

Except I am leaving my heart here.

On the way to the train station, he counted out half the money Reverend Walker had given him and handed it to his mother.

She pushed his hand away. "No, Milton. That is your money."

He placed it in her hand again. "You have given me so much. It's a small repayment for all you have done."

Tears sprang to Mom's eyes, and she took the money.

When Mr. Primm turned the wagon into the train station, Milton could see the steeple of Shiloh above the buildings. He sat very still. So much had happened there. The stampede, the money, and Massey. Very soon, Lealia would walk through those doors and get the scholarship she so deserved.

None of that kept his heart from breaking.

"She is a strong woman. She'll be all right." Mom rested her hand on Milton's arm.

"I know," he said. "I just wish things could have been different between us."

"They can be in the future."

"By the time Lealia and I meet again, we will be in different circumstances. Even more different than we are now."

"You could write to her," Mom said.

"If she writes to me at Tuskegee, I will."

Milton took one last look at Shiloh before he climbed down from the wagon.

CHAPTER TWENTY-THREE

Lealia fought to keep from fidgeting as she walked down the same hallway to the same classroom where she had met the Education Board before the stampede. Rodah chatted excitedly beside her about how she had adopted some of Lealia's bookkeeping practices.

"You are really quite smart, Lealia. When I looked at what you had done, I felt like a dunce for not thinking of doing it that way myself."

Lealia smiled. "I was just happy to help."

Rodah slowed her walk. "You and Milton helped us all a lot. I wish I had gotten to see him off."

"You can write to him. He's going back to Tuskegee. I'm sure he would appreciate hearing from you."

"I'll do that." Rodah opened the classroom door. "I know you're heading to Howard, but I hope we can meet again somewhere."

Lealia hugged Rodah. "Me too."

In the classroom sat only two of the board members, Reverend Hawks and Mrs. West. "Hello again, Miss Bevard. You have done quite a lot of work since we saw you last," Reverend Hawks said.

Mrs. West smiled. "Yes, and we are very proud of the reports we've gotten."

Lealia sat. "Thank you. It was a horrible time, and I wanted to help."

"Have you recovered from your injuries?" Reverend Hawks asked.

"Completely. I'm ready to resume my studies." *Thanks to Milton.*

Reverend Hawks' face grew serious. "Miss Bevard, I am sure you remember the promise of a scholarship we made before the conference."

Lealia nodded, holding her breath.

"Also, you of all people know the financial problems we had with Reverend Massey and his theft. We appreciate you helping to recover some of the donations."

Her mind flashed to the incident in the sanctuary with Reverend Massey. "It was the least I could do."

"We have since discovered that his crimes went even deeper." Reverend Hawks sighed. "We have discovered that he is behind the shortage of Education Board funds. He took advantage of his position here. Unfortunately, we were unable to recover the funds he stole."

Mrs. West sighed. "Before you arrived, we only had enough money to grant two students a scholarship. As we said, we had already decided to give you one."

Lealia breathed. She was going to Howard.

"But," Mrs. West continued, "with the additional missing money, we can only afford to grant one scholarship. We have decided to give it to Rodah."

Lealia blinked. "What did you say?"

"We are giving the scholarship money to Rodah. She has no support, and her injury in the stampede has hurt her wages. We felt she was more in need than you, since your family in Tuskegee can continue to support you."

Mrs. West gave her a sympathetic look. "We can, however, promise you a scholarship to Howard at next year's convention."

"I—" she started, but her thoughts were racing. She was not going to Howard. Not now anyway.

Her only option was to return to Tuskegee.

She remembered her letter from Mr. Washington. To return to Tuskegee with a full scholarship.

Milton was going back to Tuskegee.

She shot out of her seat to Reverend Hawks' and Mrs. West's surprised looks. "Thank you," she said, rushing to the door. "I understand, and Rodah is far more deserving than I am." If she hurried. . .

"Godspeed, Miss Bevard. We know you will do great," Reverend Hawks called out from behind her.

"Thank you," she yelled over her shoulder as she ran down the hall. She stopped at Rodah's office. Rodah looked up at her with surprise.

"I need your help."

Faster than she thought possible, she and Rodah were at the Rafferty house packing. When they were almost done, Rodah left to get Mr. Hamilton to take Lealia and her bags to the train station. Lealia was standing on the porch with her things when he arrived, and she handed her house key to Rodah. "Please give that to Mrs. Rafferty for me."

Rodah hugged her. "I will. I hope you catch him."

Lealia grinned as she climbed into the front seat of the wagon. She would catch him if she had to turn all of Birmingham upside down to do so.

Mom stood next to him, holding his hand. "Here we are again," she said, tears in her eyes.

"Not the same. I'll be back sooner this time." Milton squeezed her hand. "I'll write as soon as I reach Tuskegee."

"I wish you didn't have to go. I've enjoyed having my son home." She hugged him tight.

"I'll be back in a few months."

Now there was nothing left to do but return to Tuskegee. Especially since Lealia would probably stay a few more days in Birmingham with Mom after her meeting with the Education Board. He pushed his thoughts away from her. She was going to be a great lawyer someday. He would have to carry his love for her in his heart until another took her place. If another could.

"I wish you would take all the money Reverend Walker gave you." Mom said, eyeing the platform.

"You need it more than I do," Milton said. "My tuition is already paid. I took what I needed."

Mom looked over his shoulder. "I know, but it feels wrong for me to take it. You've been through so much."

He placed his hand on his mother's cheek. "Mom, she's not coming."

She looked up at him with the same sadness he felt. "I was hoping."

Milton shook his head. "Lealia was always going to go to Howard. That is her dream. We can't expect her to put that aside for me."

"I know you're right. Still, I will miss her."

Me too.

His train rumbled into the station, and Milton gave his mother one more long embrace. "Be safe. I love you," she said.

"I love you too."

He climbed aboard and found his seat. He watched his mother walk down the platform to where Mr. Primm was waiting with the wagon. A very different goodbye this time. Things had changed so much. He settled back in his seat, ready to leave. Maybe once there was distance between him and Lealia, it wouldn't hurt so much.

But after five minutes, the train still had not moved. The passengers in his car began to look out the windows. What could be the delay?

Then he heard her. "Milton!"

He whipped to the window. *Could it be. . .*

"Milton!"

He shot from his seat and rushed to the train door.

Lealia was running along the platform, her carpetbag in one hand, her ticket in the other. Occasionally she reached up to hold her hat in place.

He broke into a grin and waved at her. She bolted to the train door and in a second was in his arms. "What are you doing here?" he asked.

She grinned up at him. "Need to sit. . .catch my breath."

He led her to his seat, and she flopped down, panting. Milton's heart sang at the sight of her. She had caught her breath by the time the train started moving. He leaned over her, scrutinizing her. "How—" he began.

"You could at least look glad to see me," she said, grinning.

"Lealia."

"They do not have enough money," she said.

"Who?" He shook his head but couldn't stop smiling. "What are you talking about?"

"The Education Board. They only had enough money for two students' tuition in the first place. After Reverend Massey stole the money and spent it, they didn't have enough money to cover two scholarships."

Milton frowned. "You didn't get a scholarship?"

Her grin widened. "No. At least not to Howard."

"How could they not give you the money—" But he couldn't finish, because she put a finger to his lips.

"They told me they'll give me the scholarship at next year's convention."

Milton's heart thudded. "You are returning to Tuskegee?" This was too good to be true.

"Yes, with a certain cute future doctor I know." She took his hand. "Besides, Mr. Washington wrote to me after the stampede and gave me a full scholarship. I figure once my cute doctor finishes his schooling, he and I can make a decision on what we want to do next."

His eyebrows shot up. "We?"

She leaned closer and laid her head on his shoulder. "Yes, we."

Joy flowed all the way down to his toes. "Yes, we."

She looked up at him. "Good. Because otherwise I would have stopped this train for nothing."

He gaped at her.

She batted her eyes at him. "Don't look at me like that, dear Milton. You know I can be quite demanding when I want something. I left straight from the Board meeting, got my things from your house, and ran through the station to get a ticket."

He laughed. "Of course you did."

She adjusted her skirts. "Let's go back to Tuskegee and uplift the race and be madly in love."

Milton stilled. "You love me?"

She put her hand on his cheek and lowered her voice. "I have loved you for a while. I just lacked the courage to say it."

He leaned down and pressed his forehead to hers. "Me too."

They sat, holding hands as Birmingham faded. "I am so overjoyed you're heading back to Tuskegee." He glanced at her. "You have to help me with my agriculture classes or else I won't graduate."

She smiled. "Of course I will help you. Someone has to protect the plants from you."

He squeezed her hand. "I love you."

"I love you too."

AUTHOR'S NOTE

The Shiloh Baptist Church Stampede of 1902 was one of the largest man-made disasters of its time.

Reverend T. W. Walker was a real person. In 1902, another Reverend Walker, R.H. Walker, wrote a book called *The Trumpet Blast*, chronicling the disaster. It contains a detailed description of Shiloh and firsthand accounts of people who were in the church at the time. It is a sobering read. Shiloh was a growing, thriving church, but after the disaster, membership declined. The 19th Street location closed and was demolished in 1927. I was saddened, because it went the way of so much Negro and Black history: destroyed and its history forgotten. Judging from the photos in *The Trumpet's Blast*, it was a magnificent building, and part of it was constructed with bricks from Reverend Walker's own brickyard. Another fascinating fact about Shiloh is that it had both gas and electric lighting. Such a majestic building doomed by a night of horror.

Of all the hardships this church faced, there was no fire. There actually wasn't a 6th Avenue location. I made that up. Shiloh's congregation continued rebounding years after the stampede and still stands, with the name Greater Shiloh Baptist Church, located on Jefferson Avenue in Birmingham.

With each historical fiction novel I write, I discover something new about my history. Years ago, my father told me that my grandfather, in addition to being a sharecropper, pastored a church in the 1950s before he fell ill. For some reason, I thought my grandfather was Methodist, but during a conversation with my father, I found out he was Baptist. It was so awesome to hear my father talk about the Baptist Convention and the excitement of the members deciding which delegates were to attend. *The Daughter of Shiloh* means even more to me now.

This book was difficult to write for many reasons. One of them is that I am a little claustrophobic. I discovered that after an MRI for an arm injury. To write Lealia's and Milton's scenes required a little extra self-care when I was done. . .to include chocolate cupcakes. Milton's panic attacks also hit close to home, as I once witnessed someone I love have one. I saw the fear and terror firsthand. My goal was to have both Lealia and Milton suffer injuries—one in body, the other in mind. I wanted to present them both as serious injuries, because they are. God created us body, soul, and mind. The health of all three is part of the abundant life He promised.

Researching Tuskegee was fascinating. Booker T. Washington was truly a visionary, and many of the descriptions of Tuskegee are true. The Children's Home was real and provided schooling for young children right on the campus. The fact that the students built Tuskegee with their own hands is also true. Lealia would have absolutely known how to remove doorknobs, as the Tuskegee students built the school buildings and even had a successful brickyard on campus. George Washington Carver, the noted Black scientist, taught the agriculture classes. Tuskegee is such an amazing school that I didn't have to fictionalize anything about it.

It was bittersweet to write a book set in 1902 with Negro/Black people so hopeful for their future, to read articles and essays about how we as a race would move forward. There were times I wished I could go back and tell them that it would take much longer for their hopes for our race to be accomplished. That in 2025, we would still have our "First Black. . ." anything. The first Black female Supreme Court justice, the first Black Vice President of the United States, the first Black man to win an Oscar for costuming, the first time the United States Senate would have two Black women serving, the first Black female NFL coach to be on a Super Bowl winning team—all have happened in the past four years. As I wrote Lealia's and Milton's reality, I felt my words were tinged with the heaviness of living in my reality.

My goal for this book was not necessarily to educate the reader about Negro/Black history. It was to tell a story about when life knocks us flat and what it looks like to recover. How to live through difficult times and move forward. This was my life in 2024 and the beginning of 2025. Life threw so many unexpected and difficult sucker punches at me that I spent weeks reeling. I pivoted so much, I was just about dizzy. All the while, though, I knew that this time in my life was about a bigger story God was telling. This book is a part of that story.

ACKNOWLEDGMENTS

Ephesians 1:3 (NIV) reads: *Praise be to the God and Father of our Lord Jesus Christ, who has blessed us in the heavenly realms with every spiritual blessing in Christ.* For that, He deserves my gratitude for my life and my relationship with Him. He creates the wildest rides but always brings me to an expected end.

Thanks to my husband Abrian, a.k.a. my writing valet. His services include cooking, brainstorming, love and encouragement, feedback, and occasional light scolding for me to get back in my chair or back in the bed, whichever is needed at the moment. Thank you for supporting me. I know I'm regularly running around with my hair standing on end, but it is a comfort to know that you will keep me grounded. To my children, Jazmyne, Dartanyon, and Emmanuel. I love y'all, and we truly are the greatest family in the world. Thanks for cheering me on, encouraging me, and being distractions when I need it. I can feel that you all are as proud of me as I am of you.

To my godmother, Dyara Henderson. Thank you so much for mothering me when I need it. You are so valuable to me. Thank you for letting me call you "Mama."

To my bestie, Linda Sothern. See, my neuroses are getting better. Thank you for letting me be your "favorite author on the pedestal of your heart." Still laughing at that.

To my agent, Tamala Hancock Murray, thank you for your help in getting this book from proposal to reality. To the Barbour Books publishing staff. . .y'all still taking risks with me? Seriously, thank you for letting me write books showcasing authentic Black experiences. To my editor, Ellen Tarver, for your dedication to reminding me that I absolutely don't know how to use commas. Sheesh. At least I didn't have seven women named Mary in this one. Thank you for your patience.

To my readers, thank you for sticking with me, writing reviews, and sharing my books with your book clubs. Without you, there would be no more books. I look forward to providing you with more stories that encourage and uplift.

Terri J. Haynes, a native Baltimorean, is a homeschool mom, writer, prolific knitter, freelance graphic artist, and former Army wife (left the Army, not the husband). She loves to read, so much so that when she was in elementary school, she masterminded a plan to be locked in a public library armed with only a flashlight to read all the books—and a peanut butter and jelly sandwich. As she grew, her love for writing grew as she tried her hand at poetry, articles, speeches, and fiction. She is a storyteller at heart. Her passion is to draw readers into the story world she has created and to bring laughter and joy to their lives.

Terri is a 2010 American Christian Fiction Writers Genesis contest finalist and a 2012 semifinalist. She is also a 2013 Amazon Breakthrough Novel Award Quarterfinalist. Her publishing credits include *Cup of Comfort for Military Families*, *Crosswalk.com*, *the Secret Place Devotional*, *Urbanfaith.com*, *Vista Devotional*, and *Publisher's Weekly*.

Terri holds a Bachelor's Degree in Theology, a Master's degree in Theological Studies, and a certificate in creative writing and graphic design, meeting the minimal requirements of being a geek. She and her husband pastor a church where she serves as executive pastor and worship leader. Terri lives in Maryland with her three wonderful children and her husband, who often beg her not to kill off their favorite characters.

Website: www.terrijhaynes.com

MORE FROM THE ENDURING HOPE SERIES

When life seems weighed down by challenges, there are always pillars of enduring hope and love to be discovered.

The Angel of Second Street
By Barbara Tifft Blakey

Ida Dempsey has grown up in a privileged life of luxury thanks to her aunt and uncle. Although Second Street—where women of ill repute ply their wares—is off limits to respectable citizens, her heart of compassion compels her to frequent the area, hoping to make a difference in their lives. Ida has also befriended Qui Shau, a Chinese woman who keeps house for her family, but friendships between the whites and Chinese are taboo in Eureka. Ida tries to keep secret her forbidden compassion, but someone is watching and will use it against her.

Paperback / 979-8-89151-112-5

The Undercover Heiress of Brockton
By Kelly J. Goshorn

Henrietta "Etta" Maxwell, heiress to the Maxwell fortune, is also a hard-hitting investigative reporter, reluctantly using a male pseudonym. Leo Eriksson is a second-generation firefighter with a passion for rendering aid to those in need. When he discovers that Henry Mason is really Henrietta Maxwell, the fire department's wealthy benefactress, he agrees to keep her identity secret. But when the Grover Shoe Factory explodes, Etta's determination to get the full story behind the disaster makes him question whether her pride gets in the way of seeing the plight of the people.

Paperback / 979-8-89151-177-4